PRAISE FOR MELANIE DOBSON

CATCHING THE WIND

"Dobson creates a labyrinth of intrigue, expertly weaving a World War II drama with a present-day mystery to create an unforgettable story . . . Dobson takes readers on an amazing journey through the British-German underground alliances of World War II. Melding past and present in unpredictable ways, this is a must-read for fans of historical time slip fiction."

—*Publisher's Weekly*, starred review

"A beautiful and captivating novel with compelling characters, intriguing mystery, and true friendship. The story slips flawlessly between present day and WWII, the author's sense of timing and place contributing to the reader's urge to devour the book in one sitting yet simultaneously savor its poignancy."

—RT Book Reviews, Top Pick, 4 ½ stars

"Another captivating weave of great characters, superb storytelling, and rich historical detail from talented wordsmith Melanie Dobson. A story to remind us all that resilience springs from hope, and hope from love."

—Susan Meissner, author of *Secrets of a Charmed Life*

"A childhood bond, never forgotten, leads to a journey of secrets revealed and lifelong devotion rewarded. Readers will delight in traveling along with Quenby as she discovers that the past can change the present."

—Lisa Wingate, national bestselling author of *The Sea Keeper's Daughters*

BENEATH A GOLDEN VEIL

"*Beneath a Golden Veil* captivated me from the beginning, from the brave souls in Virginia who dared to escape slavery to those who embraced freedom along the dusty streets of promise in Sacramento City. Once again, Melanie Dobson has taken me on a journey that touched my heart. I could not put it down."

—Ann Menke, author of *Exposure to a Billionaire*

"This book is amazing! There are so many twists and turns and surprises that will keep you riveted to the pages of this book. Melanie Dobson has written a spellbinding story that will keep you up long into the night!"

—Regina, Goodreads

CHATEAU OF SECRETS

"Amazing characters, deep family secrets, and an authentic French chateau make Dobson's story a delight."

—RT Book Reviews, 4 ½ stars

"Intriguing and suspenseful, rich in secrets, hidden tunnels, and heroic deeds, Melanie Dobson's *Chateau of Secrets* weaves a compelling tale of a family's sacrifice for those in need. A beautiful story."

—Cathy Gohlke, Christy Award–winning author of *Saving Amelie*

SHADOWS OF LADENBROOKE MANOR

"Mysteries are solved, truths revealed, and loves rekindled in a book sure to draw new fans to Dobson's already large base."

—*Publishers Weekly*

"An old cherished house is like the human heart. We keep treasures safely tucked within; some conquests we proudly display, some treasures we put behind glass, some secrets we hide from sight, our own and others'. In *Shadows of Ladenbrooke Manor*, Ms. Dobson skillfully plaits the complex strands of life: golden and dark, truth and deception, love and loss into an engaging, multigenerational story of heartache and ultimate, unexpected redemption. Any reader might both lose and find herself between the covers of this compelling novel."

—Sandra Byrd, author of *Mist of Midnight*

THE SILENT ORDER

"What a wonderful book by an amazing author! In Dobson's latest offering, readers will find mystery, love, and values that have withstood the test of time. The characters are a delight, and readers get a fascinating glimpse into the underworld of gangsters during the era of Prohibition and the dangers police faced in keeping law and order."

—RT Book Reviews, Top Pick, 4 ½ stars

Enchanted Isle

Also By Melanie Dobson:

Enchanted Isle

MELANIE DOBSON

Waterfall
PRESS

Scripture quotations from The Authorized (King James) Version. Rights in the Authorized Version in the United Kingdom are vested in the Crown. Reproduced by permission of the Crown's patentee, Cambridge University Press.

Published by Waterfall Press, Grand Haven, Michigan
www.brilliancepublishing.com

Amazon, the Amazon logo, and Waterfall Press are trademarks of Amazon.com, Inc., or its affiliates.

ISBN-13: 9781503938687
ISBN-10: 1503938689

Cover design by Shasti O'Leary Soudant

Printed in the United States of America

For

Diana Berry

Thank you for sharing your beautiful world with me.

LAKE DISTRICT MAP AND INSET OF ISLAND

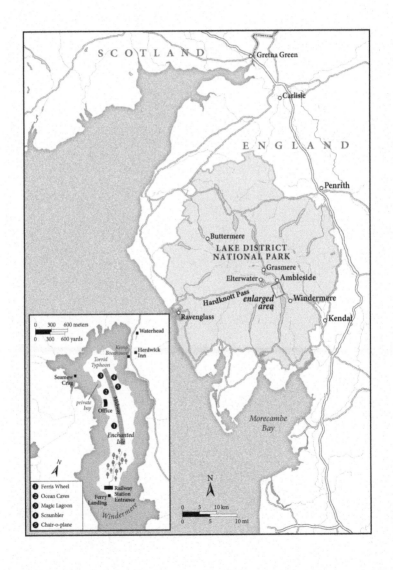

PROLOGUE

August 1935, Lakeland, England

Gilbert Kemp whistled as he trekked down the steep hill to Windermere, whistled as he circled the water's edge toward the boathouse. Not that he was happy about retrieving his older brother from the park tonight—Simon should have been home hours ago—but earlier this evening, Liz had said *yes*. Yes, she would marry him and stay here in this district of lakes. Yes, she loved him, just as he loved her.

The thought of Liz leaving for America had completely wrecked him, but now, with a simple question, everything had changed. They would be married in the spring, along these daffodil-spiked banks of this lake.

A sound—the trill of a tawny owl—echoed through the beech trees along the bank. He glanced across the sparks of starlight on Windermere's surface, toward the island where Simon Kemp and Curtis Sloan had sparked their own version of magic. An amusement park that thrived in Great Britain as the economy struggled to recover from its depression.

Most of the rides were hidden back in the trees, but he could see the light from the Torrid Typhoon, a wooden roller coaster that peaked above the forest and then plunged down toward the water, the cars surfing through the waves of trees.

Tonight the park had closed for the season, most of the summer visitors returning home after their holiday, but his brother was still on the island. Maria, Simon's wife, was worried and for good reason. Simon's behavior had been odd the past month, even for an eccentric man. His park was making money, hand over fist it seemed, but paranoia had begun to plague him. Several nights ago, he'd even told Maria that Curtis was stealing from them.

Tomorrow, he'd take Simon to a doctor over in Kendal. The man, he suspected, would tell his brother to hibernate during the winter season. Then Simon would return to his typical eccentric self when he and Curtis reopened their park next spring.

Gilbert unlocked the boathouse and stepped inside. Their motorboat was gone—Simon would have it on the island—so he lowered the canoe into the water and tossed his hat inside.

The paddle cut smoothly through water and wind as he crossed the lake, the glint of starlight reflecting on the wood. His brother was a visionary who'd broken the confines of society to build his empire, never content to settle into a boxed sort of life. Like the sheep roaming in the fells above this lake, refusing to be penned.

Even if his brother would say he didn't like boundaries, he knew the boundaries were necessary. Simon was terrible at managing money and fixing things to maintain what he'd built, but he respected those who did both.

Gilbert didn't mind the boundaries of regular life. Now that he'd obtained his degree in civil engineering, he would work alongside his brother and Curtis during the winter months as well as the summer, maintaining the current rides and building new ones.

The island wasn't far from this side of the lake, about two hundred yards from the boathouse to land, but the island's rocky shoreline on the east side was inaccessible to boats. They'd found the perfect bay on the west shore, in the harbor of a promontory that jutted out into the lake.

He rowed around the northern tip of the island, down to the private bay Curtis and the Kemp family used. Then he looped his rope around one of the posts on the landing stage, beside their family's motorboat.

The pebbles on this beach gleamed white. The electric lights were hidden back in the trees, but on nights like this, when the stars rained down their light, he preferred the silhouettes and shadows to the glare of electricity.

During the summer, visitors disembarked at a ferry platform on the south end of the island, walking up a cobblestone trail leading into a railway station with a clock tower. Lampposts flanked the elegant entrance.

There was no grand entrance on the island's west side, but the private footpath ahead of him was the direct route to the office.

"Simon," he called from the beach. His brother didn't answer, so he followed the narrow path through the trees.

Simon was probably at his desk now, bent over books containing numbers that made little sense to him. He and Curtis were supposed to hire an accountant soon to help manage their finances. Tonight, Gilbert would help him finish his work so Simon could return home to his wife and daughter. And perhaps, if it wasn't too late, Gilbert could see Liz for another hour or two.

He started whistling again as he walked; he couldn't seem to help himself. The park would be closed for the next seven months, and when it opened again, he and Liz would be husband and wife.

As he neared the small office, he expected to see the glow of Simon's desk lamp though the window, but the glass was dark; both front and back doors locked. He turned toward the midway where Simon and Curtis had built their most popular rides, the long strip ending with a boxy platform beside the Torrid Typhoon. Light from the roller coaster trickled down on the park, but all the other grand lights that sparked the enchantment of this place had been extinguished.

On his left was the Ocean Caves, modeled after the river caves at Blackpool's Pleasure Beach, except there were mermaids and sunken ships instead of dinosaurs and a gold mine on this ride. The river looked eerie tonight, trails of light snaking through the inky black water. On his right were the Chair-O-Plane, an aerial swing that twirled passengers above the trees, and the Scrambler, for those who liked to spin.

Wind gusted up the midway, stirring up the greasy smell of fish and chips, rocking the swing on the Chair-O-Plane and the buckets on the Scrambler as he called Simon's name.

It was strange to be here alone in the darkness, though there was nothing to fear, not like in the cities. Crime in Lakeland consisted of petty thievery and the pranks of youth. And the only animal to fear was a cornered ram.

Beyond the Ocean Caves was the crown jewel of the park: the Magic Lagoon, a magnificent merry-go-round plated with gold leaf and colored glass. Instead of horses, sea creatures circled the ride, and as it rotated, blue and white lights twinkled above brightly lit murals of seahorses and seashells, mermaids and mermen, and fish swimming in coral.

As he and Liz had ridden the merry-go-round this evening, hand in hand, he'd sworn it cast a magical spell, because it had given him the courage to dream as well. In that moment, circling in this park, he'd realized that he didn't want to live a life without her.

There was a sound in the trees, a shuffle near the end of the midway that jolted him back to reality. He started to shout again for his brother when he heard another sound. A screech curled down the path, coiling up his spine.

A second owl—he told himself. Surely it must be an owl, caught in one of the trees.

But the scream ebbed into a wail. Like a person trapped instead of a bird.

He removed his hat, the brim crushed in his hands as he raced toward the roller coaster. Had Simon been injured, or was someone trespassing on the land?

His entire body was shaking when he reached the platform where the strands of roller coaster cars were stored. He could see the glimmer of metal tracks in the beacon of light, between railings made of wooden beams. Then he saw a man at the base of the hill. His brother, searching for something in the grass.

Gilbert called for Simon again, rushing toward him, but Simon didn't respond. In the dim light, Gilbert saw his brother's eyes, confused and afraid.

"Come along," Gilbert said, his arm outstretched as if he were speaking to a child.

His brother didn't move.

"Maria is worried . . ." His voice trailed off as his eyes settled into the darkness again. Simon was clutching the handle of a knife in both hands.

Gilbert stepped back. "What are you doing?"

"I only came," Simon started, his voice monotone, "came to sort it out."

"Sort what out?"

Gilbert followed his brother's gaze to the ground. Someone else was there, lying in the grass. "Dear God . . ."

"I didn't do it."

His stomach roiling, Gilbert dropped to his knees beside the body. It was Curtis, the man's arms twisted in the wrong direction, his chest completely still. Gilbert couldn't see blood in the starlight, but he could smell the tang of rust in the wind, hear the silence from a man who should be gasping for breath.

5

He pressed his fingers into the man's neck, but blood no longer pumped through his veins. Curtis was dead, and Simon was alone in the park, a knife clenched in hands that didn't shake at all.

Gilbert's fingers trembled when he pulled them away from Curtis's neck, sticky.

Had Simon killed him for stealing?

"Give me the knife," Gilbert commanded, his voice trembling.

Simon complied, and Gilbert dropped it into the grass, right beside the body. Then he backed away. "Let's go home."

Like a lamb trailing its mother, his brother obeyed, following him down the path that led back to their boats. Gilbert tied the canoe to the back of the motorboat.

"I didn't do it," Simon repeated as Gilbert piloted them both toward the mainland, the canoe carving the wake behind them.

He didn't say anything.

"I swear, Gilbert. I found him minutes before you arrived. He fell—"

"Fell on your knife?"

"No." Simon shook his head. "The knife was already there."

His brother was hiding something. Something important.

Simon looked back at the island. "We can't leave him there."

"I'll retrieve his body," Gilbert promised.

But when he returned, Curtis Sloan's body was gone.

And so was the knife.

Beauty is what Nature has lavished upon us as a Supreme Gift—
it is all about us to see and use.

—Louis C. Tiffany, American glassmaker
(The Art World, 1917)

CHAPTER 1

April 1958, Lakeland, England

Windermere looked exactly as her mom had described—a glittery lake dappled with sunlight and hemmed in by emerald hills. According to her guide, fifteen other lakes dotted the region, though they weren't officially called lakes. All but one was a *water, mere,* or *tarn*.

These waters expanded and swelled together in Jenny's mind, and she saw, even if no one else could, a palace underneath them with coral spires and towers of sea glass—a castle for mermaids and their men. And a sunlit dance floor. In her mind's eye, the mermen bowed to the ladies, each mermaid dressed exquisitely in a beaded gown and jewels mined from the hidden crevices of their world.

Jenny fingered the strap of the new camera around her neck, wishing she could capture their dance on film.

Even though she was thousands of miles from home, Jenny could almost hear her grandfather scoff at such silliness. *Ridiculous,* he would say. *A waste of a mind.*

Then the disdain of her college professors followed, the men and one woman who constantly battled against her imagination to make themselves heard. With all their silent laughter mocking her, the merfolk and their palace disappeared.

Jenny carefully framed her first picture of Windermere in the view-finder of her camera. The needle swung from red to green on the scale, and she pressed the silver button on top. Here she was going to find beauty in the world outside her mind. These lakes, her mom had promised, would give her the opportunity to explore via foot instead of just wandering in her head.

Her mom purchased the Fujica Automagic camera from Bloomingdale's before Jenny had left America, an early gift for her twenty-first birthday. Then she flipped open the door on a cage that had surrounded Jenny for most of her life and told her to fly. At least until the first of June, when her ship sailed back to New York Harbor.

Upon her return to Cleveland, her grandfather expected her to step into the heels of a respectable lady and marry Robert Tripp before summer's end. But her mother—the most elegant woman she knew—hadn't said anything to Jenny about acting like a lady in England. Instead she'd told her to take lots of pictures as she explored the lakes and the moorland hills called *fells*.

Jenny wanted to see one place most of all. A magical park called Enchanted Isle. Her mom said it was closed now, but surely someone would let Jenny in the gates, if only to take a few pictures.

One more photograph of the lake in front of her, and Jenny lowered her camera. After sixteen more exposures, she'd send the roll of film in for development with the other two rolls she'd already taken on the ship between New York and Liverpool.

She glanced at her watch—almost three now.

The ten o'clock train was supposed to transport her from Liverpool to Manchester this morning before she caught connecting trains up to the station at Windermere. But another train left at nine, and she couldn't resist the earlier journey. An extra hour to explore on her own before her hostess arrived.

Stopping beside a wrought-iron bench, Jenny re-strapped the red buckle of her sandal around her ankle and coated her lips with a crimson color that matched her shoes and pocketbook. Mrs. Banks may not care about things like lipstick and pocketbooks, but best to give a good first impression when she met her mom's friend.

Jenny replaced the lens cover on her camera and began climbing the steep sidewalk back up to the railway station but stopped again when she saw a bakery. Inside the window were rows and rows of iced pastries, jam doughnuts, and cupcakes. She should greet her hostess with some sort of a gift—it was the respectable thing to do. A raspberry jam tart for Mrs. Banks and two chocolate cupcakes for herself would be the perfect cure for hunger pains and restless nerves.

When she returned to the station, Jenny dug two claim tickets out of her pocketbook and placed them on the ticket counter. "I'd like to collect my two pieces of luggage, please," she said to the counterman. "Both of them teal."

He retrieved her bags and dropped them on the tiled floor beside her. "Are these correct?"

"Yes, thank you."

"They look green to me."

She looked down at the square suitcases with their brass clasps and bluish leather. "I suppose color depends on the individual."

He shrugged. "I don't put much stock in color."

Her mouth hung open for a moment, appalled at the thought of someone not caring about color. Then her gaze shifted down to the coin purse inside her pocketbook and its assortment of bronze farthings, silver shillings, and both green and blue paper notes. She'd exchanged some of her traveler's checks for cash at the port in Liverpool but wasn't sure what to make of the currency.

When she tipped the man with two of her bronze coins, he grunted in response. She opened her purse again to give him several more, but he'd already retreated behind his counter.

Tucking her pocketbook under one arm, her bag of treats under the other, Jenny tried to lift both suitcases but felt like an awkward duck weighed down by its wings, unable to fly.

"Would you like help?"

She turned slowly to see a man in his early twenties, perhaps a year or two older than her, waiting near the door. His dark hair was swept back, like James Dean's, except Mr. Dean would have had a cigarette dangling from his mouth. A smile was the only thing that crossed this man's lips.

"Oh no," she protested, putting both pieces of luggage back on the ground.

The man tilted his head, studying her and her suitcases for a moment. "Clearly you're from America."

She stiffened. "You sound like it's a crime."

"No crime in a man or woman's citizenship." He crossed his arms over his black T-shirt, nodding at her suitcases. "How do you plan to transport your convoy?"

"It's not exactly a convoy," Jenny insisted. And she had seen convoys, notably the five steamer trunks filled with clothing and accessories that her college roommate had tried to stuff into their dormitory room. For this trip, Jenny had limited herself to seven outfits, eight pairs of shoes, and loads of color film for her Automagic in case she couldn't purchase it in England.

"Very well, then." The man leaned against the counter and watched as she secured her paper bag and pocketbook under one arm and lifted the heavy suitcases. She walked several steps before her camera strap caught on one of the suitcase clasps, and she stopped to untangle it.

She glanced over at the man, and his lips trembled as if he were trying to suppress laughter. "Is this amusing to you?" she asked.

"Quite."

"There must not be much in the way of amusement around here."

A light flickered in his hazel-green eyes. "There's plenty to be found in this station."

"From the tourists?"

He didn't reply.

She looked for a porter, but the only people who seemed to be carrying luggage were those traveling on the next train. More than anything, she'd wanted to prove to herself that she could live on her own, without her grandfather or anyone else telling her what she must do. But now she couldn't even figure out a way to transport two pieces of luggage to the curb.

Sighing, she pointed to one of the suitcases. "If you could help me carry one of these, I'd be grateful."

The man lifted both cases as if they were as light as matchbooks and hauled them outside.

As she followed him, Jenny opened her pocketbook and retrieved a shilling. After he set down the luggage, she tried to press the coin into his palm, but he yanked his hand back as if the silver burned his skin.

"I'm not a porter."

She lowered the shilling, embarrassed. "It was my way of saying thank you."

"Words work just fine."

"Thanks loads for helping me." She unrolled the paper bag and removed one of the cupcakes inside. "Surely you can't refuse chocolate."

He thanked her, taking the cupcake before pointing to the strap around her neck. "What sort of camera is that?"

She lifted it with two hands. "An Automagic. It's made by Fujica."

"Nifty," he said before taking a bite of the cake. "What's the shutter speed?"

She glanced down as if the numbers might magically appear. "I don't know."

When he leaned forward to examine her camera, she smelled chocolate and the musk from his aftershave. The world around her dimmed for the briefest moment, and then in the distance, she heard the rumbling train entering the station, its brakes screeching as people clamored through the station door.

Stepping back, the man pointed over his shoulder. "I have to fetch someone."

"Of course."

"Do you need a ride?"

"No, I'm—"

A honking horn interrupted her, and a burgundy car flew up to the curb, the woman inside wearing a peacock-green headscarf and black sunglasses, waving at her.

Jenny waved back at the woman she assumed was Mrs. Banks. "My ride appears to be here."

The man pretended to tip an invisible cap before merging into the crowd that swarmed out of the station.

"Hullo!" Mrs. Banks called as she slipped out of her car. Her red lipstick was even brighter than Jenny's. Clearly she had an appreciation for color. "Here I thought for certain I was early."

"You are early," Jenny said. "I decided to take the nine o'clock train."

Mrs. Banks reached for one of the suitcases. "You're just like your mother when she was younger, wanting to arrive before everyone else."

A twinge of homesickness pressed against Jenny's heart. "She still likes to arrive early."

The woman studied Jenny's face. "You're just as lovely as your mum too."

"Thank you, Mrs. Banks."

The woman brushed her hand across her face, the colorful bracelets on her wrist reflecting the sunlight. "Please, call me Cora."

"All right. Cora it is."

She nodded toward the station door. "Adrian wasn't bothering you, was he?"

"The man with the black shirt?"

Cora smoothed back her scarf. "He's more of a boy, really."

"He only offered to help with my luggage."

Cora's lips pressed together in disapproval before she spoke again. "Hopefully you won't see any more of him."

Jenny squinted through the window for one last glance of this Adrian, but she didn't see him in the crowd. She didn't want to debate with her host, but she actually hoped that she might see Adrian again in the next two months.

Cora's bracelets clanked together when she waved at the car. "Let's be off, then, shall we?"

Jenny grinned. "We shall."

The two of them managed to squeeze one suitcase into what Cora called the boot; the other sat on the back seat. Then Jenny slipped into the passenger seat on the left side, placing her camera, pocketbook, and paper bag in her lap.

After Cora climbed behind the wheel, she nodded toward the paper bag. "What do you have there?"

Jenny pulled out the other cupcake and the raspberry tart.

"I adore chocolate."

"Me too," Jenny said as she handed the cake to her. "Actually, I like pretty much anything that's sweet."

"I believe we're going to get along famously," Cora said after a bite, chocolate crumbs glued to the gloss on her lips. "I'm breaking my diet for chocolate and the pudding and roast beef waiting for us at home."

"I'm famished."

Jenny took a bite of the tart and savored the sweet raspberries.

Her mother was correct. She liked this land of lakes very much indeed.

CHAPTER 2

Adrian steered the boat around an outcropping of rocks that broke through the water's surface and endangered the powerboats that raced across the lake. A blue-and-rust kingfisher perched on the tallest crag, waiting to catch minnows in the clear water.

Temperatures were still cool, but visitors began trickling into the Lake District each April, bundled in their fur-lined coats and hats for a respite from the smog that curdled in the cities. Some stayed for weeks while others relocated here for the entire summer.

On the boat were five guests of the Herdwick Inn: three with binoculars and two holding cameras to photograph the cormorant, warblers, and heron on Windermere. In a few days, Adrian would forget the ladies and gentleman on this cruise, just like he'd forgotten most of the visitors at his sister's inn, but he couldn't seem to get one visitor out of his mind. The American girl with her magic camera.

Why hadn't he asked for her name?

He'd thought about asking as he'd stood dumbly on the curb yesterday, eating her chocolate cupcake. But then Cora Banks had arrived, and that woman would have no business with him. She'd probably told her guest all about him and his family already, precluding any attempts for him to befriend her.

It was unfortunate. He'd rather liked the girl and her spunk.

"What's on the sheep?" one of his passengers asked, pointing starboard.

The hillside was sprinkled with black lambs, each one paired with a gray-coated ewe. A stripe of dark-green paint colored the muddy fleece of the older sheep.

"The farmers mark them," he explained. "That way they can easily identify their sheep when they're grazing in the fells."

"How long have you lived here?" his male passenger asked.

"Most of my life."

"You're one lucky bloke."

Adrian pulled his cap closer to his eyes to keep out the rays of sunlight. Every man in Great Britain was required to do national service, so he'd left the district for garrison duty in Hong Kong when he was eighteen, and then he'd attended Durham University, north of Yorkshire, obtaining his business degree last December. But around here, all people seemed to remember were the stupid mistakes he'd made in his youth. They'd pinned a reputation on him like he was a donkey in need of a tail, but once pinned, the reputation stuck for a lifetime. Like father, like son.

While he'd thrived in the Lakes during his youth, he was more than ready to embark on a new adventure that didn't involve his sister's inn or farming or the gossip from people like Cora who'd never let him forget.

The tourists were different—they respected what he said. After over twenty years in and out of Lakeland, he had plenty of stories. He could probably tell them that a band of leprechauns had hidden gold in this lake, where a rainbow had dipped into the water, and they would believe him. But he didn't have to make up stories. There was plenty of lore to draw from with the occupation of Romans and Vikings in this region during centuries past, as well as the legends of fairies and elves and the white horse that supposedly haunted this mere.

The man turned from the hillside of sheep, pointing his binoculars toward one of the eighteen islands on Windermere. "What is that?"

Adrian didn't have to look over his shoulder. He knew exactly what had caught the man's attention. It was the tip of the Torrid Typhoon, a spire over the bramble and forest of oak and beech trees.

"An old roller coaster," he explained, just as he'd done hundreds of times over the years.

"Are there more rides on the island?"

He nodded. "There used to be about fifteen, but the park was abandoned a long time ago."

Now all his passengers were looking over the port side, as if they might catch a glimpse of another ride. "What was it called?"

"Enchanted Isle."

"I wish we could stop," the young woman with the blue coat said.

"Unfortunately, the current owner won't let anyone trek on his land."

He steered the boat close to the shoreline, circling the long island before returning his guests to the landing stage. His sister would have hot tea along with poached eggs and toast waiting for them inside the dining room. And he would take one more group out on the water this afternoon before helping his uncle at the farm.

As he secured the boat, his gaze wandered back toward the island again.

To locals, the abandoned park was a black mark, a bruise of sorts on their pristine district, but to him it was a wretched scar. Some days he wished the owner would tear down all the rides and let nature swallow up the memories, but for some reason, the man refused to let the place die.

Almost as if he wanted the world to remember exactly what Adrian's father had done.

Jenny woke to the peal of church bells ringing across the hill, accompanied by the chiming of a grandfather clock in the room below. Every clang stamped a new number into her brain, all the way up to nine.

Wind seeped through the old stone-and-plaster walls as she rose from one of the twin beds. Cora had shown her how to light the paraffin heater in the spacious guest room and then told her to sleep until her body was rested from her trip.

Outside the window, a clematis bloomed magenta on the trellis, and beyond the house, rolling green hills dipped down to a sapphire sliver of lake.

Her mom had met Cora here more than twenty years ago when she'd been visiting with an aunt who'd since passed away. At the time, Jenny's grandmother had wanted her only daughter, Liz, to experience a season overseas before she married, especially since most of their ancestors were British. Jenny's mom had loved exploring these lakes, and Jenny longed to explore here as well.

Both the upstairs bathroom and a designated water closet in the renovated farmhouse were located down the hall, on the other side of Cora's bedroom. Jenny tied her robe around her flannelette pajamas and unpacked an outfit from her suitcase. Then she rushed toward the bathroom. Cora hadn't mentioned the absence of her husband last night, and she didn't want to meet Mr. Banks until she was fully dressed.

After washing up at the pedestal sink, Jenny tied her dark-blonde hair back with a violet striped handkerchief to match the color in her blouse and zipped up her corduroy slacks. Then she retrieved her leather camera bag, pleated coat, and Wainwright's pictorial guide to begin her explorations for the day.

The carpeted steps circled down to a hallway, and she followed the drafty corridor past a second water closet, sitting room, and formal dining room into the kitchen, where Cora had left two scones and a cup of tea that had long ago lost its warmth. Jenny promptly added two sugar cubes to the tea and ate both scones.

Last night, Cora had explained that she worked as a glazier and glass artist all day and sometimes all night in her studio beside the house. When she wasn't home, she was meeting with a customer or traveling outside the Lakes to repair stained-glass windows in chapels and churches across Great Britain. She'd explained, quite graciously, that she wouldn't be able to entertain Jenny much during her stay, but Jenny wasn't in need of entertainment. All she wanted was space to unshackle, roaming as she pleased.

Cora had stocked the cupboards and icebox with food using money that Liz wired, though Jenny hadn't a clue how to operate the gas range. Long ago, her mom had instructed her on all the basics of cooking, but Jenny rarely prepared a full meal for just herself. Still, she'd manage just fine on a diet of canned meat, fresh produce, and plenty of sweets.

A side door led out of the kitchen, into an enclosed courtyard where Cora parked her Fiat. Strung across the right side of the courtyard was a clothesline with several articles of clothing, to the left a small barn her hostess had converted into an art studio. A private entrance opened from the studio into the courtyard, with a separate gate for customers opening onto the lane outside.

Jenny found Cora inside the studio, hunched over various shapes of stained glass on her worktable, a denim apron tied at the nape of her neck and a glasscutter in hand. Black-rimmed glasses framed her eyes.

The studio itself was a gallery of light. Shelves lined two of the walls, each one filled with a kaleidoscope of glass pieces—vases, lampshades, goblets, charms for jewelry. A gray kiln stood at the far end of the room, and a dozen strands of wire dangled from the ceiling beams, each one holding a wind chime made from fragments of colored glass. In the middle of the room was a second table with a messy assortment of tools and jars.

Cora set her cutter on the table and pushed her glasses back over her permed auburn hair. "Good morning."

"I'm sorry I slept late," Jenny said. "After my time on the ship, I thought I'd be accustomed to the time change."

"Lake weather always puts visitors into a bit of a stupor." Cora smiled. "Did you get enough to eat?"

"More than enough." Jenny picked up a fairy, its wings made with a pale-blue glass. If only she could make something so pretty, something to spark the embers of imagination. "This is beautiful."

"Thank you." Cora swept her arm in front of the shelves. "Most of these things I make for local shops, but every once in a while, I create something special for myself or a friend."

"The colors are incredible."

"They're made from different metals." Cora picked up a lampshade pieced together with stained glass. "Green glass is from uranium or iron, yellow from silver. And blue glass is made from cobalt or even copper."

"Goodness," Jenny said, her mind swimming with all the colors. "I could never keep all that straight."

"I think you need a special piece to remember your spring in Lakeland." Cora's gaze drifted out the window for a moment before she looked back at Jenny. "Something that embodies water and earth and perhaps a little fire."

Jenny set the fairy back on the shelf. "How do you make fire?"

"I don't make it." Cora laughed. "The earth does."

Jenny glanced at the labyrinth of orange and red on a lampshade. The colors looked like fire to her.

"A powder of gold or selenium makes the glass red, though some people say that selenium is toxic. All the components of glass are powerful in their own right."

Jenny picked up a triangular piece of red glass from the worktable and held it toward the window. The color transformed into ruby in the sunlight.

"Most glass that man makes is from soda, lime, and silica, but it's quite unremarkable until it's stained. Nature's glass is marvelous without any intervention."

Jenny put the manmade glass back on the table. "How does nature make glass?"

"In a blast of fury, at least for the most beautiful pieces. When lightning strikes a beach or lava boils over a volcano." Cora reached up to a top shelf and brought down a chunk of forest-green glass iced with layers and layers of thin ridges branched out like the fronds on a palm tree. "This was created when a meteor crashed into Czechoslovakia. It's called Moldavite."

Jenny cradled the dramatic piece in her hands, and the fury of lightning and lava exploded together in her mind, almost blinding her. She agreed—God's creation far exceeded man's ability to create.

"You must get out and explore." Cora scooted her toward the door. "I purchased a bicycle with the money your mum sent so you can ride wherever you'd like."

Jenny eyed the blue-and-cream bicycle leaning against the wall of the studio, beside a pot of budding spring flowers. Above the bicycle's front wheel was a woven basket and electric lamp, with a shiny silver bell on the handlebar.

She'd never ridden a bicycle in her life. Or driven a car, for that matter. How was she going to visit the fells without transportation?

Life isn't a game.

That's what her grandfather had told her before she'd left Cleveland, as if it was a crime to play. He'd also said she could never survive on her own, and if she did this foolish thing, either he or her mom would have to rescue her from England, as if she were too stupid to care for her own needs.

Her mom had stood up for her, saying she was more than prepared for this, but Jenny had heard the doubt in her voice as well. Jenny had failed her winter college term, after all, and opted not to return. What if she *was* too inept to care for herself?

She looked back at Cora. "Perhaps you could drive me to the village when you're finished. I can walk from there."

"Unfortunately, I can't chauffeur today." Cora refocused her attention on the scattered pieces across the table. "Follow the lane down to Ambleside—it's only about twenty minutes by bicycle. Just stay on the left-hand side of the road so you don't get plowed over by a car or motorbike."

Jenny groaned inwardly. Perhaps it might take twenty minutes if one knew how to ride a bicycle. It would take her a whole lot longer to reach the town. "Perhaps Mr. Banks could take me," she suggested.

Cora shook her head. "He's not here this morning."

"I can wait—"

"Watch for dark clouds," Cora continued. "The weather can change in an instant around here."

Jenny almost inquired again about Mr. Banks, but a shadow darkened Cora's eyes with her warning. Jenny's nosiness often got her into trouble, and she didn't want to upset her hostess if this was one of those topics that should be swept under endless reams of carpet.

"I don't mind the rain," Jenny said.

Cora eyed the box coat that dropped over the waist of Jenny's capris. "Borrow my oilskin coat, just in case. And use the tarpaulin in the basket to cover your camera bag."

Outside, Jenny examined the bicycle wheels and seat before folding Cora's coat and tarpaulin, placing them both into the basket with her other things. Then she reached for the handles and positioned the cycle on her right side.

She'd certainly seen a number of women ride bicycles, especially during the three years she'd attended college at Flora Stone Mather in Cleveland. Surely she could learn to ride as well.

Lifting her leg over the low bar, she straddled the bike frame, both feet still firmly on the ground. With one hand braced against the wall, she tried to position both feet on the pedals, but her body teetered right, one foot planting itself back on the driveway.

Slowly, she inched out of the courtyard, away from Cora's view, and tried to balance again. Her fellow students had made it look so simple, riding their bicycles with one hand while clinging to a hat or handbag with their free hand. How had they accomplished this feat?

Perhaps it was too late for her to learn. Perhaps it was like the schoolwork that her classmates understood easily, work that proved almost impossible for her.

But she didn't want to quit. At least not yet.

Clutching the handlebars, she shuffled with her feet on the ground before attempting to ride again. The brakes, she discovered on flat land, were her friend.

The twenty minutes down into Ambleside turned into an hour as she alternated between learning how to pedal and walking alongside the bicycle so she wouldn't tumble down the hill.

Even though she wanted to soak in the beauty around her, this trip was about much more than biking and taking photographs. Before she married Robert—if she married him—she needed to prove to herself that she could embrace life on her own. If something happened to her future husband and she couldn't care for herself, she'd have to return to her grandfather's prison of a house. She feared those walls would suffocate her as they'd done with her mom.

A sash of mauve and coral rhododendron wrapped around the shores of Windermere, and she parked her bicycle beside a drystone wall before walking the last quarter mile into town, glad to rely on her legs instead of wheels that had no loyalty whatsoever to her.

A steeple rose from Ambleside's center, and she snapped several photographs of the church and sprawling cemetery with its tombstones partially hidden in the overgrown grass. They almost seemed rooted in the earth, like Cora's meteor glass.

Her hometown of Cleveland basked in the modern, from the glittery lights on the theater marquees to the hundreds of automobiles that crowded the streets as locals drove downtown for the shops and popular nightclubs. Here, it seemed, the buildings had been erected a century, if not centuries, ago along the rambling back lanes, with more bicycles than automobiles rolling across the cobblestones.

Walking down Main Street, she passed a soda fountain—called a milk bar—and one theater, but no nightclubs. At the chemist, she purchased a pint of ginger beer, crackers, cheese, and a thin bar called Kendal Mint Cake that the clerk insisted she try. Jenny asked her directions to Enchanted Isle, but the girl said she'd only lived here for a year. Perhaps the park, the girl said, had been dismantled, like the flying boat factory on Windermere after the war.

Disappointed, Jenny returned to her bicycle and stored her food under her camera bag. The amusement park may be gone, but plenty of lakes and fells remained to photograph. Her confidence increased as she and her bike wobbled around the shore, her gaze wandering occasionally from her shaky handlebars to the landscape around her. Dozens of daffodils sprayed the grassy bank with yellow blossoms, and birds swept low above the rippled water.

The air was cold, but still a boat cruised near the shore, its fumes wafting inland in the breeze. She heard laughter from the passengers and the driver—for a moment, she thought he looked like the man she'd seen at the train station, though she couldn't tell the color of the driver's hair. She only caught a glimpse of his face and cap, blurry in the distance, before he turned with his passengers to look at the land on the other side of the lake. The boat reached what seemed to be the end of the lake, and then it turned left, disappearing behind the trees.

A gray heron skirted the water, and she snapped a picture of its flight before tucking her camera back into its case. The lake was beautiful, but she wanted to explore the fells behind her. Perhaps even find another lake.

Turning from the water, she glanced at her guidebook and then pedaled toward another hill, balancing and steering her bicycle as if she'd been cycling for years. The accomplishment invigorated her. Her legs ached, but pedaling uphill was much easier than trying to cruise down.

A magenta-colored heather carpeted the fell on both sides of her as she climbed, and in the distance, she saw some sort of ancient building, like one of the abbeys from her history books. Leaving her bicycle against a stone wall, she hiked to the abandoned building, both her camera and lunch in hand, and found a bench under the long portico to spread her lunch. Any monks who'd lived and worshipped here were long gone, yet a peace lingered.

In the quiet, a new freedom seemed to break through the soil inside her. No one here was telling her what she should or shouldn't do, whether or not she should be riding a bicycle or trekking on her own through the fells, whether she was acting like a lady or a tramp. In that freedom, perhaps she could discover exactly who God had made her to be, away from the daunting expectations of her grandfather.

Almost two decades ago, Stephan McAdam had carefully groomed his only son to take over the McAdam manufacturing dynasty, but the war was no respecter of persons, even for him, leaving only a daughter and granddaughter. Now her grandfather wanted both women out of his business, married off instead.

Last fall he'd urged Liz to marry a prominent businessman from Detroit, which was ironic because Grandfather thought nothing good came out of Michigan, a sentiment that went way back to her great-grandfather's raging competition with a man by the name of Henry Ford. While others were manufacturing horseless carriages run on gasoline or steam in the late 1800s, Jenny's great-grandfather had manufactured one of the finest electric cars in the country. He'd taken numerous risks to do so until Ford's gasoline cars took over Detroit first and then the rest of their country.

Her great-grandfather had to resort to building parts for his opposition's Model T. The parts made their family wealthy as Dad and Grandfather continued building them for companies like General Motors and Chrysler through the Second World War, but satisfaction hardly followed the money. Grandfather now refused to build anything for Ford's company.

Jenny's father, Jack Winter, had died almost four years ago in one of Grandfather's factories, an accident that stole away his life and the life of the foreman. Grandfather had selected Jack as his daughter's future husband before she'd even graduated from high school. Liz had married him to make Grandfather happy, but his happiness was fleeting. He'd kept Jack firmly under control, angry that the man had never produced a grandson for him, as if Jack and Liz had personally tried to thwart his plans. Then after Jack was gone, Liz had refused to marry any of the men who he'd paraded before her including the one from Michigan.

When his daughter wouldn't cooperate, Grandfather had set his sights on Jenny, deciding she should marry one of his managers, a man named Robert Tripp. Robert was a decade older than her and quite the fuddy-duddy; at least that's what she had determined after a certain ice cream social when he'd not only refused to dance but also refused to eat anything sweet.

Her nose crinkled at the memory. What kind of person didn't eat sweets? Not the type she wanted to marry. Defiantly, Jenny selected the Kendal Mint Cake from her bag and ate it first, the smooth peppermint-and-sugar bar melting in her mouth.

It was beyond her grandfather's realm of plausibility to think she might only marry for love. Robert was a man her grandfather respected, responsible and good with numbers, but he didn't seem to enjoy Jenny's company any more than she enjoyed his.

Her mom approved of a marriage between Jenny and Robert, prizing security for Jenny over love. But Jenny's parents had enjoyed both love and security for more than fifteen years. That's what she wanted. A marriage to a man more like her father than grandfather.

Even though she'd cared for her husband, her mom never seemed to really mourn her loss, burrowing down instead in a sadness that lingered like the quietness in this abbey. Sometimes Jenny wondered if her mom needed to wander a bit, if that was why she'd encouraged Jenny to visit England before she was boxed into a life of strict regulations and society rules and the kingdom that Stephan McAdam had built.

Jenny leaned her head back on the mossy stone, wind cresting over her face. And with the wind came voices.

Her mind conjured up fairies in the pine trees around her—ornery ones whispering about the human girl who'd stepped into their playground. They were hiding behind the branches, peeking out at her.

Jenny wished they were real. She'd join them in their play.

The voices continued, and Jenny packed her remaining food into her bag and wandered out from under the covering, through the trees into a field of tall grasses on the hillside. Instead of fairies, three men and a woman, not much older than Jenny, were digging in the plateau about twenty or so yards away. Jenny watched them from a distance until she felt a drop of rain on her hand. Then a drop splashed her cheek.

The group began to scatter, and when she looked up, she realized the clouds had soaked up a dark indigo color, pregnant with rain. She raced back toward her bicycle before it poured, tucking her camera case under the waterproof cloth. Then she buttoned Cora's oilskin coat over her blouse and corduroys.

Using her brakes and the basket lamp, she bounced back down the rocky path, soaking her beige Keds and ankles each time she stopped to balance herself in the puddles. But she hardly felt the cold rain on her hands and face.

When the rain subsided, she'd return to photograph the abbey and maybe find the old amusement park to photograph for her mom. Perhaps it would remind Liz of a time when she'd been independent as well.

CHAPTER 3

Water streaked through Jenny's hair as she unlatched the gate into Cora's courtyard, the rain soaking her cheeks and effectively washing away any remnants of powder and lipstick.

Cora's Fiat wasn't outside, but Jenny still called the woman's name as she hung her coat on a hook inside the kitchen door and slid off her sopping Keds and socks. She padded down the tiled hallway with her damp feet, glancing into the front room and then outside the window at the studio before moving upstairs to change. The last thing she needed was to catch a nasty cold on her second day in England.

In the downstairs bathroom, she splashed warm water on her face, washing away the cold, and wrapped her hair in the towel. With a weary yawn, she moved toward the steps, the muscles in her legs burning even as she shivered from the chill on her skin.

When Cora returned home, Jenny would inquire about a blow-dryer. If she was still awake. Her eyelids hung heavy, two curtains about to fall for the night. She just didn't want them to close until she collapsed into her bed, tired but pleased that she'd pedaled up most of the hill to Cora's house without falling.

A knock on the front door startled her, and she paused, waiting for the housekeeper to answer it like in Cleveland. But no one rushed toward the sitting room. Jenny wouldn't answer the door—no one in England would be visiting her, and she certainly didn't want one of Cora's friends to see her in this state.

Then again, what if Cora was knocking? Jenny had locked the side door after she'd found it open, and it was quite possible that her host hadn't taken a key. Perhaps she should peek outside, just in case.

She walked into the front room, but Cora, it seemed, hadn't concerned herself with locking the front door either, because seconds later it opened. A middle-aged man a good decade older than Cora stepped into the room and shook raindrops off the sleeves of his black overcoat. Rain had puddled up on top of his pomade-coated hair, dripping down toward his ears as he scanned the room. "Who are you?" he demanded.

Jenny braced herself on the arm of the sofa, a hundred thoughts colliding in her mind. In Cleveland, no one would ever walk into someone else's house unless they were related. Was this Mr. Banks? If so, why would he knock on the door before entering his home?

She eyed the telephone sitting on the end table a few feet away. Not that this man would allow her to make a telephone call, but if she could just knock it off the hook, perhaps the operator would make an emergency call for her.

She stepped toward the table. "I was going to ask you the same question."

The man removed his coat and hung it on the rack, the door still open behind him. "I'm Cora's husband."

Jenny reached up to pat back her hair but felt the edge of the towel instead. Blast it all, how was she supposed to have an adult conversation with a towel wrapped around her head? "My apologies, Mr. Banks."

"Former husband would be more accurate, I suppose, but Cora and I are on friendly enough terms." He eyed the phone near her. "Should I phone for the police, or are you and Cora on friendly terms as well?"

Why hadn't Cora told her that she was divorced?

Jenny stood up straighter, trying to feign confidence. This man may have been married to Cora once, but Jenny didn't like him much. "I'm Cora's guest."

"A paying guest?"

"I don't believe that's any of your—"

"Stop harassing her, Perry." Cora stepped through the door and dropped her wicker handbag onto the sofa. A lipstick container and wallet fell onto the rug. "Jenny is correct. You no longer have any right to my business, and you certainly don't have any right to hers."

Perry remained focused on Jenny. "Where do you come from?"

She didn't answer. Cora had already said that her business was not for Perry Banks.

"She's from America," Cora said, moving in front of her. "It's probably best for you to wait upstairs, Jenny."

"Gladly."

But she didn't go far. The top step was about fifteen feet or so above the sitting room, and she stopped there.

"How are you, Cora, love?" Perry asked.

"Don't call me love," Cora said, clearly irritated.

"But I do love you, Cora. Always have and always will."

There was a pause. "What do you want?"

"Why must I want something—"

"Money?"

Jenny heard a whooshing noise as if he'd collapsed down onto the sofa. "Have I done something to offend you?"

"I'd need hours to list your offenses."

Perry sighed. "I suppose a little money would help. I've found myself in a bit of a bind."

"You must be desperate to come begging again."

"I'm not begging. You asked what I needed, and I'm telling you."

Jenny crossed her arms over her chest, wanting to defend Cora against this snake of a man, like she wanted to defend her mom whenever Grandfather lit into her about her attire or cooking or for showing up tardy for an event without asking why she happened to be late.

"You would have plenty of money if you'd sell that blooming park," Cora said. "More money than even you would know what to do with."

"I'm not selling it."

"And why would you?" Cora snorted. "That would be the sensible thing to do."

"I have a new business venture," he said. "I will pay you back every dollar I borrow."

"And the money you borrowed for your last business. And perhaps the one before it."

"This venture can't fail, love. It's foolproof."

Cora's laugh sounded raw. "Then perhaps it will be successful."

Perry didn't respond to her slight. Jenny thought perhaps he'd finally left until she heard him speak again.

"I only need a few hundred quid, Cora. Then I'll leave you be."

From her perch on the steps, Jenny wasn't certain that Cora groaned, perhaps because she groaned for her.

"You never leave me be," Cora said.

Fog had settled over Windermere in place of rain, the mist a perfect cloak for Adrian and his canoe as he cruised quietly across the water, around the tip of Enchanted Isle. Even though he couldn't see much in front of him, he knew the exact number of strokes to paddle from his family's boathouse to the bay on the northwest side. One hundred and sixty, if he timed it right.

Tonight, he'd have preferred to use the small motorboat docked in his family's boathouse in case he needed to cruise quickly away from the island, but lately that boat had a mind of its own, starting—or not starting—whenever it pleased, and he didn't want to bother with having to fix it on the island. So, he selected the reliable canoe once owned by his father.

His dad had died during the war, and in the months after, Adrian had paddled over to the island often, as if the ghost of his father still lingered there. Often he would spend the night walking around the park, talking to his dad.

He'd idolized his father when he was a boy—until he'd discovered that his father wasn't even close to being a saint. How could someone Adrian had admired so much turn out to be a criminal? Years had passed since his uncle Gilbert had told him what happened on this island, and Adrian still hadn't been able to reconcile Gilbert's story with the man he remembered.

As he grew older, Adrian no longer sought out even the memory of his dad.

Ghosts weren't real, he'd realized, at least not the kind where someone returned from the dead to talk with his son. But plenty of ghosts still rooted around in Adrian's past, haunting him.

Once he stepped onto shore, a stack of rags in his hand, he flicked on his electric torch, the light fading into the fog. There was once a pier here, but it had collapsed years ago, along with almost everything else on this island. Instead of tying the canoe to a dock, he pulled the bow up onto the shingle beach and secured it to a tree.

More than fifty years ago, the Kemp family had purchased this island and a hundred acres on shore for a farm and the inn. Perry Banks had since acquired the island for a pittance, but why he kept the ownership was beyond Adrian. The man no longer lived in the district, and he did nothing with the island except let it rot.

Sometimes Adrian wished he could buy the place himself, redeem it in a way. Perhaps he could turn it into a nature preserve for his sister Emma's guests.

Even if Adrian had the money, Perry would never sell the island to him or anyone in his family, but it hadn't stopped him from wondering, at least until he reminded himself that such dreams were dangerous. His father had spent most of his life with his head swimming in the clouds, as if no one had ever told him that he couldn't fly.

Reality is where Adrian decided to ground himself, with a solid plan for the future.

After graduation, he'd been offered a position with a bank in London, the manager promising to move Adrian up quickly through the ranks. At one time, he'd intended to use his business degree to partner with Emma at the inn, but she was more than capable of managing the place on her own. And no good reason remained for him to stay here after the summer.

The torchlight guiding his feet, Adrian hurried up an overgrown path and then onto what was once the wide midway between rides, a path his dad must have walked hundreds if not thousands of times. Trees leaned in on both sides of the abandoned rides, as if Mother Nature was forming a canopy to protect what remained.

He stopped in front of the merry-go-round and began cleaning the debris off the platform, wiping off the seats of sea creatures that had once transported their passengers through an imaginary lagoon. Some of the creatures were missing from the platform, probably taken away by kids who snuck over here, daring each other to vandalize the place or searching for a treasure rumored to be buried here, one more legend of many in these Lakes.

He'd asked his dad about a treasure once, when they'd been searching for a lost sheep. The question startled his dad; then he'd told Adrian that he had found gold on the island long ago. Adrian inquired about it again, before his dad left for war, but that time his father denied finding anything.

Years later, his mother had confirmed what Adrian already knew: that the idea of a treasure was a farce, a figment in the scrambled mind of a man who'd lost his way. She never believed in a treasure, nor did she seem to mourn the loss of her husband, at least not like Adrian had when news arrived from Belgium that the enemy had shot down his plane.

Four months later, his mother had left him in his sister Emma's care when she'd moved to Manchester to start a new family. Emma was only eight years his senior, but she'd been much more of a mother to him than their own mum.

The war, Emma had told him repeatedly, was a horrific time for all of them. They shouldn't judge the actions of a recently widowed woman who'd already been plagued for more than a decade by rumors that her husband had stolen money and killed a man.

Still, it wasn't right to leave a nine-year-old boy without a mother. Emma was a brilliant sister who'd raised him until he left for Hong Kong. By that time, she'd had two sons of her own, and they would both grow up, he feared, under a cloud of gossip as well.

Long ago, he'd done a little digging for treasure, back in the forest on this island. In some strange way, the legend of treasure helped keep the legacy of his father alive. He'd never found anything—nor would he, chasing the mumblings of a man who'd gone mad.

But the island kept calling to him. He'd refused to succumb to its whispers of hidden treasure, but he still returned on foggy nights like this. Except instead of digging, he cleaned up some of the mess his father had left behind.

CHAPTER 4

"Now you've had the privilege of meeting my ex-husband," Cora said as she slid into the chair beside Jenny.

Jenny nodded slowly, taking a sip of the warm milk spiced with cinnamon that she'd opted to drink instead of tea before bed. "He made quite the entrance."

"I'm sorry he startled you." Steam billowed from Cora's mug until she topped her tea with milk.

"He knocked once and then walked right in." Jenny cringed again at the memory. Her hands, wrapped around the warm mug, had finally stopped shaking.

"It's been ten months since the divorce," Cora said. "Perry lives someplace north of here now, but he still thinks he owns this house."

"Mom didn't tell me that you'd divorced."

Cora sipped her tea. "I'm afraid I neglected to share that bit of news when I wrote."

"That's an awfully big item to neglect!"

"I probably should have mentioned it, but I wasn't certain how to broach the subject. Until your mum wrote about this spring, we hadn't communicated in years."

Jenny opted to change the subject. "Where is the park Perry owns?"

Cora leaned back in her chair. "I'm sorry you had to hear us quarrel."

Jenny shrugged. "I've heard worse on the television."

"Even so, I'd appreciate it if you didn't repeat it all to your mum."

Jenny swirled her drink, the milk splashing up on the sides. "Mom and I tell each other pretty much everything."

"Of course." Cora patted her hand. "I wouldn't want you to keep secrets from her."

"Before I left, she told me about a place called Enchanted Isle."

"A lot has changed since the war." Cora refilled her mug with hot water from the kettle. "Perry bought the park about fifteen years ago, but it's all rack and ruin now, begging for someone to make it pretty again."

"Why won't he sell it?"

"The judge asked him the same thing during divorce court." Cora wrapped both her hands around her cup. "I'm afraid you'll have to excuse me. My head's pounding."

"Of course," Jenny said as her hostess stood, the mug still gripped in Cora's hands.

"The headaches come whenever the weather changes."

And perhaps, Jenny thought, when her ex-husband came begging for money.

"There's leftover beef in the icebox. You can heat it up in the cooker." Cora pointed toward the refrigerator before stepping into the corridor.

Jenny found the roast beef on the second shelf but since she still didn't know how to use the cooker, she settled for the rest of the cheese from her lunch, kept dry by the tarpaulin.

After a long bath, she wrapped herself in her robe and escaped to her room. Beside the window was a small desk, and she selected a piece of blue stationery. Yesterday, she'd sent a telegram to her mom saying that she'd arrived safely, but in her letter tonight, she invited her mother on this journey with her by describing Cora's old farmhouse, the photographs she'd taken, the old abbey she discovered on the fell.

She didn't mention Perry. Not because Cora had requested silence, but because she didn't want her mom to be concerned. Hopefully Perry would return to wherever he lived and stay there until she went home.

Her pen poised over the paper, she almost wrote about the man who'd helped her at the railway station, but that might make her mom worry even more. And heaven forbid if Grandfather happened to read her letter. He'd probably send Robert across the Atlantic to retrieve her on one of those new airplane flights.

She finished the letter and licked the two postage stamps that she'd purchased in Ambleside and stuck them onto the envelope. Then she rewound the roll of film stretched across her camera and tucked it back inside its canister.

Rain splattered the window near the desk, and she pressed her hand against the cool glass. Tomorrow she'd ask Cora again where Enchanted Isle was located. Then she'd take pictures of the place and send them in the next letter to her mom. Even if the rides were gone, perhaps the park would remind her mother of a happier season in her life. Perhaps it would make her smile again.

She turned off the lamp and crawled under the thick covers of her bed, repeating her mom's familiar words: *focus on today's successes, not failings.*

Like learning to ride a bicycle and taking photographs of the lake and fells.

In the morning, she'd take her rolls of film to the chemist and then find the park so she could capture it with her camera as well.

A gust of wind rustled the pine trees near the abbey, showering Jenny with needles. She shivered and tucked her gloved hands into the pockets of her winter coat. It was colder than yesterday, but the clouds hadn't made their appearance yet. Cora had already been gone when she'd woken this morning, so Jenny hadn't been able to ask about directions to the park. Instead, she'd borrowed the oilskin coat again to store in her bicycle basket, just in case the rain returned, and headed back to the abbey.

About thirty feet away, the group who'd been digging here yesterday bore their shovels into the ground and added load after load of dirt to the growing pile beside them. Curious, Jenny stepped closer to the group, her camera dangling around her neck. The woman saw her first and waved Jenny forward. Then the three men glanced up, one of them lifting his cap and smiling at her before he resumed his work.

"No photographs, please," the woman said, her accent clearly American. Dressed in a fur-lined hat and long beige cape, she looked as if she was either in college or a recent graduate.

"Why don't you want pictures?" Jenny asked.

"We're working on an excavation." She nodded toward the oldest gentleman. "Trying to keep it hush-hush until after we head back to Cambridge."

"You're archeologists?"

"Three of us are working on anthropology degrees. Professor Thompson is from the university."

Jealousy shot through Jenny, and she fought to douse the familiar poison before it infiltrated. Unlike Jenny, the woman before her probably didn't have any issues with calculating numbers or reading words.

The woman directed her farther away from the group before taking off her work glove to shake Jenny's hand. "My name's Amanda."

"I'm Jenny, from Ohio."

"My family is in Raleigh, North Carolina."

Jenny nodded toward the site. "I suppose I can't ask what you're searching for."

"I wish I could tell you, but Professor Thompson would have my head." She looked genuinely distraught over not being able to share her secret.

Jenny glanced back at the abbey. "There must be a lot of history to excavate around here."

"Loads of it, going back before the birth of Christ. The Celts lived near these lakes, and then the Romans and Vikings."

Jenny eyed the excavation again. "I hope you find something grand."

Amanda smiled. "Thank you."

After Amanda returned to work, Jenny walked back toward the trees and her bicycle, studying her pictorial guide again before continuing up the road. To her left was a tall hedge, to her right, a stone wall about three feet high. On the other side of the wall were a flock of sheep and the peak of one of the fells.

Beyond that, she imagined there would be lakes and waterfalls and perhaps mermaids lounging on flat rocks, sunning themselves when no one was around to catch them at their play. Perhaps they were even flirting with mermen from the deep waters, trying to convince them to brave the surface and enjoy the sun.

Smiling, Jenny pedaled carefully across a mossy bridge made of stone and wood, her bicycle bumping on the planks as she crossed the creek.

Before her dad had died, he used to say her imagination would bring her more trouble than good. Her curiosity had certainly gotten her into plenty of scrapes as a child, but she'd never gotten hurt.

As much as she'd loved and respected her dad, she had never been able to figure out what was wrong with being curious when there was so much of the world to experience and embrace. So many wonderful things to see. Her friends thought it odd when she talked about the images that looped through her brain sometimes, so she guarded these pictures closely now, traveling alone in her mind journey around the world.

Grandfather feared that actual travel would ruin her, but she had perused pictures in volumes and volumes about art, history, geography, and the ancient places like Egypt and Greece. She'd loved the photographs in her books and knew every detail of them. It was reading and *remembering* all the dates and facts in those same books that had been torturous.

School had never been easy for her with all the words and numbers—her archenemies—that tangled in her mind. Her eighth-grade teacher once told her parents that they needed to adjust their expectations for her future. His words had certainly adjusted her own. For the next four years of high school, her mind had wandered as her grades plummeted far below the average. During her college years, her grandfather had plenty of things to say about her intelligence, about her treatment of life as a game. School, she'd once heard him say, was completely wasted on her. Why educate someone who couldn't seem to recall anything of use?

Still, her mother had insisted on college, and Jenny wanted to do well, truly, but her mind kept getting in the way. Life, it seemed to her, was a giant canvas waiting for an artist to dip into jars of paint and stroke the brilliant colors across its spread. Letters and numbers, on the other hand, boxed people into much smaller spaces, though most people seemed to respect the confinement of what they knew and understood.

Words and numbers weren't easy, but pictures she understood at the deepest level—the emotions of a piece, the colors, the position of every person or building or leaf within the perimeter of a frame. Art seemed like the best choice for a major, but she'd discovered last fall that she would need more than a love of pictures to finish her degree.

Robert agreed with Grandfather. College, he thought, was entirely unnecessary for her, but still the dream of it nagged at her. Like Amanda, perhaps one day she could graduate from school.

After she crossed the creek, the borders of yew and stone disappeared, opening up to the expanse of a brown field powdered a royal blue from the wildflowers. There were more sheep here—their fleece a dark gray except for the lambs. They were all black. Was this pasture once a battlefield, the Vikings or Romans fighting on these hills?

The road split, and she chose the rocky path to the right, the stones too big for a car to maneuver around. Her leg muscles burned as she pedaled up the steep trail, and she distracted herself through a new movie of her own creation.

The sheep became Romans, a legion marching over the hill with their silver armor, shields, and spears, the ground trembling from the pounding of boots. Behind her marched the fierce Vikings, their long, scraggly beards blowing in the wind, their faces entirely masked by helmets. Hundreds of wooden Viking boats filled with more soldiers arriving by sea.

When metal clashed, she shook away the image of a battle. Sometimes her imagination took her up and down the wrong trails. She wanted to see beauty in these lakes, not death—docile sheep and delicate flowers, not battling soldiers.

Even though her face was cold, sweat pooled underneath her winter coat and clothing. Still, she wouldn't stop pedaling until she reached the top of the hill. Ahead was the promise of a spectacular view and lunch served straight from the paper bag in her basket.

With her gaze focused on the ground, she dodged stone after stone in her path. But she didn't dare look up, afraid she'd lose her

Melanie Dobson

determination in the face of distance or teeter and fall. She focused on rotating the pedals, round and round, even if they didn't seem to be taking her far. This felt much more like a mountain than a moorland hill.

Finally, she crested the top, her lungs aching as she climbed off the seat. The wind was blowing too strongly to use her kickstand, so she laid her bicycle on the lichen and hiked toward the rocky ledge.

No trees stood on this peak, but a magnificent view of the valley stretched out below her. A river carved through the flowers and grass, weaving around a farm before spilling into a lake at the valley's end.

The stamp of God's beauty was everywhere—in the stones and smooth ribbon of water, the sheep dotting the landscape, the carpet of bluebells. She wished she could bike down to the lake in the distance, but cycling back up this fell again today would prove disastrous. Not only did every muscle in her body ache, but she'd never get there and back before dark. Perhaps it was the lingering images of Romans and Vikings in her brain, but she didn't want to be pedaling up this fell by the strands of light from a bicycle lamp.

A sharp gust pierced through her coat, and above her, dark clouds spread like tar across the sky. She snapped several photographs of the river before retrieving her lunch—a brown bag with two eggs, already boiled and peeled, along with an apple and two Kendal Mint Cakes.

Before she began eating, something wet dashed her nose. She thought the afternoon rains had returned until she saw white flakes powdering her sleeve.

Back in Ohio, they didn't have a heritage of Romans or Vikings, but they had plenty of snow. When it started falling, Cleveland residents holed up in their homes, sometimes for days, until the storm passed.

She glanced around again as if a shelter might appear, but there was no place to hide in a snowstorm. She tossed the tarpaulin over her remaining lunch and the camera bag in the basket. Then she exchanged her winter coat for Cora's brown one. It wasn't as warm, but it would keep the wet flakes from soaking into her skin.

Slowly she pedaled down the hill, wishing she could release the pedals and succumb to gravity, but the rocks on the path would surely catapult her, perhaps over the ledge. At this pace, she feared it would take more than an hour for her to return to the warmth of Cora's home.

CHAPTER 5

Adrian leaned into the turn on his motorbike as he sped up the country lane, icy rain flogging his cap and leather jacket. The valley hadn't seen snow in years, but if the temperature kept dropping, perhaps it would make an appearance tonight. The hotel guests would be thrilled—instead of a boat ride, perhaps he could take a group of them sledging down a hill tomorrow beside the inn.

Reaching behind him, he checked the saddlebag. Inside was a loaf of freshly baked brown bread, covered with plastic wrap, and a thermos filled with stew. Gifts from Emma to Mrs. Moore, their friend who lived alone in this narrow valley.

As much as he enjoyed spending time with Mrs. Moore, he wouldn't be able to linger long this afternoon. Oscar, the hotel's maintenance man, was out for the day, and Emma needed his help shoveling coke for the boiler. Then Gilbert had asked him to check on six ewes who were about to lamb.

As he neared the split-off to Loughrigg Fell, Adrian slowed his motorbike. Someone was alongside the wet road, kneeling by a yew hedge.

At first he thought it was a walker, though he couldn't imagine someone trying to trek through the fells in this miserable weather. But it was a woman leaning over a bicycle, an oversized coat draped over her, strands of caramel-colored hair tumbling from her wrinkled scarf.

He stepped off his motorbike and swallowed hard when she looked up at him. It was the pretty girl from Windermere.

"Hello again," he said, clutching his handlebars. "What happened to your bicycle?"

She tucked her arms into the wide sleeves of her coat as if to bundle herself away. "Flat tire."

"Luggage I can carry, but"—he eyed the bicycle—"I'm afraid I can't carry that all the way into town."

A smile slipped across her lips, underscoring the bright red in her cheeks. "I don't expect you to."

He glanced up the deserted road. "How long have you been here?"

She shivered, the rain dripping down her face and coat. "About a half hour."

"The road ends in a mile," he said. "Typically only bikers and walkers come this way for the path over Loughrigg Fell, but no one would climb the fells in this weather."

She sighed. "No one except me."

"You are certainly exceptional, Miss—"

"Please call me Jenny."

"Jenny it is. I assume Cora told you my name."

She nodded. "Adrian."

"Did she tell you my story as well?"

She wrapped her arms across her chest. "No, but she doesn't seem to like you much."

"An understatement, I'm afraid."

She tilted her head. "Why exactly doesn't she like you?"

He glanced up at the dark sky. "Perhaps we could have that conversation another time. I'm afraid we're about to get soaked."

She pointed toward the peak behind them. "It was snowing on top of Loughrigg."

"Then it's coming our way." He resumed his seat on the motorbike. "I have to make a delivery, and then I can give you a lift back to Cora's house."

"I'd be grateful for the ride, but I hate to leave the bicycle."

"I'll bring a patch and pump back in the morning to fix your tire. And give you a ride back up here as well, if you'd like."

She shivered again in the breeze. "Doubly grateful, then."

After retrieving the things from her basket, she slipped onto the motorbike behind him, sandwiching her camera case between them as she held on to the sides of his jacket.

He didn't believe in fate, like he didn't believe in ghosts, but he believed firmly in Providence. And he prayed as he drove toward Mrs. Moore's house, thanking God for sending him along this road.

Then he prayed an altogether different prayer. If Cora hadn't already told Jenny about Tom, he prayed that Mrs. Moore wouldn't tell her today. That was a story he'd like to tell Jenny on his own.

Mrs. Moore greeted Jenny with a warm smile before shaking her gloved hand. Jenny attempted to smile in return, but her teeth were chattering so hard that she nodded instead. Cold had seeped through every inch of her skin, taking hold in her muscles and bones.

The older woman wore a wraparound housedress with two large pockets in front. Her short brown hair was salted gray, and wrinkles radiated from her eyes like rays from the sun. A fire blazed in the corner of her cozy living room, and along the wall, between Jenny and the fire, stood a long bookcase stained mahogany brown. At least a dozen framed black-and-white photographs were propped up on the shelves, all displaying a boy who grew in pictures to a man about twenty years old.

Jenny studied one of the portraits as she passed it. The man was standing beside a motorbike, a confident grin on his lips, his hair buzzed short.

"Is this your son?" she asked, rubbing her hands together to ward off the chill.

A look passed between Adrian and Mrs. Moore, as if Jenny had asked the oddest of questions. "It is," Mrs. Moore replied.

Sadness settled into Mrs. Moore's pretty eyes, and Jenny wondered if the relationship between mother and son had been severed in recent years. Or perhaps he'd passed on.

"He looks like a gentleman," Jenny said, her teeth chattering.

"Indeed."

Adrian handed the older woman a thermos and a loaf of bread wrapped with clear plastic. Mrs. Moore thanked him and then stepped toward the arched opening at the side of the room. Jenny could see the corner of an icebox beyond it. "You must be famished," Mrs. Moore said.

"I'm afraid we can't stay long," Adrian said, though he removed his wet coat and cap, hanging them beside the door. His wet hair, curling at his temples, made him look more like a boy than a man. "Emma and Gilbert both need my help tonight, and I must return Jenny home before the weather worsens."

"Surely there's time for a cup of tea."

When Adrian glanced over, he must have seen the desperation on her face, because he said they'd both be grateful for a cuppa.

Jenny smiled as well, trying to stop her teeth from chattering as she moved toward the fire. "Tea would be lovely."

"Splendid," Mrs. Moore said from inside the kitchen. "So new to England and already talking like a proper Englishwoman."

Jenny placed Mrs. Moore on her mental list of favorite people.

The woman poked her head out, a kettle in one hand. "Go warm yourselves by the fire."

Adrian stepped beside Jenny, and she wasn't quite certain what else to say, already feeling awkward about having to ride with him on the motorbike. But Mrs. Moore broke the silence. As she bustled in the kitchen, she chattered about the changing weather, the upcoming election, and the red deer that wouldn't stay out of her garden.

Jenny's fingers stung as she removed her gloves, and when she reached toward the blaze, heat seared through her skin, melting the ice that had wound tightly around each and every joint. She pulled her hands away from the fire to stop the burning inside her fingers, but it kept smoldering.

She'd been foolish, bicycling to the top of that hill with the threat of changing weather. Of all things she'd tried to prepare for on this trip, snow hadn't been one of them. Or a flat tire, for that matter.

But she was pleased to see Adrian again, even if she wasn't quite certain what to say. Now hardly seemed the opportune time to discuss why Cora disliked him.

Mrs. Moore brought two cups of milky tea to the fire. Adrian took his offered cup, but when Jenny reached for the white handle of the other one, her fingers refused to curl around it.

"You poor lass," Mrs. Moore said, setting the cup on a table. "You're freezing."

Jenny's teeth chattered again. "I wasn't expecting snow up on the fell."

"Aye. You never know what the weather will be like around here. It can change without the slightest regard for a notice." Mrs. Moore took Jenny's hands and rubbed them gently between her warm ones. "What were you doing on the fell?"

"Taking pictures," she explained. "I wanted to capture the beauty for people back home to see."

"Now that is a worthy endeavor."

The burning in her fingers began to subside into a pleasant warmth. "Thank you."

When Mrs. Moore released her hands, Jenny could grasp the handle of the cup. The liquid soothed her throat, rustling some of the chill from her bones.

"Have you visited Buttermere yet?" Mrs. Moore asked.

Jenny shook her head.

"Adrian must take you there and perhaps up to Hardknott when the rain stops."

A thread of pink ribboned across his firm jaw. "Perhaps I shall, if she'd like to see those places."

When he looked at her, she nodded. "I'd love to see them."

"Then it's settled." Mrs. Moore clapped her hands. "You can borrow my car to explore, and for that matter, you can borrow it tonight to drive back into town."

"We can't take it tonight," Adrian insisted. "You might have an emergency."

"I can't imagine any reason why I'd need it." She looked at the table. "I've forgotten the biscuits, haven't I?"

"We don't need biscuits," he said, but she was already shuffling toward the kitchen.

"You don't have to tour the Lakes with me," Adrian whispered while Mrs. Moore was out of the room.

"But I'd like to go," Jenny said. "What's Hardknott?"

"An old pass with a Roman fort, all in ruins now."

"This morning I saw a group from Cambridge digging nearby, but they wouldn't tell me what they were searching for."

Mrs. Moore reentered the room with a tray of shortbread cookies. "People will say they're searching for artifacts, but most of them are treasure hunters looking for a fortune in old coins."

Jenny finished her tea as a picture pressed into her mind, a thousand golden coins spilling from an ancient chest. "It must be fascinating to find old treasure, though. Like uncovering a pirate's cache."

"Every piece of a pirate's cache was stolen from someone else," Mrs. Moore said sadly. "More loss than gain, I think, especially when it's passed along on the black market."

Droplets of blood replaced the coins in Jenny's mind, trickling from the chest like rain.

She shook her head to rid her mind of the image. Sometimes she hated the pictures that formed in her brain.

Adrian cleared his throat, nodding toward the window. "It's raining harder."

Mrs. Moore set the biscuits on the table. "Are you certain you don't want to borrow my car?"

"Quite," Adrian said as he retrieved his coat.

"Perhaps we can phone Cora," Jenny suggested. "She could come for us."

Mrs. Moore shook her head. "I'm afraid I don't have a telephone."

"I'm sorry . . ."

"There's nothing for you to be sorry about. It's simple enough to make a telephone call from Ambleside."

Adrian buttoned his coat. "And the precise reason why you need to keep your car."

Mrs. Moore hugged Jenny. "Sleep with a hot water bottle tonight."

Jenny agreed before layering on both her coats. Adrian secured her camera case in the saddlebag on his motorbike, and then she climbed onto the seat behind him, holding on to his jacket.

She tried to keep her distance, but every bump inched her forward. Each time, she'd scoot back again, not wanting him to think she was trying to flirt with him like the mermaids who'd been flirting with mermen in her mind.

Adrian steered expertly around the puddles and most of the bumps as they cruised down the hill and through Ambleside, but nothing could be done about the cold rain. If only someone could photograph her whirling across these muddy roads in England, her hair and face sopping, the passenger of a charming stranger. Grandfather would be furious. Mom, she suspected, would have laughed with her.

When Adrian stopped the motorbike outside Cora's gate, Jenny hopped off and unlatched it. "Would you like another cup of tea?"

He eyed Cora's car inside the courtyard and then the light in the window. "Another time, perhaps." He wiped the rain off his forehead with his jacket sleeve. "I can fetch you around eleven tomorrow to fix your tire."

"Thank you."

"I'm sorry that we couldn't borrow Mrs. Moore's car," he said. "If something happened to her, I could never forgive myself."

"It's very admirable of you."

"Not really."

Cora stepped out the side door. "Come inside, Jenny," she called.

Jenny thanked Adrian one last time before rushing indoors.

CHAPTER 6

Steaming water, along with the froth of lavender-scented bubbles, soothed every bone in Jenny until the chill finally drained from her body, replaced with the comfort that only a hot bath and a cup of warm chocolate could bring.

Fortunately Cora had lots of chocolate.

"I can take you to retrieve your bicycle tomorrow," Cora said when Jenny stepped into the kitchen, dressed in her warm cotton robe and slippers.

"I don't know exactly where we left it."

Which wasn't entirely true, but she was much more keen on having Adrian transport her than Cora. And he did know its exact location.

"Where were you riding?" Cora asked as she filled a stockpot with water.

"Up Loughrigg Fell."

Cora eyed her for a moment. "I'm certain we can find it."

"I already promised Adrian that I'd go with him."

Cora glanced down at Jenny's left hand as if she might find an engagement ring there. "Your mom said she wanted you to see England before you married. I assumed that you had a fiancé."

"An understanding," Jenny said, holding up her empty hand. "Not a ring." She'd been informed about her marriage to Robert, not asked. And she'd never actually given an answer. "Why don't you like Adrian?"

"It's not that I don't like him." Cora slowly added new potatoes to the stockpot with a slotted spoon. "I don't trust him."

"Did he lie to you?"

"I'm afraid it's more complicated than that."

Jenny sighed. "My life seems to be full of complications."

Cora lit a match to ignite the gas burner. "This is one complication that you don't need, Jenny. Adrian is reckless like his father, and sometimes he risks too much."

"What's wrong with taking risks?"

"Because sometimes people end up . . ."

Jenny leaned back against the counter. "End up what?"

The telephone rang in the other room, and Cora whisked away to answer it. As she waited for Cora, Jenny opened the silverware drawer and began setting the table for dinner.

She still didn't understand why taking risks was considered a flaw. She'd always admired people willing to take a chance. Try new things.

Besides traveling here alone, she hadn't really taken any risks in her life. Staying with her mother's friend was hardly a daring move, though her journey up the fell today would be considered risky in her world, as was learning how to ride a bicycle.

When Cora returned to the kitchen, she fervently stirred the pot, seeming to vent her frustrations on the potatoes instead of resuming their talk about Adrian or telling Jenny about her phone conversation. Then she removed the chicken from the oven and spooned the boiled potatoes into a bowl.

"Your mum and I hiked up Loughrigg Fell ages ago," Cora said as she filled two plates with food.

"What else did you do together?"

Cora pulled out a chair at the table, and Jenny sat across from her. "On Saturdays, we would watch the speedboat races, and then we'd meet friends afterward at the cafe in Ambleside."

Jenny tried to imagine her mother surrounded by a group of friends, spending a day of leisure watching a race and then drinking a cherry soda or lemonade or whatever they liked to drink back then.

"Mom said she enjoyed visiting Enchanted Isle."

"I suppose so."

"What was your favorite ride?" Jenny asked, slicing through butter molded into a leaf.

"The roller coaster. I screamed like a banshee for ninety seconds and then slipped back into the line to ride it again. I'd spend all my tickets on that one attraction."

"Before my father died, he used to take me to a park called Cedar Point each summer. I liked the roller coasters too." She hadn't realized how hungry she was until she took a bite of the potatoes, soaked now in the melted butter.

"You would have liked Enchanted Isle," Cora said wistfully, her smile fading. "When it was in its prime."

Jenny leaned forward. "Where was the park located?"

"The north end of Windermere, on an island."

"I'd love to see it!"

Cora shook her head. "No one is allowed onto the property. Perry claims there's some sort of curse on the island, making it quite dangerous."

"Do you think it's haunted?"

"Perhaps," Cora said. "People around here certainly think it is."

Jenny lowered her fork. "What happened?"

"Adrian's father was named Simon Kemp." Cora took several bites of chicken. "He built the park with an Irishman named Curtis Sloan, but Curtis disappeared more than twenty years ago. The last time anyone claimed to see him, he was standing at the entrance, helping funnel out visitors on the last night of the season."

She inched forward in her chair. "I wonder where he went."

"Most people think Simon killed him and stole the profits they were supposed to share," Cora said. "No one's been able to prove it because they never found Curtis's body, though sometimes people see lights on the island. Some say his ghost stayed behind, seeking revenge."

Jenny shivered at the thought. "What did Simon Kemp say about the disappearance?"

"That his partner took all their money and hotfooted it out of England."

"Did Simon stay in the Lakes?"

"For a few years. Unfortunately, he died during the war."

Jenny shook her head. "Poor Adrian."

Cora pierced another small potato, holding it on the fork in front of her. "I used to feel sorry for him as well when he was younger, but we each choose our own path in this life. Unfortunately, Adrian has chosen a rocky one."

Jenny's mind wandered to the path she'd pedaled today. It was full of knots and slippery pebbles, but sometimes the rockiest of paths led to glorious things, like rivers and lakes and treasure buried in the ground.

Then again, sometimes they led to storms.

She sneezed.

"I'll clean up here." Cora stacked her silverware on her plate. "You go to bed and sleep as late as you'd like."

"I'm not ill, just cold."

Cora continued, "And no more bicycling until you're well again."

Jenny bristled. "I don't need a chaperone, Cora."

"It's a good thing because I don't have time to be one." When Cora stood, Jenny followed suit. "But Liz will never forgive me if I don't take good care of you—and for that matter, make sure that you become acquainted with people a bit more respectable than Adrian Kemp."

The words made her cringe. Cora surely didn't mean it in the same way as her grandfather would, but it still reminded Jenny of him.

Where was the dividing line between associating with the right and wrong people? For her grandfather, it had more to do with business than anything else, not the moral character of an individual.

"Did Mom know Adrian's family?" she asked as she lowered her plate into the sink.

"I think Liz knew most everyone who lived in Ambleside before summer's end."

"What year did Curtis Sloan disappear?"

"It was 1935."

"Mom was here that summer."

Cora reached for the kettle on the stove. "She was."

If her mom knew most everyone in Ambleside, perhaps she knew one or both the park owners. "Is Mr. Sloan's family still in the area?"

Cora filled a hot water bottle, shaking her head as she worked. "His parents were from Northern Ireland, and he never married."

"But Mr. Kemp had a family—"

"You met Adrian, and Simon's daughter and brother both live in Ambleside." Cora handed her the rubber bottle. "We need to focus on getting you well again, not on things of the past."

Cora turned her attention to the sink, adding a few drops of soap as she streamed water over the dishes. But Jenny couldn't keep her mind from wandering back to what had happened more than twenty years ago, while her mom had been visiting the Lakes.

When she returned to her room, a cup of chocolate in hand, she started another letter to her mother, but she crawled into bed before she finished writing.

That night, she dreamed of a fire raging in the fells.

And giants in armor trying to scale a rocky path.

Vanilla icing, smoothed over a tray of cupcakes. That's what the hills outside Jenny's window looked like when she rubbed a circle on the glass, the frosting of snow flowing down to the lake below.

There'd be no retrieving her bicycle this morning, but perhaps she could still walk to Ambleside and photograph the snow wreathed around the lake. Perhaps the chemist had developed her photographs as well.

Instead of interrupting Cora's work, she left a note on the kitchen counter and bundled herself in dungarees, a woolen sweater, and earmuffs. She'd laughed when her mom suggested that she bring the earmuffs and gloves, but she wasn't laughing now.

No tires had plowed through the snow yet, but plenty of footprints marked the dirt road. The sky was a crisp blue again, and she passed several farms and a general store as she plodded down toward the lake in boots borrowed from Cora's stash of winter clothes.

The surface of Windermere pierced the snow with its midnight-blue sheen, and she snapped several pictures of the water before rewinding her film and threading another roll into her camera. Then she took pictures of a ewe and two lambs cuddled together on the snow.

Near the village was an elegant two-story building called Herdwick Inn, about twenty yards from the water's edge. After hiking down the hill, she decided that hot tea was a necessity before photographing the snowy banks.

Inside, the man behind the counter directed her toward a corridor that doubled as a photo gallery, both walls covered with black-and-white pictures of the hotel, pier, and steamers full of passengers during earlier years. At the end of the hallway were dozens of nature photographs. One of a fell lush with bluebells, a waterfall trickling down between the flowers. Another taken of a brilliant moon rising in its fullness over a lake.

Oh, to be able to shoot photographs like these, framed windows that welcomed in anyone willing to step outside their world into another.

In her pocket was her next roll for the chemist. She had no illusions that her pictures would look like these on the wall, but she'd be thrilled if one or two of them welcomed others into the world she'd seen through her viewfinder.

The corridor opened into a dining room with an expansive view of the lake, two dozen tables arranged neatly on the asphalt-tiled floor. She glanced at the clock near the entrance. It was already almost noon. No wonder she was hungry as well as cold; she'd been walking in the snow for more than two hours.

Two waiters bustled between tables, and a pretty, petite woman in her early thirties approached her from the kitchen door wearing a white blouse, black skirt, and sensible leather pumps. Her dark-umber hair was cut in a pixie, her green eyes glistening.

"I'm Emma, the proprietor of this inn," the woman said. "Are you meeting someone for lunch?"

Jenny's stomach rumbled. "No, but I was hoping for a cup of tea and perhaps a sandwich on my own."

"We have plenty of both." Emma held out her hand. "Could I hang your coat?"

"Yes, please." Jenny unbundled herself from her sage scarf and coat before passing them to the woman.

"It's dreadfully cold out there." Emma nodded toward the window. "We'll make something to warm you right up."

After Emma showed her to a table, Jenny watched a group of determined children outside rolling mounds of snow along the narrow lawn that separated the hotel and lake. They seemed to be trying to make a snowman, but each time their creation grew large enough to be of any use, one of the children would collapse into the pile of snow, returning it to powder.

What if they actually managed to build a man out of the snow? And what if he decided to roll one of the kids around in the snow instead? The children could build more snow people, dozens of them. A colony of snowmen and women laughing and dancing and pelting each other with snowballs.

Minutes later, Emma slipped beside her with a plate of miniature white sandwiches, some filled with sliced cucumbers, others with thinly sliced ham. On her tray was a teapot painted with delicate yellow flowers and two matching cups with a milk pitcher to accompany it.

Jenny smiled. "It looks smashing."

Emma pointed at the empty seat beside her. "Would you mind if I shared tea with you?"

"Not at all."

Emma filled both cups. "My family owns this place, but I rarely get to sit and enjoy the food."

"It's a beautiful inn," Jenny replied, splashing milk into her tea, like her hostess.

"Thank you," Emma said. "My grandfather opened this place decades ago, and it's been a blessing to continue his work."

How fascinating, Jenny thought, for a family's business legacy to be a blessing instead of a curse.

"I like taking care of people." Emma sipped her tea. "My husband says it's a good thing I have the inn, or our home would be bulging with strangers. Here I can host guests all spring and summer long, and everyone has plenty of space."

Jenny smiled. "I'm sure none of them want to return home."

"If that's the case, then I've succeeded at my work," she said with a laugh. "What is your name?"

"Jenny Winter."

Emma nodded at the blanket of snow on the other side of the glass. "A timely name."

"And an ironic one too as I grew up in northern Ohio, where it feels like winter half the year. I much prefer spring and summer."

Emma nudged the plate of sandwiches forward, and Jenny took one. "Are you staying in our district for long?"

"Almost two months."

"Then you shall have both winter and spring in the Lakes and perhaps a few days of summer as well."

As Jenny ate the ham sandwich with mustard, the sound of laughter trickled into the dining room. The children had managed to create two lumps of somewhat circular snow for their snowman. One of the older boys turned and waved.

"That's my son," Emma said, waving back at him. "Do you think we should take him and his crew a carrot for the nose?"

Jenny nodded. "Every snowman must have an orange nose."

"Quite true, and a few pieces of coking coal for the mouth and eyes." Emma turned back toward the restaurant's entrance and waved again, this time at someone inside the dining room. "I'd like to introduce you to my brother."

Seconds later, Adrian stepped up beside them. His curly hair was combed back, and his eyes lit with a smile when he saw her.

"Hello, Jenny."

Emma glanced between the two of them. "Apparently, you two have already met."

"Briefly," Jenny said, looking back at Emma. "He helped me with my luggage at the railway station and again yesterday, when I punctured my bicycle tire."

Emma smiled. "Then you're old chums by now."

Jenny shook her head. "Not exactly . . ."

"Acquaintances, Emma." Adrian reached for one of the sandwiches on the plate. "Amiable ones."

"Amiable," Jenny repeated with a nod.

He glanced out the window before turning back toward Jenny. "I'm afraid we'll have to wait until the snow melts to return you to your bicycle, but no one will bother with it in this weather."

Emma seemed to examine Jenny before speaking again. "Have you ever been sledging?"

She tilted her head. "What's sledging?"

Emma looked as if Jenny had lost her mind. "It's when you ride a sledge down a hill."

Jenny smiled. "You mean *sledding*?"

"I mean sledging," Emma replied, as if the British version always trumped the American word.

"I've never been sledding or sledging before."

"Surely you have snow in Ohio," Adrian said as he reached for a second sandwich.

"Plenty of it, but my family spends most of the winter inside."

"Don't you like being outdoors?" Emma asked.

"I like it very much," she said. More than she had ever imagined.

Adrian pointed toward the window. "I'm preparing to take a group in the next hour. The slope might be more mud than snow, but we'll have fun."

Jenny eyed the snow again. She'd certainly seen children sled down the hills back home, but she'd never been invited to do it herself. What would it feel like to whisk down a snow-covered hill on some sort of board?

"I'll need a lesson first."

Emma stood from the table. "I'm certain Adrian would oblige."

He shot his sister a look that Jenny couldn't quite define. "You just hold on to the rope handle and push off the ground. The hill does the rest of the work."

Jenny leaned back, wondering again at the thought of it. Could she do that, simply hold on to a rope and slide?

Emma lifted the plate of sandwiches. "I wish I could join you."

Adrian kissed his sister's cheek. "Perhaps later."

She turned back to Jenny. "Adrian provides the entertainment around here. It's my job to keep the rooms clean and everyone fed."

Jenny nodded toward the window. "And find carrots for a certain young man."

Emma winked at her. "I won't forget the nose or the eyes."

After his sister stepped into the kitchen, Adrian asked, "Do you really want to try sledging?"

Jenny eyed the children playing in the snow again. "It can't be much harder than riding a bicycle."

"There's no skill needed, though it's good to have a decent set of lungs."

"For breathing?"

He shook his head. "For screaming."

Even if Cora was right, and Adrian was trouble, no harm could come from playing a few hours with him and his guests in the snow. Like he'd said, they were only acquaintances. She could be amiable with both him and his sister.

"Can I leave my camera at the hotel?"

He nodded. "Emma will lock it away."

She thought for another moment. "Do I have to slide down the hill more than once?"

"Of course not."

"Then I suppose my lungs and I will try it."

Adrian grinned again.

CHAPTER 7

Adrian couldn't remember the last time he'd laughed so hard. Jenny didn't stop after sledging once. She rode at least a dozen times before deciding to thaw inside the inn with the other guests, her coat and scarf caked in snow.

He'd never forget those screams of hers, pure glee as she flew down the hill, across the snowy lawn. And her smile after rolling off the sledge as it neared the road, the smile that remained whenever she looked over at him, inviting him to celebrate with her.

Instead of trying to return Jenny home on his motorbike, Adrian had borrowed two pairs of snowshoes his dad and Gilbert had crafted decades ago, back when they were two brothers wondering about their future. He and Jenny trekked up the lane to Cora's, laughing as they hobbled along in the clunky shoes. Nothing could come of their friendship, he knew that, but he planned to enjoy every minute spent with her.

The snow had finally melted, and his leg that ached with the weather changes had stopped hurting. Now he sped back up to Cora's house on his motorbike, thinking about the woman who'd laughed with him in the snow and pointed out all manner of things she found beautiful both on the lake and in the surrounding hills.

Had Cora told Jenny about his father? Or what had happened to Adrian two years back? If Cora hadn't already told Jenny about his past, he needed to do so before she found out from someone else.

After parking his motorbike, he glanced inside the courtyard. Thankfully, the Fiat was gone. Part of it was cowardice, he supposed, this avoiding of Cora Banks, but part was purely sensible. If Jenny needed a ride to her bicycle, he was more than pleased to accommodate her, but no good reason existed to further irritate her host.

Jenny answered the front door after his knock. She looked pretty in her light-yellow blouse and plaid skirt, but instead of laughter, her eyes were swollen.

"What happened?" he asked, deeply concerned.

She held up a large envelope. "Cora retrieved my photographs this morning." Then she dabbed a crumpled tissue to the edge of her eye, catching a tear before it streaked down her cheek.

"Was there an accident?" Perhaps that's why Cora's vehicle wasn't here.

"Oh no," she said. "Nothing like that."

"But something is wrong."

She handed the envelope to him, and he opened it. Inside was a set of photographs taken around Windermere and up near the old abbey. Some of the pictures were slanted at odd angles, others overexposed. Still others were dusted with sunspots in all the wrong places, and a few were double or even triple exposed, as if she'd forgotten to advance the film and taken several photographs on the same frame.

Her tears began to fall again. "I'm incompetent."

"You're an amateur," he said. "Not incompetent."

She shook her head. "You don't understand."

He tucked the pictures back into the envelope and handed them to her. "How long have you been using a camera?"

"My mom bought it for me before I came to England."

"You didn't take lessons?"

She shook her head, sniffling again. "The man at Bloomingdale's said all I had to do was push the button."

"No one takes perfect pictures on their first roll."

"This is my second roll," she said. "The first was worse."

"Even so, it can take months to learn photography. Sometimes it takes people years."

She pulled the envelope back to her waist, clutching the edges with both her hands. "That's pure speculation."

"It's fact, written someplace in stone. At least six months to learn how to use a camera well."

"The instructions to my Automagic said anyone could use it."

"Perhaps you're not anyone, Jenny."

Her blue eyes filled with tears again. "What's that supposed to mean?"

"You seem to find beauty in the places other people don't look. Now you just have to learn how to transfer what you see onto a photograph."

She glanced down at the envelope. "That's very generous of you."

He shrugged. "It's how I see it."

She looked back up at him. "Do you know of anyone in Ambleside who offers photography lessons?"

"I can recommend a good book."

She shook her head. "I need someone to teach me."

"I'll inquire for you, then."

She wiped the corners of her eyes again. "Thank you."

He pointed back toward the door. "In the meantime, I have a tire pump strapped to the back of my motorbike and a rubber patch and cement to fix the leak. Shall we retrieve your bicycle?"

"If the snowmen didn't ride off with it."

His eyes scrunched with confusion. "Snowmen?"

"Never mind." She waved her hand. "I need to change my clothes."

"I'll wait outside." He glanced toward the studio. "Where's Cora?"

"Visiting one of her customers."

Hopefully Cora wouldn't return until they were on the other side of Ambleside.

Jenny and Adrian found her bicycle half-buried in mud. While she cleaned the frame with a rag, he patched the hole in her tire. Then he refilled the inner tube with air.

"Thank you for helping me." She stepped over the bar and clutched both handlebars. Now to remember how to balance, pedal, and steer at the same time. She much preferred the simplicity of sledding.

"It was my pleasure to help."

As he tied the tire pump to the back of his motorbike, Jenny gazed up at the azure canopy of sky. The weather was much warmer today, with no sign of clouds. But she wasn't planning on taking pictures. Her photographs had been a complete disaster, and she feared it had nothing to do with the camera. It was her—she was incapable of following even the simplest of technical instructions.

Failure.

Her grandfather's slight echoed in her mind, a reflection of the grades mauling her transcript. Perhaps photography would be an impossibility for her, like most of her college classes. An enormous *F* so everyone could see exactly how inept she was.

In her leather satchel, she carried colored pencils and paper. If she couldn't use her camera, she'd attempt to capture the essence of these lakes today on her sketchpad.

When he finished his task, Adrian dug his hands into his pockets and glanced back at the road leading down into Ambleside. "Do you and Cora have plans tonight?"

"I'm not certain."

Adrian climbed onto his motorbike. "I was wondering if you'd like to join me for a movie in Ambleside."

Jenny inched her bicycle back, her mind spinning. She'd like to spend the evening with Adrian, but what would Cora say? Not that Cora could stop her from seeing a movie with him or anyone else. Here, Jenny was free to spend time with whoever she liked.

When she didn't reply, Adrian continued. "It's an American film with Cary Grant and Deborah Kerr."

"*An Affair to Remember?*"

His smile fell. "You've already seen it."

"Just once, but . . ." Her gaze fell to her handlebars as she tried to formulate a response.

Adrian yanked the throttle, his motorbike roaring to life. "Never mind."

"I'm sor—"

"There's no reason to apologize, Jenny. I want you to speak your mind."

She dug the toe of her Keds into the soggy grass. "My mind is all tangled up."

He nodded toward the road. "I'll follow you down to Ambleside in case your tire goes flat again."

Her fingers tight around the handlebars, she bristled at the thought of him watching her wobble all the way down this hill, wondering why she couldn't do something as simple as take photographs or ride a bicycle. He'd probably been riding a bicycle since he was three or four.

She nodded in the opposite direction. "I'm actually going to ride awhile before I return to town."

Disappointment flooded his eyes. He'd been nothing but gracious to her, transporting her and her luggage, helping her fix her bicycle, teaching her how to sled. Then she'd rejected the common courtesy of his offer to be an escort.

He kicked his motorbike into gear. "I'll see you around."

"Adrian—" she started, but her voice was lost in the engine's rage. He was already gone, the motorbike spitting chunks of mud behind him.

Frustrated at herself, she tried to balance the bicycle against a low wall near the road. Then she pushed off, attempting to pedal and steer in the mud. The bicycle teetered, and she climbed off again, moving into the middle of the deserted road as she reoriented herself with the art of riding.

She pedaled slowly away from Ambleside, up to the split in the road before circling back around. It was almost four now, and she'd probably need more than an hour to ride home in the mud.

She hadn't meant to hurt Adrian Kemp, not at all. Perhaps, in fairness, she should tell him what Cora had said about his father and ask him directly if he knew what had happened to Curtis Sloan. And perhaps she should just be honest with him as well and tell him that she rode a bicycle about as well as she took photographs. At least he'd know that she was disappointed in herself instead of him.

As she descended the hill, she slowly maneuvered around the rocks, trying to steady her handlebars and shaky limbs. About halfway down, she stopped for a break and scanned the horizon of sky, lake, and trees. She couldn't see Ambleside from this point, but beyond the lake, she spotted some sort of structure gleaming in the light, an arrow of sorts piercing the sky. It was much too narrow to be a building. In fact, from here it looked like some sort of amusement park ride.

Her heart raced as she scanned the trees under the structure, wishing she could see what was hidden underneath the leaves, but all she saw was the crest of wood and metal.

Was that Enchanted Isle?

She wished she could ask Adrian to take her there, but after what had happened to Curtis, Adrian might avoid the place. For that matter, he might avoid her as well for the next two months if she didn't tell him the truth.

It was time for her to be honest with Adrian, and perhaps he would be honest with her as well.

CHAPTER 8

Adrian stomped through the back door of the inn. His leg no longer ached, but his entire body burned from the rejection. He'd thought Jenny had begun to enjoy his company as much as he'd been enjoying hers, but clearly he'd only imagined the connection between them.

It was warm enough to take guests on a boat excursion this afternoon, but he wouldn't linger on the lake. He needed to check on the ewes for Gilbert to see if any others had begun lambing, then perhaps he'd go out on his own for a motorbike ride.

It had been ages since he'd ridden around the lakes—even longer since he'd asked a girl out to the cinema. Jenny needed his help, but that didn't mean she wanted to spend time with him. Or perhaps she was being much more practical than he was. The end of her visit here would be the end of any friendship between them.

He'd never been the type of person to journey halfway into anything, including relationships. When he made up his mind to pursue something, nothing deterred him. *Intense* is what one girl he'd met during basic training had called it. They'd only gone to the cinema twice before her calendar was flush with commitments she couldn't break. He'd taken the hint and moved along, not fond of the concept of dating in general anyway. It all seemed so superficial to him, a strange dance where no one was quite certain who was supposed to lead.

Why couldn't he be honest when he liked someone, telling them up front that he enjoyed their company instead of doing a silly dance? If nothing else, he respected Jenny for refusing to accept his offer. If she didn't want to spend more time with him, she shouldn't be obligated to do so.

Before he reached the lounge, his sister stopped him in the corridor. "I thought you were with Jenny."

His jaw clenched as he folded his arms over his chest. He wished he could dive into the lake and swim off his frustration like he used to. "We fixed her bicycle, so she decided to spend the afternoon riding it."

"You should go bicycling with her."

"Blast it, Emma," he said, not caring one wit about the anger that fired through his voice. "I can't just cruise around on a bicycle. I have to take our guests out on the boat."

Her eyebrows climbed. "You can't take out anyone in your state."

"What state is that?" he demanded.

"A dreadful one." Emma leaned forward. "I like her, Adrian."

He passed by her. "Then you should ask her out to a movie."

"Perhaps I shall," Emma called before he turned the corner.

When Jenny walked into the inn's lobby, Emma welcomed her at the reception desk. "Are you returning for more sandwiches and tea?"

"Not today." Before she ate or drank anything, Jenny wanted to speak with Adrian.

"My brother said you enjoyed sledging."

Jenny nodded. "It's the most of fun I've had in ages."

"The snow is probably gone until next winter, but you're welcome to take a stroll out on the pier. Some of our guests are fishing."

Jenny fidgeted with the edge of her sleeve. "I'm actually looking for Adrian."

Emma's eyebrows slid up. "Indeed."

"Do you know where he is?"

Emma pointed toward the back of the inn. "He's helping our uncle with the sheep."

"Do you think he'd mind if I interrupted him?"

"I don't believe he'd mind. I can direct you there in a moment."

As Emma helped a guest, Jenny sipped water from the drinking fountain before stepping up to the window. The remnants of snowmen had been replaced by mud and a host of geese on the bank. On the dock beyond them, a crowd of men and women dangled fishing rods into the water.

When Emma finished her conversation, she beckoned Jenny to the other side of the lobby. "Gilbert's farm is on the hill behind the inn."

Instead of turning right toward the dining room, Emma led Jenny down a corridor on the left. Photographs lined these walls as well, between the guest room doors, but Emma's brisk pace allowed no time to stop and examine them.

"Adrian came barging through here about an hour ago," Emma said over her shoulder. "Unfortunately, he might still be in a foul mood when you find him."

"I'm afraid that I might have sparked his temper." Perhaps it seemed pompous of her to take credit for his mood, but she didn't want Emma to blame Adrian when it was Jenny who'd rejected his offer to help.

Emma stopped beside a door at the end of the hall. "Dare I ask what prompted it?"

"A misunderstanding."

A tentative smile crossed Emma's lips. "One I hope you are about to clear up."

"If he'll listen to me."

"He'll listen, though it may take him a few hours to process. Some around here say my brother's a hothead, but he's the kindest man I know. And he's faithful to the people he—" Emma stopped herself, seeming to rethink her words. "To those he cares about." She opened the door and pointed at a stairway on the far side of the parking lot. "You'll find him up that hill."

Jenny maneuvered around the cars in the narrow lot and began climbing the slate steps on the other side. She certainly hadn't known Adrian long enough for him to care about her, at least not more than any other visitor who spent their holiday in Ambleside, but she liked the idea of having him as a friend instead of just an acquaintance. Friendship could last beyond just the spring. It could last for a lifetime.

Then again, she liked the thought of him caring for her beyond friendship as well.

She shook her head, trying to clear that thought before it took hold.

When she was at Flora Stone Mather, she'd attended plenty of dances with the male students at the nearby Western Reserve University, but none of the young men understood her love of art and beauty. They'd wanted to box her up into a neat, compact case designated for their wife. Smart and silent. But she was neither smart nor silent.

Her last boyfriend before Robert was a fellow by the name of Evan. She'd met him five years ago at their church youth group, and she'd worn his class ring for three months until her grandfather saw Evan's dad at the Silver Grille driving one of Henry Ford's Mainlines. Instead of demanding that she break off the relationship, her grandfather somehow convinced Evan to end it. All because his father supported Ford.

She wanted to marry someone who wasn't intimidated by the senior McAdam or enamored more with her grandfather's fortune than with her, but her grandfather wasn't giving her a choice. She and Adrian could only be friends, but after rejecting him today, Adrian might not be interested in even a friendship with her.

A hedge separated the inn's property from the farm, and the gray slate turned into a dirt pathway as it wove up the hillside. On the right was a wooden fence, and in the sloped field, several sheep with brown fleece grazed between rocks that studded the land, their backs striped with blue.

A rugged slate barn stood at the top of the hill, but before she reached it, she saw Adrian in the field about ten feet from the path, kneeling beside one of the sheep. The animal lay on its side, bleating in pain, but it didn't struggle.

Jenny paused beside a gate in the fence. When they'd gone sledding, she had admired his confident way with the hotel's guests as he helped and encouraged them. Now he seemed to encourage this sheep as well. Working with the guests may be his job, but he had a natural way with people and animals alike.

The animal bleated again.

"Come on, girl," Adrian said as he stroked his hand across her wool. A pair of dogs sat in the grass nearby, watching over them.

Jenny lifted the gate's latch and stepped into the pasture. Several sheep glanced up at her indifferently before returning to feed on the grass. Adrian didn't seem to notice as she approached, his gaze focused on the ailing sheep as he probed its sides. A pink balloon swelled from the animal's abdomen, lying in a mound on the grass.

The timing was all wrong for an apology, so Jenny knelt beside him instead. "What's the matter?"

"Her lamb is breeched."

Jenny's stomach clenched when the animal bleated in pain again. "How can I help?"

He nodded uphill. "Please find Gilbert."

Standing, Jenny raced toward the top of the hill. Beside the barn was a two-story house with neatly trimmed holly bushes below each window. When she knocked on the front door, a man in his early forties answered, a country gentleman wearing a tweed cap and pressed khaki shirt, the sleeves rolled up to his elbows. His hands were stained with grease.

He glanced over her shoulder as if looking for someone else. "We don't get much company up here."

"Are you Gilbert?" she asked.

He nodded. "I am."

"My name's Jenny." She pointed back to the field. "Adrian is having trouble with a breeched lamb."

He winced. "Where is he?"

"Near the path to the inn."

He stepped back into the corridor and returned seconds later with a brown towel and a bottle of lotion.

Jenny trailed him back down the hill, to Adrian and the ewe and the two dogs that were pacing now nearby.

Gilbert knelt beside Adrian. "Do you want me to pull the lamb?"

"No." Adrian's eyes were focused on the ewe. "I'll take care of her."

He doused his hand and forearm with the lotion, and Jenny gasped when he reached inside the animal. But the ewe didn't make a sound, as if she knew Adrian was trying to help her.

"I've got the back legs," Adrian said. Leaning back, he began to slowly pull.

Gilbert held out the towel as a black lamb emerged, and when Adrian set the animal on the towel, Jenny wanted to cheer for this new life.

Wilbur, she silently named the lamb, after the famous pig in a book she'd been required to read in school. A fighter who needed others to become a hero.

With the lamb in Gilbert's arms, the ewe slowly pushed up to lick her offspring clean. Adrian's arm was slimy, but his smile was triumphant as he stood. "She'll take it from here."

Jenny glanced warily at the ewe. "Are you certain?"

He nodded.

"I didn't know if she would make it."

Adrian watched the ewe caring for the lamb. "Me either."

"Well done," Gilbert said before turning to Jenny. "We've had four ewes lamb since the snow. Thank God we haven't lost one."

"I've never seen a sheep give birth," Jenny said, overwhelmed.

Gilbert folded the towel. "It's a beautiful thing, isn't it?"

Not the muck and blood, but the new life. "I suppose it is."

"I've got to clean up and see to the stew waiting on the stove." He lifted his hat. "It was nice to meet you, Miss Jenny."

"You as well."

Adrian motioned for her to follow him, and they trekked side by side across the hill. The setting sun rippled color across the sheen of sky, the scent of wood smoke warming the air. Across the field, a spring bubbled up under the umbrella of a tree, then trickled down toward the lake on a narrow bed of rocks and twigs. Adrian dipped his arms into the water and cleaned them off.

"How did you find me up here?" he asked when he stood again, shaking his arms to dry them.

"Emma told me you were working with your uncle."

"I help him when I'm not at the hotel," he said. "Or assisting American girls with their bicycle tires."

A breeze drifted across the hill, and she shivered. "I didn't thank you as I should."

He shrugged. "It was proper enough."

"Still . . ." She took a deep breath, watching another ewe hop over the brook and then turn, waiting for her lamb to follow toward the shelter of trees. "Is the offer for a movie still open?"

"I don't need a sympathy date, Jenny."

"Your invitation"—she folded her arms over her chest—"it caught me off guard."

"I didn't think it would be such a shock."

And now she was blaming him when she'd wanted to apologize. "I'm sorry, Adrian."

"You should speak your mind," he said again, and while she was grateful for the sentiment, she hadn't been honest with him.

"I didn't exactly speak my mind." She fidgeted with her hands, searching for the right words. "It was kind of you to offer to follow me down the hill, but the truth is, I'm just now learning how to ride a bicycle. I didn't want you to think less of me for it."

He leaned back against the tree, suspicion cutting through his gaze. "You rode the bicycle up the fell."

"It wasn't pretty," she said, trying to smile.

He looked down at the lake before turning back. "There's no reason for you to be embarrassed."

She sighed. "That's because you know how to ride a bicycle."

"I certainly don't think less of you. In fact, I think it's admirable you've decided to learn."

She glanced at the path but didn't move, hoping he would extend his invitation for the cinema tonight one more time. But in his silence, it seemed he'd changed his mind.

It was too bad. She would have enjoyed spending the evening with him.

A dark streak inched across the parking lot below, the shadow of nightfall. "I should return home for supper," she said, stepping toward the path. "Your uncle was right. You did a fine job delivering that lamb."

"Jenny . . ." He moved up beside her. "There are a few things I haven't told you either."

She stopped, turning back to him. "What sort of things?"

"I'll tell you tonight. That is, if you'll still go out with me."

She nodded. "I'd like that very much."

"But I think we should skip the movie."

She cocked her head, searching his face. "And where would we go instead?"

"Someplace you'll like much better than the cinema."

"What's better than a movie?"

"My secret place."

She glanced down at the sunlight fading over the lake. "I'm intrigued."

"Dress warm," he said. "And bring your camera with you."

It was strange, she thought as she walked back toward her bicycle. The man unnerved her, and yet she wasn't the least bit afraid.

CHAPTER 9

Jenny swept her hair back into a neat ponytail, but it didn't stay neat for long. Wind stole away her yellow ribbon as she and Adrian sped through Ambleside on his motorbike, passing the milk bar and small cinema, then following the shimmer of reflectors as they rode out beyond the houses and stores into the countryside.

The full moon crept up the expanse of sky, casting bronze across the river valley and the fells above them. It was surreal, the quiet beauty around her, like the hand of God had carefully sculpted, glazed, and fired this land.

Adrian parked the motorbike in a grove of trees. A waterfall gushed nearby, splashing into a pool, and in the distance, she could see lights on one of the fells. But not a single car had passed them since they'd left Ambleside.

He unloaded two leather satchels from his motorbike. He handed Jenny her camera bag, and the second one, he strung over his shoulder.

"Where are we?" she asked, her Keds sinking into the soft peatland.

"Near Elter Water."

She glanced back at the trees. "One of the lakes?"

"Exactly. The 'lake of swans,' according to the language of Old Norse."

"Is there also a land of swans nearby?"

He chuckled. "The village is about a mile up this road, but only locals know how to access the lake. Years ago, my best mate and I used to come out here and nick the cat's eyes."

Stunned, she struggled to process what he'd said. "What did you do?" she pressed, her voice stiff.

"We'd steal the cat's eyes."

She rubbed her arms. It didn't seem like this man, who'd been so gentle with the sheep, would hurt any animal, but she knew well that things weren't always as they seemed. "That's terrible."

"Not actual cats," he said, pointing at the road. "Those."

"All I see is black."

Laughing, he removed a flashlight from his bag and shined it on the pavement. A red square, the size of a wallet, gleamed back at them.

"Reflectors?"

Adrian shook his head. "No one here calls them reflectors."

"Why, pray tell, would you steal reflectors from the road?"

He shrugged. "So tourists can't see."

She crossed her arms. "I'm glad the cats are safe, but now I'm concerned about me."

He flinched as if she'd stung him, and she dropped her arms back to her sides. "I'm only joking, Adrian. I'm not really worried."

He clicked off the flashlight and then reached for her hand, leading her back through the trees. The moonlight dripped through branches like silky raindrops, and leaves crackled under their feet.

As they neared the edge of the forest, the trees eclipsed the moon. Then the forest broke open onto a magical display of light. The moon hung above a fell, spilling embers of light across the lake. Liquid fire.

One day, her father used to say, someone would walk on that moon. But perhaps some form of life was already up there, reveling in the beauty of earth.

"It's spectacular," she whispered.

"Better than a movie?"

"Immensely."

He smiled. "I believe the moon just might be showing off."

Like it was a starlet on the big screen. "I wish I could take a picture of it."

He squeezed her hand. "You can."

"I would never be able to capture that on film."

"Only if you don't try."

She turned toward him. "You've seen my pictures."

He released her hand and retrieved the flashlight. Then he shined it on her camera bag. "Let's see if we can work on the auto portion of your camera."

She unlatched her bag. "You know how to work an Automagic?"

He grinned. "We'll figure it out together."

She held it out to him, the metal edges cool in her hands. "The man at the sales counter said I wouldn't have to make any adjustments."

"The best things in life usually take a bit of adjusting," he said. "Can you hold the torch?"

"The what?"

He held out the flashlight. "The electric torch."

She took it from him. "In America, a torch can burn you."

As she shined the flashlight, Adrian examined the dial and levers on each side. "This is where you switch to manual control."

"I don't know how to use it manually."

"If you can learn to ride a bicycle, you can certainly learn how to operate your camera."

His encouragement bolstered her confidence.

"The lower you set the shutter speed, the more natural light will come through the lens." He glanced over at the moon mirrored on the water. "And you'll want as much of this light as possible."

He showed her how to turn the dial, changing it to the lowest speed. "Now it will stay open for a full fortieth of a second."

"That doesn't sound very long."

"Plenty long to capture this moon." He studied the camera. "The aperture changes on its own, based on the shutter speed."

"Do I want this aperture to change?"

"It will make things a bit less complicated." He turned off the flash-light. "Now you just have to focus the lens."

She took the camera from him and lifted the viewfinder to her left eye. Adrian stood over her shoulder, his chin bent down near her ear. "Can you see the moon?"

"It's all blurry," she said, her voice sounding as fuzzy as the moon looked in the viewfinder.

"Adjust the focus here." He gently pressed his fingers over hers, showing her how to turn the black dial that encircled the lens. "Is it getting clearer?"

"A bit."

He turned it a notch. "Better?"

"Yes," she said, shivering at his closeness.

Even though she'd gone steady with Evan Gray for three months, he'd never kissed her except on the cheek. And she'd never encouraged a kiss from him or Robert. But her body was screaming now, on alert, like a fangirl at a Ricky Nelson concert. All she could think about was the man beside her.

What if he tried to kiss her?

Part of her wanted him to kiss her, and yet she was terrified.

The moon sharpened in the viewfinder, a brilliant bulb hanging on the bough of sky. "It's crystal clear," she said, trying but failing to breathe again.

"You have to keep the camera as still as possible. Hold your breath."

"I already am."

The shutter button clicked when he pressed it, opening and then closing. "What's next, Jenny?"

"Breathing."

He laughed softly, his hand dropping back to his side. "Don't forget to advance the film."

"Of course." She turned the advance wheel to move the film forward on the spool.

"I want to show you something else," he said, turning on the flashlight again.

She nodded, still struggling for the fullness of her breath. They needed to move along rather quickly now.

Her heart quaked when he took her hand again, guiding her toward the water. When they neared the shore, he cleared a path through the reeds until she saw an overturned rowboat, two wooden oars lying at its side.

"Is this yours?" she asked.

He flipped it over. "It belongs to a friend."

"Will your friend mind if we borrow it?"

He shook his head. "She lets me use it whenever I like."

With that statement, the tension seemed to fizzle between them. Who was this friend? And how many times had she and Adrian rowed on this remote lake together?

Jenny eyed the rickety-looking boat, trying to calm the frustration growing in her heart. It was completely unreasonable for her to be jealous—she was supposed to be marrying another man—but still it swelled. "How often have you taken this out?"

"A number of times," he said. "The boat's plenty seaworthy, but even if it wasn't, the lake is shallow near the shore. We could wade if necessary."

"It's too cold to wade."

He picked up an oar. "And I have no intention of doing so."

Together they pushed the boat into the lake, and Adrian secured it close to the grassy bank so she could climb inside. It rocked as she sat on the bench, but her feet remained dry. The boat swayed again as he stepped inside, facing her. Then he began rowing, staying near the edge like he'd promised. The whisper of lapping water brushed against the shore, and the reeds rustled in a breeze that made the light on their lake dance as well.

When they neared the far side of Elter Water, Adrian slid the oars into their rowlocks and opened his leather bag again. But instead of the flashlight, he removed his own camera, and she watched in fascination as the lens folded out like an accordion.

"You're a photographer?"

"Purely amateur," he said.

"Did you take the photographs hanging in the inn?"

"Some of them."

No wonder he knew so much about operating her camera. The pictures at the Herdwick Inn looked as if they'd been taken by a professional.

She leaned toward him. "What type of camera is that?"

"An Agfa Isolette."

"I've never seen a lens unfold."

"It was my father's," he said. "Many of the photographs at the hotel were taken by him."

When the wind gusted again, she tugged her collar together to warm her neck. "It's fascinating, how you can freeze a moment in time on paper for the rest of the world to see."

"I suppose it is frozen. In silver salt."

"You can remember someone through a photograph, long after they're gone." A tear slipped unbidden down her cheek. "For the briefest of moments, it's almost as if they're still with you."

He lowered his camera. "You've lost someone close to you."

"My father died almost four years ago in an accident."

"I'm sorry."

She wiped the tear off with her sleeve. "Cora said your father is gone as well."

He nodded. "His plane was shot down during the war."

"Now I'm sorry."

"He . . ." Adrian glanced back up at the moon. "My sister said our family actually lost him around the time I was born. After that, he wasn't . . . quite himself."

"How old were you when he died?"

"Almost nine, though I didn't see him for several years during the war. There are so many things I wish I could have asked him."

How sad, Jenny thought, for him to grow up without knowing his father, only through stories and pictures, really. For his questions to still linger. At least she'd known her dad, trusted him. And she'd heard most of his stories firsthand.

"Did Cora tell you about Enchanted Isle?" he asked.

"A little. She said your dad built the park."

Adrian nodded. "When he was younger, my dad used to sketch all sorts of magical structures and then paint them. The park was only a dream until he saw the pictures of the island in America called Coney. Then he was hooked on creating a similar park, except he wanted one inspired by the ocean."

The moon seemed to split open in Jenny's mind, a dozen sea creatures peering through the chasm as if waiting for curtain call. "It sounds amazing."

"My dad always loved the sea because of the endless treasures he thought were hidden under its surface. And he loved how the fells around here are filled with treasure as well."

The breeze lapped water along the sides of their boat, rocking it gently. "Did your father ever find a treasure?"

He hesitated before answering. "Nothing of value."

"He was a courageous man to pursue his dream."

Adrian dipped the oars into the water, propelling them forward. "No one except Curtis Sloan thought people would travel up here to visit an amusement park, but he helped finance my father's dream and people came by the thousands. It was a great success until . . ."

She rubbed her arms. "Until Curtis died?"

"Cora told you."

"She told me the rumors."

A frog croaked nearby, interrupting the silence. "Curtis disappeared after the summer of 1935, and the profits from the park seemed to disappear along with him. People think my father killed him and took the money."

"What do you think?"

Adrian stroked the oars through the water again to keep the boat from catching in the reeds. "A few years after the war, Gilbert told my sister and me that he'd found my father with Curtis's body at the park, but when he went back later, Curtis was gone."

"Oh, Adrian . . ."

"Gilbert thinks my dad's mind snapped, and he didn't even realize what he'd done. But he must have been present enough to return for the body."

"That's so sad."

"Gilbert went to the police after he told Emma and me, but my dad was gone by then, and there was no evidence to convict anyone. The police weren't supposed to say anything, but you can't keep a rumor like that completely quiet."

"Did anyone find the missing money?"

"No. After my father died, my mum sold the island to Perry Banks. Some people think she took the money with her when she remarried, but her new husband had more than enough for both of them."

Resting the oars in their locks, Adrian lifted his Isolette and adjusted the dials. Then she heard the clicks as he snapped several frames. The moon was perfectly arced in the sky, the fells looming underneath.

He pointed toward the pool of light. "You'd better take some pictures before we row back."

With the shutter speed on low, an open door for the light, she adjusted the focus on her camera. Then she photographed the moon and reeds and the regal-looking trees that circled the lake, emeralds dangling from a necklace made of gold.

"Why are all your photographs in the inn taken with black-and-white film?" she asked.

"I like the contrast."

"The color in these lakes is exquisite!"

"True, but sometimes too much color distracts from the patterns in the grain."

She'd never thought about color as a distraction before. To her, color created the threads in a pattern, the beauty of a piece.

Adrian began rowing the boat back toward their path. "Don't tell Cora, but some of my best photographs have been taken on Enchanted Isle."

Her heart raced. "I'd like to see them."

He dug the oars into the water again, grinning at her. "Perhaps one day I'll show them to you."

CHAPTER 10

Adrian stabbed his fork into a chunk of potato and circled it through the vegetables on his plate. Bubble and squeak, that's what his uncle had fried up for breakfast, but Adrian's mind kept wandering away from the food back to the evening he'd spent with Jenny Winter.

Gilbert eyed his plate. "Is something wrong?"

Adrian ate the potato before replying. "Everything is splendid."

"At the pace you're eating, a sloth would lap you."

Adrian glanced at his uncle's clean plate. "I'm not very hungry."

Gilbert laughed. "You must like her a lot."

"Who are you talking about?"

"I believe she said her name was Jenny."

Adrian tossed his cloth serviette on the table. "She's only here for a few weeks."

Everything rounded back to that one disastrous fact. It didn't matter how much he liked her; Jenny was leaving the first of June.

"A few weeks is plenty of time to get to know someone."

"But what happens after June?"

Gilbert rapped his knuckles on the table, eyebrows raised. "It must be serious if you're already thinking about the after."

"It's nothing yet." Adrian drank his black coffee. "Nor will it be when I tell her about Tom Moore."

"I thought you were going to tell her last night."

"She asked about Dad, and then I lost my nerve."

Gilbert's gaze wandered toward the first rays of light that slipped through the window. They couldn't see the island from the house, but sometimes the memory of the park seemed to haunt his uncle, like the memory of Tom haunted Adrian. His dad and Gilbert had been more than brothers. They'd been the best of mates.

"Did you tell her what happened with Curtis?" Gilbert asked.

"I'm sorry. I should have asked you first."

"It's your story to tell, Adrian, to whoever you want." Gilbert turned back to him. "You can't keep beating yourself up about your dad or Tom. Just be honest with her about the past and what you want for the future."

Adrian leaned back in his chair, mulling over his uncle's words. When the timing was right, he would tell her about the night on Grasmere that he wished to God he could take back. Give anything to take it back, really.

"Your Jenny reminds me of an American girl I used to know before the war," Gilbert said. "I'd hoped to marry her."

"Did she return home?"

He nodded. "Sadly, she married someone else."

It was unfortunate for this woman in America that she hadn't married Gilbert. He was the most devoted person Adrian knew.

"Jenny and I are nowhere close to talking about marriage," Adrian said. "I just like spending time with her."

"You should invite her over for supper."

"And scare her off?"

Gilbert laughed. "I'm not that frightening."

Adrian stood, snatching his plate from the table.

"Do you care about her?" Gilbert asked.

"It doesn't matter. Once she finds out the truth about Tom, she'll leave on the next boat to America."

"Or not," Gilbert said, leaning into the table. "My guess is that she's stronger than you think."

Adrian eyed the telephone. "Maybe I will ring her."

"I fear you'll regret it if you don't."

Jenny left Cora a note on the kitchen counter telling her that she'd accepted the invitation to dine with Adrian and his uncle. Then she set her hair with rollers and dressed in a navy–blue-and-red skirt, white blouse, and scuffed saddle shoes with bobby socks folded neatly down to her ankles.

She hoped she'd captured the moon in all its glory last night, the light reflecting in the lake. But even if the pictures didn't work, she'd created a moving picture of the evening in the theater of her mind, the frames rolling over and over again so she'd never forget the memory of the beautiful night, the attentiveness of her companion.

The movie only stalled when the question crept back—whose boat had they rowed across Elter Water? Surely Adrian would have mentioned if he had a girlfriend. Or at the very least, his sister should have said something.

Or perhaps not. Jenny hadn't told him yet about Robert. She'd simply requested a photography lesson, and Adrian had given her one. And now she'd practically invited herself in her inquiry about Enchanted Isle.

She rubbed her hands over her bare arms, savoring the memory of standing so close to him in the moonlight, his help with the camera. She hadn't concentrated as well as she should have on the lesson, but she hoped her pictures were in much better focus than her state of mind.

When the doorbell rang, she scrambled down the steps to meet Adrian. He looked quite handsome in his suit and plum-colored necktie, the shadow of a beard darkening his jawline. So different from the man yesterday kneeling beside the ewe in dungarees and a stained shirt.

He shifted on his feet, flashing her a tentative smile. "You look lovely."

She dipped one leg behind the other in a faux curtsy. "Thank you."

"I borrowed my uncle's car."

"I don't mind riding your motorbike."

"That's what I told Gilbert, but he didn't believe me."

They walked off the stoop, toward the vehicle parked on the narrow drive. Jenny laughed when she saw it. A blue Ford Consul, the convertible top down.

"What's so funny?" he asked as he opened her door.

"My grandfather won't let me ride in a Ford."

His eyebrows arched in concern.

She laughed again. "It's good that my grandfather is back in Cleveland."

"I suppose it is." He closed the door and climbed into the driver's side. "I hope you're hungry."

"Very much. Did you make the meal?"

"No. Emma's convinced I would ruin dinner if left to my own cooking devices. She asked to prepare food for us tonight, but it seems she prepared a banquet instead."

Jenny smiled. "Is she joining us?"

He shook his head. "She kept half the meal for her husband and two boys. They live in a flat behind the inn."

"I hope it wasn't too much trouble for her," she said as he shifted into first.

"Emma makes it all seem quite effortless. She takes good care of everyone in the family."

"And it seems as if you take good care of her too."

He shrugged. "That's what family is supposed to do."

The sitting room in the Kemp family farmhouse was clean and orderly, with its upholstered chairs and beige davenport. Two pictures hung on the wall, both oil paintings of a lake, as well as a tapestry with the embroidered words from Psalm 23. Beside the davenport was a clock and a bookcase filled with titles about agriculture, botany, mechanics, and British history. Everything in the room, it seemed, had its proper place.

Gilbert stepped out of the kitchen, drying his hands on a towel. "Welcome to our home."

"Thank you," she said. "How is Wilbur?"

He looked back and forth between her and Adrian. "Who's Wilbur?"

She blushed. "The lamb born yesterday."

"You named it?"

"I hope you don't mind," she said. "Every person and animal should have a name."

Gilbert smiled. "Wilbur is quite well, thank you, though I've never known a ewe lamb with such a name. She's taken to her legs like a child to a bicycle, following her mama all over the pasture."

Jenny glanced at Adrian, but he gave a quick shake of his head indicating that he hadn't told his uncle about her newfound bicycle skills. They moved into the dining room and sat in three of the six bentwood chairs that rounded a polished table.

"Most of our lambs don't need to be pulled like that, but Adrian is a hero. He saved both the ewe and the ewe la—Wilbur."

"Wilbur's mama is the hero," Adrian said.

Emma had indeed prepared a banquet with corned beef hash, cabbage, and a bread pudding. Jenny tried not to seem overly hungry, but besides Cora's chicken and potatoes, she'd been subsisting mainly on Spam, eggs, and crackers. Along with Kendal Mint Cakes and chocolate.

Gilbert prayed a blessing over their meal, and she tried to eat slowly, but the food tasted light years better than anything from a can.

"Adrian says that you're a photographer," Gilbert said before taking a bite of cabbage.

"Only he would be kind enough to categorize me as such."

"You have an eye for it," Adrian said.

"Just not the skill."

"We'll decide after we develop your next roll of film."

Jenny blinked. "We?"

Gilbert laughed. "He didn't mention that he turns the kitchen into a darkroom about every other week."

"No, he didn't mention that."

Gilbert took another bite of food. "So, you're visiting from America."

She nodded. "My family's in Ohio."

He lowered his fork. "Where in Ohio?"

"Cleveland," she said. "Along Lake Erie."

His face paled, and for a moment, she thought he might be ill. "How exactly do you know Cora?"

"My great-aunt rented a summer house on Windermere eons ago, and my mom came to visit. She and Cora became fast friends." Jenny ate more of the hash before speaking again. "Perhaps you met my mom."

He hesitated before asking. "What's her name?"

"Liz McAdam, until she married. Then her last name changed to Winter."

Gilbert's fork clattered on the plate. "I believe I did meet her."

Jenny smiled. "Where did you meet?"

"I don't remember exactly." Gilbert pushed back his chair and stood. "I'll leave you two to get acquainted."

Jenny glanced at Adrian, startled. Gilbert had only eaten a few bites of his meal. "You don't need to leave."

"The evening chores are waiting for me."

When he left the room, Jenny turned toward Adrian. "How many chores does he have?"

"Only a few."

The sky had darkened, and raindrops were streaking down the dining room window. "Should we help him?"

Adrian shook his head. "It was just an excuse for him to leave."

"Did I say something wrong?"

"No," Adrian assured her. "Sometimes he just needs some space."

She looked at the empty doorway. "You two seem to get along just fine."

"After the war, we were the only men left in the Kemp family. He's been like a father to me."

After dinner, Jenny helped Adrian with the dishes, and then he retrieved a manila envelope with several dozen black-and-white photographs inside. Side by side at the table, they rifled through his pictures of Enchanted Isle. Most were taken in a haze of eerie fog, so she couldn't see many details. Weeds overtook the benches, and an old food stand was tipped on its side. At the bottom of one picture, the tracks of a ride disappeared into the mist.

A cavern—that's where Jenny thought those tracks must lead, into a magical wonderland with dancing snowflakes and candy canes. Flutists and sugar fairies. Perhaps even a nutcracker who transformed into a handsome prince.

"This park must have been a beautiful place in its time."

Adrian leaned back in his chair, looking up from the pictures. "It's sad to see all the destruction."

She examined the next photograph, of a miniature boat sunk in a pond. "How do you access the island?"

"The main entrance is on the south side."

She glanced up. "I suspect that you don't enter from the south."

"You suspect right," he said with a grin. "There's also a clearing on the west side, with a path through the trees. Perry would have me arrested if he found me on his property, though."

The next image looked like the ribbing of a giant seashell leaning against a tree. "What is that?"

He lifted the photograph. "A piece from the merry-go-round. It was called the Magic Lagoon, though Emma calls it my father's crowning jewel. He designed it when he was a boy."

The carousel with the magical sea creatures and shells began rotating in her mind. "I'd like to see your father's magic."

He shook his head. "Unfortunately, there's not much left to see."

She pushed her chair out a few inches. "Do you have pictures of the park when it was still open?"

"My father took a number of photographs in its glory days."

"Where are they?"

"In the garret, I believe, but I must warn you, it's a disaster up there."

She smiled. "I'm not afraid of attics or disasters."

He motioned her out of the kitchen, toward a narrow staircase. "What are you afraid of, Jenny Winter?" he asked as they climbed the steps.

"Of being alone." The words slipped out unfiltered, and she wished she could stuff them back inside where they belonged.

"But you traveled all the way from America by yourself."

She smoothed her hand over the metal railing. "Not alone, I suppose, in an everyday sense. Alone for a lifetime, like—"

"Like what?"

She shook her head in response. She'd almost said "like my mother."

He stopped in the corridor above her, turning back. The silence, along with his proximity, made her nervous.

"What are you afraid of?" she asked.

He reached up overhead and pulled down on a rope. A ladder unfolded toward them. "Mind your head."

"Adrian?"

"I'm afraid of night creatures."

She shook her head. "I don't believe that for a moment."

"Something happening to my sister or my nephews, I suppose." He started climbing. "And finding out the truth about my dad."

CHAPTER 11

Gilbert sloshed down the muddy hillside beside Winston, one of his sheepdogs, as if the two of them had important business to attend to in the pouring rain.

The weather caught him unawares at times, but circumstances rarely surprised him anymore. And he liked it that way. He'd experienced plenty of turmoil during the Second World War, ambushes and other unwelcome surprises as he and his section had marched across France, right into Germany. The perimeter of his farm shielded him from the havoc of the outside world, from memories he'd fought hard to forget.

He'd always been a man who liked to build things, including the toys his brother had designed on paper when they were children. Simon was five years older, but they'd grown into the best of friends, at least until Curtis lured Simon away with his grand plans and fluid cash. Simon still wanted to work with Gilbert during the park years, but under Curtis's influence, he'd no longer seen Gilbert as a partner or even really a friend.

During the first part of the war, Gilbert had helped build flying boats at the factory on Windermere, but during its last year, he'd been shipped across the Channel to destroy almost everything in his path.

Since then, he'd attempted to shoot down memories like they were the *Boche* he'd been conscripted to kill, but his stomach churned this evening as memories of the war mixed with those that had crushed him long before he'd stepped foot on French soil.

Over the years, he'd tried to forget Liz, but she kept returning to him in his dreams. And now Jenny Winter had arrived in the Lakes, the daughter of the woman he once loved. Still loved, if he were honest with himself, though he'd never tell anyone that his heart hadn't fully relinquished the woman who'd captured it. The war of his heart and the war of his country were long over, but he was still a prisoner, in a sense. His country had been victorious, he and his heart soundly defeated.

Instead of trying to forget Liz, he should have fought for her as he'd fought for England. But on that fateful night in 1935, everything shifted for his brother and him. He had respected his older brother more than anyone else until he'd found Simon standing with a knife beside Curtis's body. In that moment, he'd realized that Simon had lost his mind. And Gilbert stopped idolizing a troubled man.

If he hadn't been so smitten with Liz, he might have noticed his brother's failing mind long before Simon killed Curtis. Maria had certainly noticed something was wrong, but he thought it was only a passing strain from the burden of the park. If his head hadn't been stuck in a cloud, he would have taken Simon to the doctor in Kendal straightaway.

After that night, Simon had refused to see a doctor. Adrian was born a week later, and Maria fully immersed herself into raising two children and running their family's inn even as Simon slipped into himself like a turtle hiding inside its shell. He'd puttered around the inn and farm for the next four years, but he lost interest in creating anything new. Then the RAF had posted Simon to their station in Wiltshire. Apparently, they'd thought his mind sound enough for him to be a gunner. Or they'd overlooked his mental state in their urgent need for recruits.

The moon lit the lake below Gilbert, forcing him to recall the night he'd tried so hard to forget. He had returned to the island hours after he'd found Curtis's body to confirm the reality that Simon had killed his business partner, but the body had disappeared.

Either Simon somehow returned that night, or someone else disposed of it. Or Curtis hadn't really been dead after all.

His own memories of that night weren't as reliable as he'd hoped, the shock erasing some of the details. There was a chance, albeit slight, that Curtis had walked away.

He wished it all had been a figment of his imagination. A nightmare. But more than twenty years had passed and no one ever found Curtis Sloan.

He and Simon had had one more conversation about Curtis, his brother claiming again that he didn't know who hurt his partner. Instead of slipping into a shell like his brother, Gilbert had gotten himself drunk and pelted Liz's window with rocks, splintering the glass. He didn't remember exactly what he'd said that afternoon, but the words were foul.

In hindsight, in the pure madness of youth, he'd almost wanted to scare her away so she would never know the truth about his family. And he'd succeeded, sent her running straight back to Cleveland and into the arms of Jack Winter, the luckiest man in the world.

It was the stupidest thing Gilbert had ever done, except perhaps waiting to tell the police what he'd seen on the island.

Without a body to indict anyone, he hadn't told a soul about Curtis until after Simon died. Sometimes he wondered what would have happened if he'd gone to the constable the night he'd found Curtis, twenty-three years ago. A confession from Simon might have cleared them of their weight of guilt, ultimately freeing both brothers.

Liz had left for America the day after he'd battered her window, and his new job as an engineer for Enchanted Isle was gone as well. So he and Simon worked together on the farm before the war, his brother taking the occasional photograph, Gilbert tinkering on his boat and car. Neither of them talked beyond the necessary.

Winston turned away, scampering back up toward the sheep. And in that moment, Gilbert craved the fire that once drowned bloody images of war in his head. He clenched his fists together, increasing his pace. He hadn't touched a drop of alcohol since two months before V-E Day.

In the ruins of a village outside Berlin, he'd had an encounter akin to Paul's on his journey to Damascus. He and Allied comrades had wreaked havoc across France and Germany, done things he regretted in spades, but during watch that night, he'd seen a brilliant light that was no dream. Whether or not the voice spoke out loud, he couldn't say, but in the light was an ultimatum. Follow God into life or follow his own path straight to hell.

God hadn't called him to be an evangelist like Paul the Apostle. Instead, Gilbert served weekly in the church and worked quietly at his farm. His was a simple life with a complex faith in that he was still learning to trust when he didn't understand, still learning to forgive himself for all he'd done. He couldn't take it back, but he wished he hadn't terrified Liz after he'd succumbed to his own fears.

What was God doing now, bringing Liz's daughter to his supper table?

Even though Gilbert wanted to know what had happened to Liz, he didn't think he could bear to hear the stories. He wished for her happiness, for a whole heart instead of one that had been broken. A lifetime of love instead of pain. But the thought of her with another man still haunted him, the thoughts of what might have been if they'd married.

He and Liz had both been so young, naïve in their affection for one another—and completely ambivalent about the differences in their families and cultures. Love, they'd thought, would cure every woe, but perhaps their marriage would have been a disaster.

The craving for a drink welled up in him again. He'd walk all night if he must, up and down the fells in the rain, instead of succumbing to his old demons.

"Uncle Gilbert?"

Turning, he saw his niece up in the doorway of her family's flat, a pink floral apron tied over her dress. Without realizing it, he'd walked into the parking lot behind the inn.

"What are you doing out in this rain?" Emma asked as he climbed the narrow staircase, joining her under the stoop's sliver of roof.

He straightened his sleeves, struggling to focus his mind back to the present. "Just taking a walk."

She kissed his cheek. "How was the food?"

"It was splendid, Emma, but we can cook just fine on our own."

"I like to cook for you."

He smiled. God had blessed him immensely with his niece and nephew, who were like a daughter and son. "I certainly won't argue if you insist."

"Do you like Jenny?" she asked, leaning back against the doorpost.

He nodded slowly. "She seems quite nice."

"I think she'd be good for Adrian." Emma glanced over at the steps leading up to his house. "And perhaps he just might be good for her too."

"Matchmaking can be a nasty business."

"I only want to help light the fire," Emma said with a grin.

He shook his head. "I don't think they need your help."

Swimming—that's what Adrian had almost told Jenny he feared as he climbed up into the garret.

Except for the bit about night creatures, the other things he'd said were true. He did worry about his sister and her family. Worried that evidence would emerge to convict his father of thievery and murdering Curtis Sloan. But if he told Jenny that he was afraid of swimming, he'd have to explain straightaway what had happened to his best mate.

He groaned inwardly, his right leg throbbing as he switched on the torch in his hand, waiting for Jenny to climb up the ladder behind him. He'd sworn that fear wouldn't run his life, yet some days it seemed to overtake it.

Light drifted across the old furniture and cobwebs, a weathered steamer trunk, and dozens of boxes. Then the light seemed to settle into the crevices of the cluttered room.

When he was about ten, he'd found the Enchanted Isle album hidden in the trunk. His father was gone by then, and he'd learned that questions about the past pained his uncle. The album, Adrian hoped, was still up here.

He unlocked the trunk's clasp and lifted the lid, Jenny peering over his shoulder. He didn't see the photo album, but he pulled out a small leather box and set it on the floor.

"What's that?" she asked.

"Some of the artifacts my family has dug up over the years." He tipped back the lid, showing her the bits of iron and stone inside. Then he lifted out a piece about six inches long. "Gilbert thinks it's some sort of cutlery, like a fork or knife."

She ran her fingers over it. "From the Romans?"

"Perhaps. My dad and I found it together when I was four."

"It's so well preserved." She reached for an ivory-colored disc that tapered into a long needle shape. "What is this?" she asked, stroking her finger down the point.

"Probably a spindle whorl."

She smiled. "I've never heard of a spindle whorl."

He cradled her hand in his, spinning the top of the spindle whorl in her palm. "The Norse would have used it to make cloth."

"Is it stone?"

"No." He paused. "Bone."

She placed it quickly back into the box. "Does your government let you keep what you find?"

"Sometimes," he said. "The coroner takes artifacts to review for what we call Treasure Trove. If an item is deemed valuable, he'll conduct an inquest to decide if it was lost by its original owner or deliberately hidden. Then the British Museum has the option to acquire lost items as long as they pay a reasonable sum to both the landowner and the person who found it."

"What if someone doesn't tell the coroner?" she asked.

"If they're caught, they lose whatever they found and are probably fined as well for hiding it."

She brushed her hand across the open box. "Did the coroner deem any of your artifacts treasure?"

He nodded. "The museum took a Roman coin."

"Why didn't you sell the rest?"

"It's not worth much," he said as he replaced the lid.

"And the pieces remind you of your dad."

He nodded before rifling through the rest of the steamer trunk. Then he dug through the box beside it, but the album wasn't in either place. "I'm not certain what happened to it."

Jenny pointed to another box. "Can I help you search?"

"Of course."

"Perhaps we'll find more treasure."

The pain in his leg eased as they pored through boxes of chinaware and linens, old books, and some farming tools. Neither of them found the album on Enchanted Isle, but Jenny discovered a Kemp family photo album wrapped in newspaper. Adrian brushed off the steamer's lid to use as a bench.

The ring of the telephone filtered upstairs, but he ignored it, carefully opening the album's cover instead beside Jenny and pointing to a sepia-toned photograph of a baby in a long gown. "My father," he said simply. "He was born a few years before the First World War."

On the next page was a studio photograph of his grandparents, when Simon and Gilbert were about ten and five years old. "My father and uncle lost their parents when they were teenagers. Gilbert took over the farm, and my father was supposed to oversee the Herdwick Inn. Dad was never good at farm work, or business for that matter, but my sister said the guests enjoyed his company."

Jenny uncurled a bent edge on the album, then smoothed it out with her fingers. "How did your parents meet?"

"When the Herdwick closed for the season, my dad would search for other work while Gilbert managed the farm. He met both my mum and Curtis working near Buttermere."

"How far away is Buttermere?"

"About an hour or so north. My mum moved to Ambleside after they married. She thought they were going to run the inn together, but when Curtis offered to finance a park, Dad quit everything else and focused on building his dream. He told Gilbert and my mum that the park would bring business to the inn as well, and he was exactly right."

"Until his dream died," she said softly.

"It was almost as if his entire life was a failure."

"No one who dares to pursue their dreams is a failure."

He glanced at her, curious. All these years in the Lake District, he'd never heard anyone except Emma and Gilbert say something positive about his father. "Not everyone appreciates the realization of a dream."

"You may never know what happened at the end with your dad, but you can always be proud that he created something special with his life." She smoothed her hand over the vinyl-covered photographs. "A place where other people could dream as well."

She turned the page again, to a picture of his father on the island before Enchanted Isle was built. He looked triumphant, as if he'd conquered an army on his own. "You look like him."

"Do you think so?"

She nodded. "Same hair. Same smile. Same confidence in your eyes."

A piece of hair fell across her face as she examined the photograph, and he pushed it gently away. When she looked up, her blue eyes were wide, questioning him.

He slowly lowered his hand, but neither of them looked away. His heart pounding, he wanted nothing more than to take her in his arms, kiss her, but he couldn't do it. Not until he found the courage to tell her the whole truth.

The floor creaked as if taking a breath for him. God help him, he had to tell her what happened to Tom. "There's something I need to say."

"What is it?"

Below them, the doorbell clanged, but he ignored it, taking a deep breath to steady himself. "Two years ago—"

"Adrian?" Gilbert called from the corridor below.

Confound it! He'd finally unearthed the courage to tell her. He couldn't stop now.

He started talking faster. "Something happened."

Gilbert called his name again.

Jenny nodded toward the opening in the floor. "He sounds worried."

Sighing, Adrian set the album on his lap and called back. "We're in the garret."

His uncle peeked up through the hole. "Should I ask what you're doing up here?"

Adrian lifted the album. "Looking at some old photographs."

Gilbert's gaze fell to the cover. "Perhaps we should let the ghosts of the past rest in peace."

"I don't think ghosts ever rest."

"Cora's at the door," Gilbert said. "She's looking for Jenny."

Jenny sprang up. "What time is it?"

"A few minutes past ten."

She shook her head. "Surely not."

"I'm afraid so."

Adrian followed Jenny down the ladder, to the front door. "I seem to have lost track of time," she told Cora.

Cora glanced at Adrian before refocusing on Jenny. "Your mother would have my head if she knew you were out so late."

Jenny smiled at him one more time before Cora whisked her away.

CHAPTER 12

"You're playing with fire," Cora said as she drove Jenny back up the hill.

"Adrian is hardly fire."

"What would your fiancé say?"

Jenny shrugged. "I don't know him well enough to know."

"If you continue seeing Adrian, I'm afraid you're going to get burned."

Jenny thought about Cora's description of natural glass, how fire molded and colored it. "Some of your prettiest pieces were formed by heat."

"That's true, but the components are completely different when they emerge from the fire." Cora parked the car in the courtyard. "Colored glass changes or even hides light. Adrian might seem nice enough on the outside, but—"

"Adrian isn't hiding anything," Jenny insisted, though she wondered what he'd been planning to say before Gilbert had called them. Perhaps he was going to tell her about the female owner of the boat on Elter Water. When he did, she'd tell him about Robert.

"So he finally told you what happened to Tom?"

Jenny's heart stirred at the gravity in Cora's tone, and she braced herself. "No."

"Come along," Cora said, stepping out of the car. "I'll explain inside."

Cora scooped coal into the stove before sitting on the sofa. Jenny shifted in the chair across from her, not wanting to hear what Cora had to say, yet feeling like she must.

"Adrian has always been a good swimmer," Cora began. "He and his friend Tom were hoping to compete in the Olympics, but only one of them could be chosen to train with other athletes at the Academy in Birmingham. Two years ago Adrian dared Tom to race across Grasmere, but Tom . . . he never made it to the other side."

Jenny's heart lurched. "He drowned?"

Cora pressed her hands together in her lap, sighing before she spoke. "It was an awful day."

Jenny wrapped her arms across her chest as the image of a young man broke through the depths in her mind. He was flailing in the water, trying to catch his breath. And her own breath seemed to fail her. "Adrian must have grieved terribly."

"I don't know if he grieved at all," Cora said. "Some people thought he was trying to get rid of his competition."

Jenny stiffened, every muscle in her body clenched into an angry mass. "Adrian would never do that."

"You just met him, Jenny." Cora glanced out the dark window and then looked back at her. "Unfortunately, he has a long history of trouble."

"What kind of trouble?"

"When he was younger, he used to sneak away and wreak havoc around Ambleside while the other kids were in school. As he grew older, he and Tom became known for speeding around on their motorbikes. Adrian wrecked his a couple of times, but never hurt himself enough to slow down."

Jenny wrapped her arms across her chest and leaned back against the cushions on her chair. She could imagine Adrian as a strong competitor, racing on his bike, but the picture returned of him helping the sheep, so tender in his care. Surely he wouldn't hurt his friend, even if he were vying for the same slot. "He'd never intentionally kill someone."

"I don't know that he was trying to kill Tom. Perhaps injure him or make him question his ability."

Jenny glanced down at a colorful vase on the coffee table, trying to reconcile the man she'd been getting to know with a man willing to injure another to get ahead.

"Did Adrian compete in the Olympics?" she finally asked.

Cora shook her head. "He didn't make the team."

Jenny picked up the vase and rotated it in her hands. With square edges, it had been pieced together with lead came and dozens of stained-glass pieces; the larger chunks of red and green at the bottom looked like steps, narrowing up into smaller pieces.

Each of their stories were made of hundreds of pieces like this, some fragile, others as strong as the lead that glued it together, some parts clear, and others opaque. She couldn't imagine that the man who'd been so nice to her had intentionally hurt his friend, but perhaps he was hiding his past behind some sort of facade. Perhaps, in her ignorance, she would get hurt.

"I fear he's following in his father's footsteps," Cora continued. "If he is, his choices will devastate everyone in his path."

"He's been kind to me." Jenny set the vase back on the table. "And his sister has been nice to me as well."

Cora nodded briskly. "Emma's the only sane one in that family."

"She doesn't seem to see Adrian as a threat. In fact, it seems she adores him."

"Love blinds people, Jenny." Cora patted her knee as if the words extended far beyond Emma.

The telephone rang, and Cora scooted to the end of the sofa.

"I've been out," she said simply after answering it.

The clock ticked beside Jenny, filling in the silence before Cora spoke again.

"Perry—" Cora stopped as if he'd interrupted her. "I don't have that amount of money."

Jenny retreated toward the corridor to give Cora some privacy.

She hoped Cora would tell Perry to find a way to earn some cash instead of sponging off her, but Jenny suspected she would cave in to her ex-husband's demands, blind as well in what she thought was love.

Cora, it seemed to her, was the one playing with fire.

In his years of swimming, Adrian had meticulously kept time on the clock, but whenever he was with Jenny, he seemed to lose track of hours. Cora had swept her away tonight without even a cursory recognition of his presence, like a fierce wind capturing a sail, forcing it in a different direction. Jenny seemed as stunned as he by the interruption, but she had no real choice except to concede. Cora, after all, was her host for the season.

After the women left, Adrian slipped out the door to Emma's home. Even though her kitchen light was on, Adrian tapped lightly on the door, not wanting to wake Frank or his nephews if they were asleep.

Emma answered his knock wearing a terry bathrobe, her short hair twisted with ties. The kitchen table was still covered with plates and crumbs from their meal. As much as Emma enjoyed preparing food, she was averse to picking up the aftermath. He suspected that Frank would clear all the dishes in the morning.

She waved Adrian toward the table, and he pulled out one of the chairs. "Uncle Gilbert said supper was a success."

"Because of the corned beef hash and pudding."

"I think it was because of the company." She smiled again. "Something pressing must be on your mind for such a late visit."

"I wanted to show Jenny the photographs that Dad took of Enchanted Isle, but I couldn't find the album."

Her smile fell. "Why do you want to show her those?"

"She's curious. I think her mother visited the island when she was in England."

"Ah," Emma said, stepping into the kitchen beside the table. "I would hate for her to get wrapped up in that mess."

"She doesn't see it as a mess."

Emma reached for a saucepan on the stove. "I'd also hate for Jenny to get her heart wrapped up with you if you're not interested."

He brushed a mound of crumbs into his hand and dumped them onto a plate. "That is none of your business, Sis."

"Touché." Emma poured the contents of the pan into two cups and brought them both to the table. He smelled the milk spiced with cinnamon and sugar. "Are you going to ask her on another date?"

"I'll ask, but Cora might convince her to make alternate plans."

"If you're honest with Jenny, Cora's words will have no power over either of you."

But some words, he knew, could be extremely powerful.

"Do you have the album?" he asked.

She nodded. "It's stored with my things for the inn. I was afraid that Uncle Gilbert might not keep it."

"Wise of you to hide it away." He paused, sipping the cinnamon milk. "Some days I want to forget as well, but other days . . ."

"You're a lot like Dad, Adrian. In the best sense."

Part of him wanted to be like the man he'd so admired as a child, but part of him wanted anything else. "Do you think about him much?"

"Occasionally, whenever Mum rings."

"How often does she phone you?"

"A couple times a year," Emma said. "You should ring her."

He leaned back in his chair, shaking his head. "David will answer, and he's not particularly fond of me."

He'd only seen David Brown once since the man had married their mother. After the war, she'd been more than ready to rid herself of the memories of her deceased husband, ready to start a new family. She'd once told Adrian that she'd stopped caring for Simon Kemp long before Adrian had been born.

While his father hadn't liked to talk, his mum sometimes said too much.

"She always asks about you," Emma said.

"That's awfully kind."

"It's hard for her, Adrian. You remind her of Dad as well."

"That's a lousy excuse for deciding not to parent."

Emma sighed. "I don't excuse her. Only trying to find a reason for her behavior."

He glanced around the dining room where he'd spent much of his childhood, where he and Emma had laughed as children, where his parents had quarreled. Emma and Frank had reclaimed this room and this whole flat, filling it with a family who loved one another.

Ever since Jenny had asked about his father, a memory niggled at him. "Years ago, you told me that you heard Dad and Curtis here, arguing about something."

Emma nodded slowly, her head bowing as she wrapped her hands around her mug. "They were fighting about money."

"But what about money?"

"I'm not certain. They woke me up from my sleep with their shouting, but I never got out of bed." With a sigh, she looked back up at him. "I wish I'd gotten up, really I do. Wish I would have told Mum."

"Where was she that night?"

Emma shrugged. "Probably working."

He nodded. Even though the Kemp family started the inn, the place had been a refuge for his mother before and during the war. While she was married to Simon, she'd spent at least six months of the year managing the business.

He leaned forward. "Did you hear anything else they said?"

"They were talking about losing money." She rotated the mug in her hands, reflecting back on that night long ago. "The man accused Dad of stealing."

"Do you think he stole the park's money?"

"It doesn't matter what I think. Dad already suffered for whatever choices he made. We can remember the good in him, though. The love he had for his family."

One of Adrian's nephews, seven-year-old Ronnie, stuck his head out of the corridor, his hair messy. "Hello, Uncle Adrian."

Adrian held out his arms, and the boy gave him a hug. They'd been the best of mates since Adrian had returned from the Academy. Emma wouldn't allow Ronnie to be a passenger on Adrian's motorbike, for good reason, but the boy loved to fish with him from the dock. Together they'd caught schools of perch, charr, pike, and trout. The chef paid Ronnie for his catch and then baked, broiled, or fried the fish for the evening's diners.

Emma shooed her son back to his bedroom, but Adrian's gaze lingered on the corridor, his own memories of boyhood flooding back before he turned toward her again. "What else did the men say that night?"

"That was all I heard. When they lowered their voices, I went back to sleep."

If Adrian had heard someone accuse his dad of stealing, he would have snuck out into the corridor like Ronnie, if he must, to hear what they were saying. He wouldn't have been able to go back to sleep even if he'd tried.

"When we were searching for the album, Jenny and I found the box of artifacts that Dad and Gilbert dug up around the farm. I remember carrying my shovel around as a kid, searching for artifacts like them."

"You were Dad's shadow," Emma said.

"He told me once, when I was about five, that there was a treasure hidden on the island."

She flinched. "He wasn't thinking clearly."

"I know."

"But—" She shifted in her chair.

He inched forward. "What is it, Emma?"

"After Dad died, I was the one who went through his things. I found the photo album . . . and something else."

He drummed his fingers together, his nerves feeling as if someone had hot-wired them. "What did you find?"

"An old coin," she finally said.

The hair on the back of his neck prickled. "What sort of coin, Emma?"

"I stored it away, afraid . . ."

He slowly processed her words. "Why didn't you tell me before?"

"When we were younger, I feared you'd go mad searching for a treasure that's not there."

"Like Dad?"

"I think the treasure was a fantasy, Adrian. One of Curtis's grand schemes to drum up business or interest potential investors in the park. He probably planted a coin on the island to make Dad believe something was buried there."

His heart raced. "Can I see this coin?"

"I'll look for it when I search for the album."

"Perhaps there are more coins hidden on the island," he said, the words directed more to himself than to Emma.

She shook her head. "That's exactly why I never told you or Gilbert."

"Because we'd wonder?"

"Because the possibilities might consume you."

He considered her words. "Perhaps Dad killed Curtis over something still buried out there."

She pushed back her chair and stood. "You have a life to live, Adrian. Seize it. Get to know this Jenny and plan for your future beyond these lakes instead of rummaging around in the past."

He blinked, surprised at her words. "You'd be okay if I moved to London?"

"No, but I want what's best for you . . ." She paused. "Going away may be the very best thing."

He kissed her cheek. "Thank you."

"Embrace what you have now."

But he couldn't stop thinking about the coin as he walked back up the hill. What if his father had found something of value? Something that Curtis had tried to steal—along with Simon's life.

Instead of murdering his partner, perhaps his dad had only defended himself against the man who'd planned to kill him first.

CHAPTER 13

As bells tolled across the damp hills, Jenny found herself standing outside the arched doorway of a sandstone church below Cora's house, in the valley opposite Windermere.

A plaque beside the imposing door said Normans had built this sanctuary around 1150. Jenny read the date twice, mulling over the thought of people walking across this porch and into the nave eight hundred years ago.

There was strength in history, woven through plaster and stone, but there was also sorrow. Tears when reflecting on loved ones from the past. In some cases, the barbs of history could be like a ball and chain dragged through life, the key thrown away. One couldn't always escape, even if they wanted to be free.

Jenny had invited Cora to attend a morning service with her, but Cora declined, saying she needed to finish cleaning a piece she'd brought home from a cathedral in Carlisle. The profit from her work, Jenny assumed, would line Perry's pockets.

Did Perry really need her money? Perhaps he felt threatened in one sense, if he'd once controlled Cora. Threatened that she might have a mind to step completely away.

"Welcome," the parson said, waving Jenny inside with the small congregation. She selected a wooden pew on the left side. In front of her was an embroidered kneeling cushion, the colorful needlework breathing life into a rabbit that held a bright-orange carrot. Like Peter or Benjamin in Beatrix Potter's books.

The windows to her left were stained with dozens of colors, the glass portraying Jesus during the Last Supper as well as His crucifixion and ascension into heaven. Sun filtered through the stain, its rays brushing a rainbow of color across the pews. Stained glass did hide things, like Cora said, but it transformed the simplicity in this sanctuary as well, changing the wood and stone into a garden of light.

Organ music wafted through the nave, soothing her soul. She had traveled to England in search of beauty and identity, and both seemed to fuse together in this room.

The parson directed the congregation to turn to the book of Isaiah, chapter sixty-four. She reached for the Bible in front of her and flipped through the pages with the rest of the congregation until she found the chapter.

"'But now, O Lord,'" the congregation read together, "'thou art our father; we are the clay, and thou our potter; and we all are the work of thy hand.'"

The parson began speaking about Daniel, the Hebrew man who was forced into captivity, but he respectfully resisted in his captivity, refusing to conform like those around him. The rector spoke about how God molded and shaped Daniel even as His servant remained faithful to Him.

As the parson continued speaking, Jenny's thoughts receded back to the verse in Isaiah. She missed her earthly dad dearly, but she still had a father who cared for her. He'd created her to love His creation, like Adrian said, to see beauty in places others might miss. Her gifts may be different than those of her fellow students talented in words or numbers, but instead of fighting those gifts, perhaps she needed to accept them, embrace who He made her to be even as He continued to mold her.

Daniel hadn't known what his future held either, but he had honorably stood for what was right. Could she stand up to her grandfather and tell him that she couldn't marry Robert Tripp, that she felt as if God had an entirely different plan for her life, cemented in Him?

She prayed silently that God would anchor her no matter what she faced. Shape her into the person He, not her grandfather, wanted her to be.

At the end of the sermon, Jenny stood with the congregation and opened her hymnal to join a song worshiping the Creator of the world, a song about the sweetness of His home.

The sun was shining over the valley when she walked outside, calling for her to explore. She needed to get out this afternoon and clear her mind. Let the light, His light, filter through her as well.

Back in Cora's house, she changed her clothing and retrieved her camera. Before she pedaled away on her bicycle, the telephone rang, and she answered it, hoping it was Adrian. But instead it was Perry.

"I must speak with Cora," the man demanded.

"She's not here," Jenny replied, glancing down at the coffee table. The stained-glass vase she'd seen before was gone.

"When will she return?"

"I'm afraid I'm not privy to her schedule, Mr. Banks."

"Tell her to ring me when she returns."

Jenny wrapped the telephone cord slowly around her arm.

"Hello?" he demanded.

"I'm still here."

"I need to speak with Cora immediately."

"Where should I tell her to ring?"

He huffed. "She knows my number."

Jenny scribbled a note and left it by the phone; then she pedaled back down to Windermere. Instead of using color film today, she threaded the black-and-white film that Adrian had given her into the spool, her thoughts wandering back to the man who'd taught her how to use her Automagic. He too sought to capture the wonder of creation.

A mallard paddled across the lake in front of her, and she snapped a photograph of it. Then she wandered farther down the lake, glancing back at the stone front of the Herdwick Inn. And she wondered again about what happened between Adrian and Tom.

Had Adrian been about to tell her about Tom last night?

She prayed he would be honest with her now. And that the truth was much different than what Cora had said.

On his walk home from church, Adrian eyed two swimmers who braved the icy waters of Windermere. Even though the daffodils had made an appearance in their district, the water still stung of winter.

As a swimmer, the cold had only bothered him in those first moments after plunging into a lake, heckling him until he flung his arm overhead and pulled through his first strokes. Once he'd started swimming, nothing else mattered. Not the cold or his family. Not what people whispered about his father, pretending that he didn't hear. Swimming, in a sense, had saved him from destroying himself. Its salvation was fleeting, but he'd found significance during those years as he moved through the water, pressing toward his goal.

He wrung his hands together as he turned from the shore. That season was over for him, but some days he wondered what it would be like to overcome this fear that shackled him and dive back into one of these lakes like he used to, the fire inside warming the cold on his skin.

He and Tom had begun swimming together at Elter Water when they were nine and ten. A teacher had encouraged them to swim before school during the warmer months, in the hopes it would keep them out of trouble. The swimming hadn't eliminated their mischief, but it certainly helped curb it during those earlier years. And in the midst, he'd discovered that he loved gliding through the water like a bird caught up in the wind. And Tom had discovered that swimming breathed life into him as well.

For years, they'd worked together, challenging and pushing each other to grow stronger and faster in their sport. Then Gilbert had taken Adrian to the summer Olympics in London, back in 1948. He'd been mesmerized by the precision in the swimmers' strokes, their incredible speed and determination to struggle for something great.

After their stints with the national service, he and Tom had both returned home, as fit as the day they'd left and with scholarships waiting for them at separate universities, monies to ensure they'd join the swimming teams. He and Tom had resumed their routine on holidays, swimming together every morning and some evenings as well, until the nightmare that would haunt Adrian the rest of his life.

The water they'd both loved had swallowed his best friend.

He shivered as he climbed the steps up to his sister's flat.

Some people might think he was strong, a rebel even as he'd been in his youth. The truth was, he was terrified and tired of living in fear. Nothing, he imagined, could ever force him back into the water, but he wanted to dive into life like he'd once done with his swimming, immerse himself into his plans for the future like Emma had encouraged him to do.

What would Jenny think about living in London?

Instead of fear, that thought made him smile.

After a meal of tea and his sister's rarebit, Adrian hopped on his motorbike and rode back into the hills to Cora's house. He'd enjoyed his time with Jenny last night, showing her the family photographs, but he needed to speak with her about Tom before another thought crept in about the future. *Their* future.

He rang the bell beside the front door and waited. When no one answered, he turned to leave, but he hadn't walked far before the red door leading into Cora's studio opened.

Cora stood in the doorframe, her forehead beaded with sweat and her curly hair wild, as if she'd been up all night. "What do you want?"

"I'm here to see Jenny."

"You need to leave her alone."

He slipped his hands into his pockets but didn't move. "Jenny hasn't asked me to leave."

"Why would she?" Cora said. "You haven't been honest with her."

He stiffened. "What did you tell her?"

"She doesn't want to see you again, Adrian."

He glanced up at the windows, hoping that Jenny might be looking back at him, but no one was there. "Because of Tom?"

"Because she's engaged to marry someone back in Cleveland."

It felt as if she'd punctured him. "What—"

"A man by the name of Robert."

Every muscle in his body tensed, threatening to snap within him. Of course Jenny was engaged. He'd been such a dunce, never even thinking to ask about a boyfriend or fiancé. Assuming . . .

He backed away as Cora closed the door, shaking as he heard her slide the bolt across it.

His mind whirling, he shifted his motorbike into gear and rode down past the hotel, then north through the valley, reeling from the slap in her words. Wind blew through his hair, stung his eyes as he sped through the fells.

Jenny was getting married.

Once again, he'd dived headfirst into unknown waters without checking for rocks below the surface.

It didn't matter what had happened in his past or what he had planned for the future. Didn't matter if he cared about Jenny. She was already in love with someone else.

Fells rose above the lake on his right like a pod of blue whales, their backs curled above the surface and padded white with the lingering snow. He slowed the motorbike, trying to frame the future in his mind.

Perhaps he wouldn't wait until the end of the summer to leave these lakes. Emma didn't really need his help, and Jenny would be returning soon to the man she'd marry. He needed to leave this district and its memories behind, create a life for himself where no one knew his story. Where people like Cora Banks weren't anxious to tear him down.

Tomorrow he'd send a letter to Mr. Webb, the man who'd offered him the bank position. He could move to London right away if they needed him.

He slowed the motorbike as he neared Elter Water, his racing heart beginning to settle as he walked back through the trees. He'd spend an hour or two rowing this afternoon, at the place where he and Tom had begun their pursuit of a dream. It wasn't the same as swimming, but he loved pressing the oars through the water, feeling the flame heat his body.

But when he reached the reeds, the rowboat wasn't there. Shading his eyes, he scanned the small lake until he saw a speck of a figure rowing on the far side.

Had Jenny borrowed the boat to take more pictures? Or had someone else found his hiding place?

Unlike many of these lakes, there was no real shore around Elter Water. In order to circle it, he'd have to duck under low-lying tree limbs that curtained the surface and stomp through the muddy fringe of reeds. There was no reason to do that. If Jenny had decided to borrow the boat, he was glad to let her use it. He should just slip away now and leave her alone, like Cora had said.

But then again, that's probably what his father would have done, slipped away into himself instead of being honest with the people he cared for. If only his dad had told the truth and been honest about whatever plagued him. It might have healed the wounds between his parents, scars that remained long after his father's death.

He'd already run far and long enough. He should be honest with Jenny today.

But as the boat drew closer, he realized it wasn't Jenny. It was Mrs. Moore rowing, the woman who'd been like a mother to him after his own mother had left. He didn't realize she still used Tom's old boat.

He brushed twigs off a lichen-stained rock and sat on it, waiting for Mrs. Moore to finish her journey. When she was about fifty feet away, she wiped her eyes with the back of her hand. Somehow she'd managed to find strength in her grief, but still her tears made his heart lurch.

He often wondered what would have happened to him and Tom if his friend hadn't drowned. Would one of them have gone on to compete in the Olympics? Would Tom have moved away by now, perhaps even married?

It was senseless to wonder what might have been, but they'd dreamed so much about their future. Neither of them had considered the possibility that they wouldn't be forging into it together.

When Mrs. Moore drew near the shore, he helped her steady the boat, reaching for her hand as she stepped back onto grass. Then he pulled the rowboat out of the water and tipped it so the rains wouldn't fill the hull.

Turning back to her, he dug his hands into his pockets. "I didn't mean to intrude."

"You're not intruding," she said. "On the days my memories seem to be slipping away, I visit here or the schoolhouse."

"I come here to remember too."

She glanced toward a rocky fell in the distance capped with white. "This was Tom's favorite place to swim."

He nodded. "In all our years here, we never met another swimmer."

She teetered for a moment, like the needle on a compass trying to change direction. He reached out his hand to steady her, and she clutched it. "He liked nothing more than swimming with you, Adrian."

"I'm so sorry."

Fresh tears slipped down her cheeks, but she didn't bother wiping them off this time. "It wasn't your fault," she said, as if she hadn't already assured him of that multiple times.

His gaze slipped back over the water. "I miss him."

"I'm glad," Mrs. Moore said, patting his hand. "It makes it easier to have someone to miss him with."

He squeezed her hand before releasing it, both of them lost for a moment in their own memories. Even though Mrs. Moore had assured him repeatedly that the accident wasn't his fault, Tom wouldn't have swum in Grasmere that night if Adrian hadn't urged him to go. He would still be alive and perhaps training now for the games in Rome.

Adrian trekked back with Mrs. Moore through the trees. Her car, she said, was in the nearby village, and she preferred to walk instead of ride on his motorbike.

She stopped when they reached the end of the path. "I enjoyed meeting your Jenny."

He shook his head. "Jenny's not mine."

Her eyebrows climbed. "Have you asked her to be?"

He couldn't tell her that Jenny was already promised to someone else. "Cora told her what happened to Tom."

"Why didn't you tell her first?"

"Each time I started, it didn't seem right," he said. "Cowardly of me, I know, but I . . . well, I rather like her."

"No one thinks you're a coward, Adrian."

This time, his eyebrows raised in protest. Plenty of people thought he was a coward and worse.

"Well, I certainly don't think you are a coward," Mrs. Moore insisted, buttoning her jacket.

"But Jenny might—"

"Then she doesn't belong with you after all."

CHAPTER 14

An incessant ringing forced Jenny out of bed and down the steps. She almost didn't answer the telephone, not wanting another confrontation with Perry, but Cora was in Carlisle today, working on the cathedral window. She might need Jenny to find something for her.

Her voice groggy, Jenny picked up the receiver. "Hello."

The line crackled in response before she heard a woman's voice. "Is Jenny Winter available?"

She sank onto the sofa, wondering who might be calling for her. "This is Jenny."

"Oh, good," the woman said, sighing with relief.

"Who is this?" Jenny heard laughter in the background, children singing. Then the honking of a horn.

"Mrs. Moore," the woman replied. "You visited my home with Adrian before the snowstorm."

"Of course." Jenny swirled the phone cord like a jump rope, skirting the floor with it. "You were very gracious to welcome me, but I thought you didn't own a telephone."

"I'm at a kiosk," Mrs. Moore explained. "Did Adrian help you retrieve your bicycle?"

"He did."

"He's a kind soul."

She stopped swinging the cord, feeling awkward about the direction of their conversation. "How can I help you, Mrs. Moore?"

"I wanted to invite you back for tea. The last time you were here, I failed miserably as your hostess."

"You didn't fail."

Mrs. Moore pressed on. "Would you be available at two?"

Jenny glanced at the clock on the mantel. It was a few minutes before nine. She'd have plenty of time to retrieve her photographs from Ambleside before biking up toward Loughrigg Fell. "I believe I could do that."

"Very good," Mrs. Moore replied, and Jenny imagined a large smile on the woman's face. "I love company. Would you like me to fetch you from Cora's?"

"Oh, no. It's the perfect day for a bicycle ride."

"I live at the very end of the valley."

"I remember." Jenny scooted toward the receiver. "I will see you in a few hours, then—"

"Jenny?"

"Yes, Mrs. Moore."

"It's probably best not to tell Adrian."

Jenny thought her request strange, but she agreed.

"Or Cora."

"Cora's working in Carlisle."

"Excellent, then. We'll have a splendid time together."

For breakfast Jenny sprinkled sugar over a bowl of Weetabix and fresh milk. Then she dressed and rode her bicycle down to the lake, unaware until she reached the bottom of the hill that she hadn't wobbled once. Finally, she'd mastered the bicycle, and she hoped that soon she'd master her camera as well.

She eyed the Herdwick Inn as she passed it, but kept pedaling to the chemist to retrieve her roll of color photographs. Later she hoped to develop the black-and-white film in her camera with Adrian.

The gentleman at the counter handed her a cardboard envelope with her pictures, and she clutched it between her hands, refusing to open it in the store. The excitement over seeing them warred with her concern that she'd failed yet again, even with Adrian's help.

If so, she'd hide her camera away for the rest of her visit and sketch the scenery around the lake. Perhaps Cora would let her help with the glass as well.

The photographs tucked under her arm, she pushed her bicycle toward the center of town until she found a bench near the church. The bells tolled from the tower above her, the vibrations rippling across her skin. She sat for a moment on the bench and stared down at the envelope in her lap.

Failure.

The word flashed in front of her again, blinking like the lights on a marquee. Blinding her.

Taking a deep breath, she tore the edge of the envelope with her fingernail and carefully opened it. Then she slid the pile of photographs onto her lap and lifted the first one, a smile moving slowly across her lips.

Her camera had captured the silvery reeds in the moonlight along the shore, the moonlight dusting their tips with gold. What she'd seen in her viewfinder had been inscribed onto this paper. In color.

She rubbed her hands together, her enthusiasm mounting.

The next photograph was a soupy mess, but the one after it was focused on the stern of their little boat, the light playing on the trees behind it. And the next photograph was the rippled reflection of orange moonlight on the lake's surface, the dance of flames on water.

She leaned back against the bench and closed her eyes to replay the memories in her head. It had been a magical night at Elter Water. The boat ride with Adrian. The moon. The beauty all around them.

Now she could take pictures wherever she liked, capturing the sunlight in the day or the glimpses of moon at night.

Part of her wanted to race to the inn to show Adrian the pictures, but she wasn't certain what exactly she would say. He hadn't called after their meal together, at least not when she was at home. Perhaps he was with the owner of the rowboat or working extra hours at the farm.

She finished thumbing through the photographs and then looked at her watch. It was almost noon. She'd begin pedaling up toward Mrs. Moore's house, taking photographs along the way. Perhaps she would stop at the inn on the way back to hear Adrian's story. If he wanted to tell her.

The air cooled her skin as she pumped up the hill, the scent of spring reviving her. Blackbirds filled the air with melody, a chorus of nature with the bleating of sheep and gentle rumble of the brook tumbling over stones.

She'd write her mom again tonight and enclose a copy of one of the photographs. Or perhaps she could compile an entire album to show her mother the highlights from the Lakes, places Liz had visited more than two decades ago.

Slowing her bicycle, she stopped to photograph a ewe with its lamb, grazing among an outcropping of rocks. Near them was a single daffodil that had unfurled its blossoms in utter defiance of the snow.

She snapped pictures of the lamb sipping water from the grass-lined stream, the ewe keeping watch as if Jenny were a badger ready to hop the fence. When the lamb finished drinking, the ewe glanced one more time at Jenny and then hopped over the stream, the lamb following at her heels.

A few minutes before two, Jenny stepped up to Mrs. Moore's ivy-clad house and knocked on her front door.

"I'm glad the sun is here to greet you this time," Mrs. Moore said, shaking her hand and inviting her inside.

"I love the sun and the snow."

"We're kindred spirits, then." Mrs. Moore took Jenny's coat and hung it on a rack. Then she directed Jenny to sit at a table set with tea and two plates, a slice of sponge cake served on each one.

"Thank you for inviting me," Jenny said as she spread a linen napkin over her lap.

Mrs. Moore poured tea into both cups. "Do you like stories?"

"Good ones." Jenny savored a bite of the sweet dessert glazed with lemon and sugar. "Almost as much as I like cake."

Mrs. Moore shook her head sadly. "Unfortunately this one doesn't have a happy ending."

Jenny lowered her fork. "Are there good people in it?"

"People that I love." Mrs. Moore stirred sugar slowly into her tea. "It's a story that will stick with you."

"Those are the best kind."

"My husband died in 1938," Mrs. Moore said, "and I hosted two evacuees from London during the war. A lovely girl who was nine when she arrived and a seven-year-old boy. In 1945, the girl returned to her family in London, but the boy's parents were both killed in the Blitz. I raised him as my son."

Jenny glanced back at the photos of the confident young man lined up neatly on the shelf. "What was his name?"

"Tom," she said proudly. "Tom Moore—I officially adopted him when he was fourteen."

"Cora told me about Tom," Jenny whispered.

Mrs. Moore nodded. "Everyone around here seemed to know Tom and Adrian. Both of them had lost their fathers, so they bonded in junior school and discovered their love of swimming together.

"Tom was fiercely loyal, but he was also brash at times." Mrs. Moore stirred a second spoonful of sugar into her tea, but she didn't drink it. "At the age of eighteen, he was sent to fight in Kenya for his national service. He returned in the spring, like one of the swallows that winters in Africa." She paused, staring down into her tea. "But like so many after a war, he didn't come back the same man. It was as if he didn't care much about his own life and never seemed to realize how his choices impacted those of us who loved him."

"Cora said he and Adrian were competing to be in the Olympics."

She nodded. "They both pushed themselves and each other for years, a healthy competition that kept them focused on the straight and narrow until . . ."

"He drowned."

Mrs. Moore winced. "Ultimately, yes, but that wasn't what killed him."

Jenny braced herself, ready for Mrs. Moore to confirm that Adrian had somehow contributed to Tom's death. But then again, why would the woman associate with the man who'd schemed against her adopted son?

Mrs. Moore sipped her tea before speaking again. "A swimmer at a meet in London introduced Tom to a narcotic called cocaine. Tom thought it made him faster, but Adrian and I both told him that it would harm him in the end. A few months later, Adrian challenged Tom to a race across Grasmere, not knowing Tom had taken the drug."

A tear fell into Mrs. Moore's cup, and this fragment of pain, of deep loss, etched itself into Jenny's heart. The woman had loved and then lost the boy who had become her son. "Tom never made it back to shore."

"I'm so sorry . . ."

"Adrian injured his leg trying to rescue him."

"Some people," Jenny said, "think Adrian wanted to hurt or even kill Tom."

"The people who say such things"—Mrs. Moore straightened her napkin—"they don't know Adrian, and they don't know about the cocaine. Adrian has guarded that secret for both Tom's sake and mine, though I think it's time to tell people the truth. Adrian would never have hurt his best friend."

"How do you know?" Jenny blurted. The question seemed inconsiderate, but what if Adrian had deceived Mrs. Moore?

"I found Tom that night with the cocaine. I tried to stop him from going out, but nothing would deter him. Just like there was nothing Adrian could do when Tom's heart failed him in the water."

"What happened to the swimmer who gave him the cocaine?"

"He won a bronze in Melbourne."

Jenny cringed. "You must hate him."

"Some days I get angry, and other days I'm incredibly sad, but I have had to learn to forgive him, or the drug of hatred would kill me too." Mrs. Moore nudged Jenny's plate of cake toward her. "Please eat."

Jenny took several bites as she mulled over her hostess's words. It was easy enough to talk about forgiveness, especially from the confines of a pulpit, but the act of forgiving must be heart-wrenching as Mrs. Moore tried to forgive daily the successes of a man who'd contributed to the death of her son.

"Have you forgiven Adrian as well?" Jenny asked quietly.

"There isn't anything to forgive. What happened wasn't his fault, but even if it had been, I would try, God willing, to forgive him."

"That's a gift."

"Indeed. I don't have the power to do it on my own, but when I forgive others, I experience God's forgiveness for my own past."

Jenny settled back into her chair. "Adrian told me a bit about his past. About his father . . ."

"Simon Kemp and Curtis Sloan were a bit like Tom and Adrian before they started Enchanted Isle."

"Did you know Mr. Kemp?"

"Not well, but my Eddie and I visited his park every summer for the three years it was open. The attractions spoke of a man who saw the extraordinary in his ordinary life. I suppose it endeared me to Adrian and his sister even more."

"You are a remarkable woman, Mrs. Moore."

The woman smiled again. "I see remarkable in you."

"I'm not remarkable. Anything but."

"Adrian sees the remarkable in you too."

Jenny looked back at her hands. No one had ever commended her before for stepping outside the ordinary. "How do you know what Adrian thinks?"

"I saw him yesterday, when I was rowing on one of the lakes."

Jenny blinked, the realization dawning slowly. "Elter Water?"

"Yes." The woman looked surprised. "Have you been on my little boat?"

"Adrian took me out on the water to take some photographs."

"Very good," Mrs. Moore said, patting her hand. "Very good indeed."

Adrian packed two glass containers, cushioned with dishcloths, and a loaf of bread in the leather saddlebags on his motorbike. Every Monday and Thursday, Emma sent whatever was featured on the inn's dining menu up to Mrs. Moore, even though Mrs. Moore insisted that she didn't need charity. He always insisted it was a gift, not charity. Emma sent an identical meal up for him and Gilbert on those nights as well.

After she lost her husband, the government provided Mrs. Moore with a small pension. She took in sewing to supplement her income, and Tom had worked on weekends and during the summer to help provide. In the months following Tom's death, her dwindling resources were reflected in the lack of coke for her furnace, the skin on her face taut from grief and the lack of food.

Even though Mrs. Moore never complained, the parish began delivering coke to heat her home, and Emma started sending meals. Whenever Adrian visited, he assisted her with the chores, chopping firewood, changing light bulbs, planting or harvesting the vegetable garden. And when necessary, he fixed her Austin motorcar, a skill his uncle had taught him long ago.

She always left him a few pennies on the table, coins he always ignored. It was a bit of a game, he supposed, born out of respect. She appreciated his work, but he suspected that she enjoyed the company even more. He certainly enjoyed seeing her.

He didn't know how long Mrs. Moore could continue here after he left for London. The thought of her being alone, without someone to check in every few days, was the biggest deterrent to him leaving, but he would come back often to visit. Perhaps Gilbert could stop by at least once a week to help with chores while he was gone.

When he reached her cottage, Adrian removed both glass containers from the wrappings of cloth and carried the food toward her house, along with a bundle of flowers secured under his arm.

Her tears yesterday at the lake had reminded him again of how much she'd sacrificed to care for Tom, expecting nothing in return. If he'd known the full extent of what cocaine could do, Adrian would've stolen Tom's supply, buried it in a trench somewhere and faced his friend's anger straight on.

He rapped the doorknocker, and Mrs. Moore opened it with a smile. He was glad her tears were gone today.

After kissing his cheek, she pushed the door open wider. And he saw Jenny Winter sitting inside.

He blinked several times, trying to recover from his shock before he spoke. He'd already rehearsed what he would say to Jenny if he happened upon her in town, but the words escaped him now.

"I'll return later," he muttered.

"No, no," Mrs. Moore said, reaching for his arm. "Please come in."

But he didn't step into the cottage, instead holding out the containers and bread. "Emma sent you beef Wellington and cabbage."

"It smells wonderful," she said, but she didn't take the food.

He nodded back toward his motorbike. "I must go."

She leaned toward him, then inched the door closed behind her before whispering, "Courage, Adrian."

The line in the sand.

Instead of debating with him, Mrs. Moore opened the door again, and he saw Jenny's tentative smile—no hostility in her face like he'd seen with Cora.

He stepped into Mrs. Moore's living room. "Hello, Jenny."

"Hello," she said, seeming uncomfortable as well. "Mrs. Moore invited me over for tea."

"I'll pour a cuppa for you too," Mrs. Moore said before disappearing back into the kitchen, like she'd done the afternoon of the storm. Apparently, she'd taken a page from Emma's book of matchmaking.

"I stopped by to see you yesterday," he said as he sat beside Jenny. "Cora was home."

"Did she tell you not to come back?"

"She said that you didn't want to see me again."

Jenny huffed. "Cora doesn't want me to see you again, but I never said that."

"And she told me something else . . ."

"What?"

He glanced toward the door and saw Mrs. Moore peeking out of the kitchen entry. When he waved, she ducked back inside. "About the man you're supposed to marry."

"Ah." Her gaze fell to the empty cup encircled in her hands.

"Are you really engaged?"

"It depends on who you ask."

He stared at her, bewildered. "I'm asking you."

"All I am is confused," Jenny said, her voice barely above a whisper.

He wasn't certain exactly what to say, but he was relieved that this engagement wasn't final.

She looked up at him. "Mrs. Moore told me what happened to Tom."

"I meant to tell you before anyone else."

"She said he was taking a drug when he drowned."

He nodded slowly, surprised Mrs. Moore would tell her about the cocaine. "If I'd known, I would never have allowed him into the water."

"You couldn't have stopped him," Mrs. Moore said as she stepped back into the room, carrying another cup and plate of cake. "He was bigger than you and completely irrational."

That horrific night flashed through his mind again. At first, he'd egged Tom on, telling him he'd never beat him across Grasmere, but then the tables turned. It wasn't the darkness that had bothered Adrian—they'd both swum often in the evening—but he'd known something was off when his friend shoved him into the water. He just didn't know until much later what was wrong.

He called off the race, but Tom began jeering, chastising him, really, for his reversal. Then Tom had taken off, swimming toward the other side. When he couldn't stop his friend, Adrian should have gone for help, but he'd followed him instead.

Mrs. Moore sat beside Jenny again. "Are you still taking your photographs?"

Jenny nodded. "Adrian taught me how to use my camera."

"Splendid." She glanced between them, seemingly oblivious when he knew she was anything but. "Adrian, you should take her back out on Tom's boat during the day."

He glanced over at Jenny. A smile stole across her lips, and she winked at him. "If Adrian has time, I would enjoy seeing the lake again."

Her words pressed through him, pushing aside his own insecurities. "I believe I could make the time."

Mrs. Moore nodded. "Then it's settled."

Adrian shifted in his chair, turning toward Jenny. "Emma found the album from Enchanted Isle."

She clapped her hands together. "I'd love to see those pictures."

"Perhaps you could come for supper again tomorrow night?"

Thankfully, she agreed.

CHAPTER 15

Colored segments of glass, cut into a dozen shapes, were arranged like puzzle pieces on Cora's worktable. Jenny stood at the doorway, watching Cora hold an emerald piece up to the light. "The cathedral wants me to work a miracle."

Jenny scanned the gallery of glass art displayed around the studio. "It seems to me that you're already a miracle worker."

Cora shook her head. "All of these pieces were simple compared to this." She sighed. "Repairing a damaged window is almost as difficult as repairing a relationship."

"Are you talking about your former husband?"

Cora shrugged as she realigned a piece of glass. "People are even more complicated than glass."

"He phoned this evening."

Cora glanced up again. "Only once?"

"I stopped answering the telephone after his second call."

Both times, she'd told Perry that Cora wasn't home, which was true—when Cora had returned home from Carlisle, she'd hurried straight into her studio. He had been angry, as if Jenny had been barring Cora from the phone. She wouldn't even have answered the call except she'd hoped that it was Adrian, confirming their dinner for tomorrow.

Cora reached for her cutter and scored a piece of blue glass in half. "Did he ask about money?"

"No. He just asked about you."

Cora tried to fit the blue piece against a red triangle. "It's the money he wants."

Jenny leaned back against a crate. "Why do you give it to him?"

"I don't care about the money, really." Cora looked up at her, her eyes sad. "I gave him my heart a long time ago, and I haven't quite been able to get it back."

Jenny felt sorry for the woman working feverishly to fix the pieces of window, a talented, successful woman in her own right, and yet she couldn't seem to free herself from a man who appeared to use her for his own gain. Perhaps it wasn't that Cora disliked Adrian in particular. Perhaps she equated all men with Perry Banks.

"He insisted that you return his call tonight."

Cora picked up another blue piece, showing Jenny the broken edge. "Do you think I can fix this?"

"I don't know."

"Neither do I. I want to fix things, but I can't always do it."

Cora shuffled around the table and stepped toward one of the crates, rifling through plates of blue glass, each one a different shade. "Perry only contacts me if he needs something."

"I noticed."

Cora glanced up at her, a piece of glass in her hands. "If he stops needing me, he'll stop calling."

Jenny contemplated her words, confused. "I thought you wanted him to stop calling."

"Of course," Cora said, though her tone wasn't the least bit convincing. "Most of the time."

"You don't really want him to go away, do you?"

She shrugged. "He wants money, and I don't have the money to give him yet, at least not the amount he wants. He'll keep calling until he gets it."

"And then?"

She focused on the table. "He always returns."

Cora slid another sheet of glass out of a crate, the color almost identical to the broken blue piece. "I'll trim the broken edge and solder a piece of lead here," she said, pointing at the fractured corner. "If I do my job right, only the most discriminative eye will be able to spot the damage."

Jenny watched Cora work for several minutes as she cleaned and repaired the window, piecing the glass and lead back together again. But it seemed there was nothing Cora could do to repair the relationship with her former husband, no matter how much money she gave him.

Cora glanced at her again. "Did Adrian phone as well?"

"No." At Adrian's request, she planned to keep the story of what had really happened to Tom close to her heart.

"It's for the best."

"I know you don't like him, Cora, but I do. And I enjoy spending time with him."

"In hindsight," Cora said slowly, "I wish someone had warned me about Perry."

"Would it have made a difference?" she asked.

Cora didn't answer.

Jenny couldn't sleep. Around midnight she wandered back downstairs and stepped onto the front porch, an afghan wrapped around her. Several lights flickered in the valley, and the light from Cora's studio stole through the windows, flooding the front lawn.

Cora was obsessed with her work, but even more than that, she seemed obsessed with the man who'd shackled her heart. Perry clearly didn't love Cora, at least not the kind of love willing to give up anything, but in some strange way, she still cared for him.

At one time, Cora must have thought Perry was a good man. Surely she wouldn't have married him if she'd thought he would suck her dry, like a leech on her skin. When did Cora realize that Perry wasn't the man she'd thought? Or had he changed over the years?

Sitting in a rocking chair, Jenny slipped back and forth, reflecting about her afternoon with Mrs. Moore. The woman had grasped Adrian's hand on the tabletop as she spoke. Instead of being angry, Mrs. Moore treated Adrian as if he were her adopted son as well.

Cora and Mrs. Moore had such vastly different perspectives. One thought Adrian was a hero, the other a villain. But how did one really know if a man was good or bad?

If only her mom was here to help her distinguish the truth.

She closed her eyes and rocked again.

These weeks were supposed to be about getting away from Cleveland, out from under the thumb of her grandfather. Yet she wasn't just vacationing. It almost seemed as if she were finding herself here, outside the confines of home. Clarifying what had been muddied.

Adrian appeared in her mind, smiling at her.

No matter what happened here in these beautiful lakes, she knew one thing for certain. She could never marry Robert Tripp. That man, she suspected, wouldn't have any sort of appreciation for the beauty in her pictures or her desire to explore. If they married, he would require her to settle into a tidy regimen of dinners, church socials, and society meetings. Always moving inside firmly established walls. No time to create or dream.

The thought of running her life solely by a clock, hopping from one place to another, bowed under expectations—she couldn't bear to think about it. Her mother had wilted under the pressure of it all, and Jenny refused to do so as well. She wanted to thrive wherever she lived.

A breeze rustled the glass chimes hanging on the porch, the melody playing to an audience who'd been dimmed by the spotlight of stars. She imagined hundreds of crickets and tree frogs hidden among the grass and trees, enraptured by the music. Or perhaps they were singing. A choir of them and their melodies, scoring a cantata of night song.

There'd been no elaborate planning for this concert. No exhausting practices or expensive ticket sales. Yet there was something magical about glass chiming in the wind.

She rocked again as the breeze cooled her face. Such beauty could be found in simplicity, but so few people seemed to stop and appreciate it. They were always moving, this creation of people. Always making new things instead of enjoying the old.

She prayed she would never stop appreciating the new and old alike.

CHAPTER 16

Gilbert stepped up to the door of the bathroom, knowing he must tell his nephew about Liz. He should have told Adrian about her long before Jenny Winter had shown up in England. He'd wanted to bury that loss with his other memories, but it seemed that God wouldn't let it remain in its grave.

Standing in front of the mirror, Adrian struggled to comb back the unruly mess of hair that he'd inherited from his father. Simon had never been able to corral his hair either, no matter how long he'd wrestled with it.

"I need to speak with you," Gilbert said.

Adrian turned. "What's the matter?"

He pointed toward the corridor behind him. "Let's talk downstairs."

Minutes later, Adrian joined him in the dining room, glancing at the clock above the table. The house smelled like pepper and fresh thyme from the ham and split pea soup that Adrian had made against Emma's protests, and the table was set with the Worcester china passed along from Gilbert's parents.

His nephew had worked hard to make sure this night would be a success. Gilbert didn't want to spoil his plans, but Adrian should know the reason he'd be eating his meal down at the inn. And why he wanted Adrian to pursue Jenny if he loved her like Gilbert had once loved her mother.

He pulled a chair out from under the formal table and sat on it, crossing his arms as he leaned back. For two decades, he'd worked with sheep, and he knew one thing well: when confronted with their fears, sheep froze. They were smart animals, incredibly smart, but they refused to react in the face of danger. Even the possibility of fear disabled them.

It frustrated him when the sheep did this, particularly when he needed them to move, but that's exactly how he felt now, a debilitating fear mounting inside him, threatening to shut him down once again.

He'd never told anyone except Maria Kemp that Liz had agreed to marry him. When he'd found Simon on the island, shell-shocked, it had taken him months to step back onto a solid sort of ground. Almost a decade later, during the war, he'd faced death multiple times, but he'd never felt as devastated as he had watching his brother unravel.

To his knowledge, Maria hadn't told anyone about Liz, and Cora was the only one Liz had confided in. After that night in 1935, they'd all been jolted into a new reality. Even though Simon was still alive, Maria had lost the essence of her husband. And he'd lost both his brother and the woman he'd planned to marry.

Adrian tapped his foot. "I'm supposed to pick up Jenny in fifteen minutes."

Gilbert took a deep breath. "There's something I haven't told you."

"Just one thing?"

"Let's start with the most pressing."

Adrian pulled out a chair and sat across from Gilbert. "That seems reasonable."

Gilbert slumped back against the seat. Sometimes it felt as if the burden he shouldered added another decade to his forty-five years. "When I told Jenny that I'd met her mother—"

"The summer Mrs. Winter was here," Adrian said, trying to spur him forward.

Gilbert nodded. "Liz and I spent a lot of time together."

One of Adrian's eyebrows slid up. "You knew her well?"

"Quite well." He straightened the silverware set on the table before him. "In fact, I asked her to marry me."

Adrian blinked, and his lips pressed together before he spoke. "She was the one . . ."

Gilbert nodded slowly before his gaze wandered to the window, as if he could see through the wreath of fog to the island on the lake. The details of that night weren't necessary, but he wanted to be honest with his nephew about what he'd done. And how he'd changed.

"Initially, Liz agreed to marry me, but after I found your dad with Curtis's body, I turned into another person overnight, a man she couldn't—shouldn't—have married." He took a breath. "I apologized to Cora long ago and tried to apologize to Liz. I fear Cora's anger at you is borne out of how I treated her friend."

"Did Mrs. Winter return back to America soon after?"

"Ran back, really."

Adrian scooted forward in his chair. "And you never asked anyone to marry you again."

"I never met anyone else quite like Liz," he said, glancing back out at the fog. "I should have followed her across the ocean right away, tried to explain my actions, but by the time I'd garnered the courage, she'd already married."

"You never stopped caring about her."

"My feelings don't matter," he said, shaking his head. "She's been married to someone else for more than twenty years."

"But Mrs. Winter—"

Gilbert shook his head again. "I don't want to hear any stories about Liz."

"But—"

"It's too late to change the past now, but you have to understand my awkwardness around Jenny."

Adrian glanced up at the clock again and then stood up. "You should still join us for supper."

He followed Adrian out to the kitchen. "Emma's invited me to eat at the inn."

"Jenny is going to think you dislike her."

"It doesn't matter what she thinks about me."

Adrian reached for the motorbike key hanging by the side door. "Can I tell her what happened?"

"Do what you think is best."

"I don't want to keep secrets from her anymore."

Gilbert managed a smile. "You're a wise man."

When Adrian opened the door, Gilbert spoke again. "Eventually, Cora will tell Liz that a member of the Kemp family is interested in her daughter. I'm sorry—it's not fair to you."

"We all have regrets. There's no reason for you to apologize."

"Liz might . . . I don't know what Liz will do."

"Jenny has a mind of her own."

As Gilbert walked down the hill, he wished he could do more than just apologize to Adrian. He wished he could tell Liz that he was sorry too.

Adrian slipped into the kitchen and pulled the bubbling custard cups out of the oven, the top of each one sprinkled gingerly with nutmeg. Over soup and bread, Jenny had told him that her grandfather wanted her to marry Robert Tripp, but she wasn't going to marry the man. Then she told him about her three years in college, about the dances and socials and her grades—the grades, she said, had been a disaster.

He had told her about his time in Hong Kong working to keep the peace in heat stifling to the British troops and about his years at the university pursuing a degree in business, though he'd spent more hours in the swimming pool than in the classroom. He also told her that he'd made enough poor choices in his youth to earn a bad reputation for life around here.

An oven mitt on both hands, Adrian carried the hot cups of egg custard back to the dining room. Then he brought them two glasses of milk. "We need to let the custard cool."

Jenny used the oven mitt to inch her dessert closer to the edge, sniffing the sweet steam that wafted from it. "Did you make these?"

He nodded.

"I don't believe I've ever met a man who knew how to cook."

"My sister made sure that I knew my way around the kitchen, though she still thinks I'm completely incompetent when it comes to food preparation."

Jenny reached for her spoon and dug into the custard.

"You're supposed to wait—"

But she wasn't deterred. "This is fantastic," she raved as she ate the custard that would resemble soup until it cooled.

He watched her as she enjoyed the dessert, fascinated by her love of sweets. It was almost as if she could taste the same beauty she sought on film.

When they finished eating, he reached for a brass knob on the cabinet drawer beside the table. Emma had found the Enchanted Isle album in her basement storage, but before he showed it to Jenny, he took out the gold coin that he'd secured in an envelope.

"What is this?" Jenny asked, reaching for the piece.

"Emma said it was my father's."

She held the coin up to the light, studying it like he'd done when Emma had given it to him yesterday. On its face was a portrait of a crowned king seated on a throne between two leopards, both of them crowned as well. The coin was newer than the bronze one he'd found on the farm and probably of interest, he feared, to the Treasure Trove.

"You should keep it with you," Jenny said, folding it into his hand. "A good luck charm."

He didn't believe in luck, but he tucked his dad's find into his pocket before removing the album from the drawer. Emma had wrapped the album with brown paper, and he quickly untied the string.

Taped to the leather front was a postcard with a ferryboat and an artist's colorful rendition of the island, the Torrid Typhoon in the background. *Enchanted Isle, Windermere, England* was printed along the bottom.

Adrian moved around the table to sit beside Jenny. "I haven't looked at these pictures in a decade."

"How could you wait all day?" she asked, straightening the hem of the sweater she wore with her wool skirt.

"I didn't want to look at it without you."

Jenny carefully opened the cover. On the first page was a photograph of the immense sign that once curved like a rainbow over the ferry dock. A grand welcome to every adult and child who stepped off the boat.

He tapped one of the photo corners that secured the picture onto the stiff page. "Gilbert helped build the landing stage for Curtis and my dad."

"I wish your uncle would tell us some of his stories."

"He doesn't like to talk about the past."

"It's too bad," she said. "There must be wonderful stories to tell."

Jenny turned the album page, and it seemed as if they stepped back more than twenty years onto the crowded midway. Children and adults alike were carrying balloons, and several necks were craned, park guests pointing up as if critiquing the breadth of sky.

She traced the edge of the page with her finger. "They look as if they've never had a care."

The next photograph was of three men—his father, Curtis, and Gilbert—standing arm in arm by the train depot at the front entrance. His mum had hated Simon's amusement park, though she'd appreciated the significant income it had generated during the boom years. With Curtis's investment and management skills, Enchanted Isle had ballooned, the growth of it straining and bulging every side.

"To think," Jenny said, "my mom might have known your parents as well as Gilbert."

He fidgeted in his chair. If Jenny had known her mum had been engaged to marry Gilbert, she certainly hadn't even hinted at it. Perhaps he should guard this secret, like he'd guarded the one about Tom for Mrs. Moore, but any more deceit, he feared, would destroy his relationship with Jenny. The last thing he wanted was for her to think he'd been keeping something else from her.

"Gilbert remembers your mum," he said slowly.

Her blue eyes questioned him. "What did he say?"

Adrian glanced down again at the picture of his uncle. "Did she never mention his name?"

Jenny shook her head. "The only people she talked about were Cora and my great-aunt."

"While she was here, Gilbert said . . ."

She rested her elbows on the edge of the table, leaning toward him. "What did he say?"

Adrian sipped his milk. "He proposed marriage when your mum was visiting the Lakes, and according to him, she accepted."

Jenny collapsed back in her chair, seemingly speechless for the first time since he'd met her.

"I didn't know until this evening," he said.

Jenny studied the picture below her, the black-and-white reflection of the man who'd once loved her mum. "Are you certain?"

"I don't have any reason to doubt my uncle."

She traced the edges of the photograph. "But why wouldn't my mom have told me?"

"Perhaps she was protecting your father."

"Does Gilbert know that my dad passed away?"

Adrian shook his head. "I tried to tell him, but he didn't want to discuss it."

Jenny flipped the page. A half dozen pictures crowded together as a collage on the spread of pages. She studied the gallery of black-and-white photos and then turned again. This time, she pulled the page up to her face, examining it.

He leaned closer to her. "What is it?"

Her eyes wide, she looked over. "That's my mom."

She lowered the album, and he glanced at the photograph taken in front of the Ocean Caves.

"Is that Gilbert?" she asked, pointing at the man standing beside her in a white shirt, his sleeves rolled up. They were both smiling in the sunlight.

"It is."

"She looks so happy."

Adrian sighed. "So does he."

Jenny looked at the last two pages and then closed the album. "I want to see the island."

"It no longer looks anything like these photographs."

"But I still want to see it," she insisted.

"Perry would have you arrested if he caught you on his property."

"Have you ever seen him there?" When he shook his head, she straightened her shoulders. "I'm not afraid of Perry Banks."

"Don't underestimate the man, Jenny. He'll do whatever suits him best."

Her back straightened against the chair. "Please take me."

"No one is supposed to be on the island."

A sly smile crept across her lips, her voice lowering. "But you still go."

"Only on foggy nights."

She glanced out the window. "Like tonight."

"Yes," he said slowly. "Just like tonight."

She reached for the camera bag she'd stored on the seat beside her. "I'll need my coat."

CHAPTER 17

A dense fog curtained the entire valley, cold droplets of mist dancing in its seams. Jenny shivered as Adrian clipped the buckle on her lifejacket, though she wasn't certain of the exact cause—the cool air or her excitement or the proximity of the man next to her.

The lifejacket was his one stipulation, he'd said, if they were going to do this fool thing. Crossing Windermere was much different than rowing around the shallow perimeter of Elter Water. This lake was more than two hundred feet deep.

She'd readily agreed to wear the jacket.

Jenny rubbed her hands together to ward off the cold, her camera bag resting in her lap as Adrian paddled south through the fog, toward the old entrance.

Everything had changed between her and Adrian since their meeting with Mrs. Moore. Like Simon Kemp, she could dream about the future. There were no confines on her dreams here, no one to dismiss them as absurd. Or dismiss her as a failure. Perhaps her mom had experienced that freedom as well while visiting the Lakes. Perhaps she had loved Gilbert Kemp before she'd returned home to marry Jack.

Jenny closed her eyes for a moment, the chill of fog resting on her face. What would she do at the end of her stay, when she had to return to America like her mom had once done?

The paddle dipped into the water again, the sound pulling her back to the boat. "Some say there's a great white horse that watches over Windermere," Adrian whispered.

"Have you ever seen it?"

"No, but sometimes I wonder if he hides in the fog."

She shivered again as a wall of trees emerged into view. Their boat circled the trees until the bottom grated on land. She could see weeds overgrown on the shore, the remaining pieces of a pier on their left, but she couldn't see beyond the weeds or the pilings.

Adrian hopped out of the boat, his feet bare and trousers rolled up, his shoes secure in one hand. With his free hand, he pulled up the canoe; then he helped her onto shore, her saddle shoes settling into the pebbles on the shingle beach.

"Now close your eyes," he said.

"But I can hardly see anything as it is."

"Pretend you've just arrived on the ferry," he whispered. "Twenty-three years ago."

So, she closed her eyes, her camera bag strung over her shoulder, and pretended that sunshine flushed across her skin instead of the damp, that a crowd of people chattered around her, anxious to play for the day. Adrian took her hand and carefully led her away from the beach, her feet curling over the rocks on their path.

Then she heard the click of a flashlight.

"Welcome to Enchanted Isle," he said.

When she opened her eyes, her arms prickled with goose bumps.

An old train depot stood in front of them, and she followed the path of light up to its brick tower. The Roman numerals of III and VII still clung to the clock, though both hands had broken in the weathering passage of time. Below the tower was a round window made of stained glass.

"The main sign used to be up there," Adrian said, pointing above the tower. "Thousands of people entered this station during the glory days."

The photograph from his dad's album grew in her mind until she could almost see the crowds arriving on the ferry, ready to either step on the train or walk into the heart of the park.

They climbed up steps together and crossed over a cement platform inside the depot. The opening on the other side led to an eerie corridor walled in by gray-cloaked trees.

She hesitated by the doorway. Had something happened to Curtis Sloan in these trees? Their branches swelled into arms, the trunks an army of soldiers in her head. Or druids with their long beards and draping gowns.

Cora's words echoed back to her—the ones about a curse that hung over the island, stealing Curtis's life and perhaps the lives of others who ventured back here.

She tried to blink away the images, but they wouldn't leave.

"There's no one here," Adrian assured her, but he couldn't see the ghosts like she did.

When she still didn't move, he urged her ahead. "It isn't far to the rides."

The calm in his voice comforted her. Adrian had been here multiple times and hadn't encountered a single ghost or druid. She would be furious with herself tomorrow if they didn't explore.

Clutching his hand, she walked slowly up a pathway paved with cobblestones, both sides lined with rusty lampposts. As they moved away from the lake, the fog began to fade.

When they reached the strip of abandoned rides, Jenny swallowed a scream. A giant clown was gazing down over a door, his mouth open as if he were laughing at them.

"The funhouse," Adrian explained. "Would you like to go inside?"

"Seriously?"

"No." He laughed. "The ceiling caved in years ago."

She took a deep breath. "I can't say that I'm disappointed."

"I thought you wanted adventure."

"Adventure in a beautiful sort of way."

"There's beauty here," he said. "You just have to search for it."

They moved forward on the overgrown stretch, hand in hand. Tree limbs hung across the rusted cars on the Ferris wheel ahead of them, but she began to see what he did, the worn beauty in this ride and the others. Decades ago, she imagined, this park had been the pinnacle of artistry.

Farther down, Adrian shined his light on another ride. *Ocean Caves*, the sign read. The place where Gilbert and her mom were photographed.

Had her dad known about Gilbert? Her parents had met before her mom graduated from high school, and Jenny always assumed they dated for several years before they'd married. Perhaps Gilbert was the reason her mom never talked until recently about her summer in England. Perhaps she'd wanted to keep that season with him tucked quietly away.

"There's the merry-go-round," Adrian said, turning his flashlight to the next ride.

A worn sign beside it, partially covered with branches, read *Magic Lagoon*. Instead of horses on the platform, like the ones on carousels Jenny had ridden back home, there were seahorses and shells molded from wood. And playful fish, glazed with bright colors. She imagined them circling the platform and then taking flight, swimming through a magical lagoon.

Perhaps on nights when no one else was here, they came alive.

She inserted a flashbulb and snapped a picture of the carousel before tucking the camera back into the bag.

"This was my dad's favorite ride."

She touched the rippled edge of a shell. "Strange that he didn't include a photograph of it in his album."

Then she blinked as if she were taking another picture, an image to keep forever in her mind.

Adrian turned off his flashlight, but they could still see the seahorses in the dim light. Wind blew through the park, the cars on the Ferris wheel swaying in the breeze, metal clanging together.

"Cora said something about a curse on this island."

Adrian stepped forward, and she walked beside him. "Sometimes people see lights out here at night. Even if Perry wanted to sell the island, he'd be hard-pressed to find a buyer, at least from the Lakes." He pointed up the strip. "The roller coaster is at the end."

He lit his flashlight again, and she followed him toward the ride, but before they reached it, the sound of pounding echoed through the trees.

Adrian stopped, his hand tensing around hers.

"What is that?" she whispered.

"I don't know."

Another light sparked in the trees ahead, a ray chiseling through the mist.

When she gasped, Adrian released her hand to extinguish their flashlight.

"Someone's here," she hissed, turning back toward the beach. Her foot snagged on something, and she tried to catch herself in the darkness, but a sharp edge sliced her hand as she fell, the pain piercing her arm when she rolled away in the grass.

Adrian's light flashed back on, and she shrieked when she saw two black eyes glaring back at her. It was an octopus, split in two. An iron crown on its head.

"It's from the merry-go-round," Adrian whispered.

She sucked in air, trying to steady her breathing.

"Who's there?" a man shouted, and she held the air in her lungs, silencing the scream that pressed against her throat.

Click—Adrian's light vanished before he reached again for her hand. Together they fled through the trees, moving toward what she hoped was the canoe. Several times, she thought she heard someone running behind them, but it was impossible to tell with her ragged breath deafening her, her camera bag banging against her wounded hand.

An eternity seemed to pass before she felt the beach pebbles again under her shoes. She helped Adrian push the canoe out before they both climbed inside.

As Adrian paddled into the fog, someone shouted from the shore.

She willed her mind not to conjure up a new image.

It was a voice. A man. Nothing less or more.

CHAPTER 18

Adrenaline rushed through Adrian's veins like water in a fire hose trying to extinguish the flames. His arms shook as he paddled toward the boathouse, back to a safe place. Since he was a boy, people had told him that he wasn't safe. His recklessness, a teacher once said, harmed other kids.

The gold coin seemed to burn in his pocket, mocking him. He'd tried desperately to overcome the part of him that flirted with danger, but now he'd risked too much again by taking Jenny over to the island. She could have gotten hurt or—

He couldn't bear to think of what else might have happened.

Jenny clenched the side of the boat in front of him, both his lifejacket and hers tossed between them. There'd been no time to buckle it around her—all he could think about was getting her off the island.

Who was there tonight?

He'd heard sounds at the park before, but never a voice. Any visit from Perry he assumed happened during the daylight hours.

If it was Perry, why was he there so late? And what was that pounding noise?

A sound roared across the water. The engine of a powerboat coming to life.

He thrust the paddle through the water, his muscles burning as the lake lapped against the canoe. He wouldn't let the boat find them in this fog. Wouldn't let anyone hurt Jenny.

When they reached the boathouse, she lifted the door far enough for him to paddle underneath. Then he rolled the door closed.

Reaching into his pocket, he dug out his dad's coin and hurled it at the door of the boathouse. The coin pinged off the wood before dropping into the water.

"Oh, Adrian," Jenny said, her voice trembling as he helped her onto the dock in the torchlight.

"You're safe here."

She fell against him, and he wrapped his arms around her, pulling her close. Her head nuzzled into his chest, and he wished he could keep her here all night, protected. He wished he could erase her fear. "I shouldn't have taken you over there."

She stepped back, shaking her head. "I shouldn't have asked you to go."

"No—"

"I wrangled you into it."

He wanted to pull her close again, but he reached for one of her hands instead. It was still shaking—or perhaps it was his hand shaking on top of hers. He'd wanted her to see the beauty left on Enchanted Isle and revel in the wonder of it, even if most of the paint was gone, but still he'd been foolish to take her.

She nodded toward the door that led up to the street. "I should go home."

"Yes, you should."

But neither of them moved.

"Jenny . . ." What was he supposed to say? That he wanted to marry her, like Gilbert had wanted to marry her mother? Asking a question like that was almost as reckless, mad, as taking Jenny over to the island.

Perhaps reality is what had separated Gilbert and Mrs. Winter. Jenny belonged in another place, and while he may no longer belong in these Lakes, he belonged in England. Love could cross a divide, but it would take more than love to bridge an entire ocean.

He needed to think, and he certainly couldn't do it here, alone with Jenny.

A siren wailed in the distance. "Cora's probably knocking on my door."

"And I suspect Gilbert is wondering where we went."

Adrian wanted to kiss her there, in the boathouse, but he forced himself to turn. Not walk away, exactly, but lead her out to a place where she would be safe from island ghosts and powerboats. And most of all, safe from him.

The lights inside the house and studio were darkened when Jenny returned home, the Fiat missing. Had Cora stayed late to work in Carlisle? Perhaps she would stay the entire night.

At least Jenny wouldn't have to explain where she'd been.

Her first stop was the bathroom to clean the gash on her hand. Blood drained down the sink, but her hands still trembled. She wasn't certain if it was because of her injury or their race from the island. Or the memory of Adrian's arms around her.

She'd wanted to stay in that boathouse forever with him. He'd spoiled her for life, she feared. Neither Robert Tripp nor any other man her grandfather might have in mind would do.

Adrian hadn't asked her to become someone new. Instead, it seemed as if he liked her for exactly who she was.

She leaned back against the door, her mind spinning.

Perhaps she should phone her mom tonight. Collect. The cost would be astronomical, but her mom had said to call if there was an emergency. This was close enough. She wanted to find out about Gilbert and tell her about Adrian. And she simply wanted to hear her mom's voice.

She swallowed two aspirin before moving downstairs to the sitting room. It must be close to one in the morning now. Ohio was five hours behind, making it eight o'clock in Cleveland. As good a time as any to find her mom at home.

Instead of turning on a lamp, she reached for the telephone in the faint light that slipped through the window. Then she asked the operator to make a collect call home.

Minutes later she heard Demi—her family's housekeeper—answer, but Demi couldn't accept the charges for Mrs. Winter. So Jenny tried again, asking the operator for Demi this time.

"Miss Jenny," Demi said, answering after the first ring. "We've missed you."

Jenny smiled as she sank into the lounge chair beside the phone. "I've missed you as well."

"Unfortunately, your mother is out for the evening."

Jenny flinched. "Who did she go out with?"

"I'm afraid I can't say."

Jenny wound the phone cord around her wrist. Demi cared about her, but after practically raising Liz, she was intensely loyal to Jenny's mother and her confidentiality. Perhaps her mom had finally agreed to a dinner date.

"Your grandfather is home."

Her heart lurched. "Demi—"

"He'll want to speak with you."

She almost replaced the handset, but as it straddled the cradle, she hated herself for cowering. Her grandfather was stern, intensely focused on the future of their family's business. He'd never harm her, but words could cut as well, the pain lasting much longer than any cut on her hand.

She pulled the phone back to her ear. If her grandfather wanted to talk tonight, she would listen.

Something clattered in the background, and then he picked up the phone. "Hello, Jennifer."

She reluctantly returned his greeting.

"Are you ready to return home?"

"Not quite."

"Robert's been asking about you," he said. "I told him he'd be receiving a letter soon."

"I haven't had time to write him," she said, hoping that her grandfather might ask what occupied her time.

"Jennifer," he scolded. "You need to wire him first thing tomorrow."

She almost groaned but restrained herself.

"I've been much too occupied to write or wire anyone except Mom."

"Lizabeth needs you here," he said.

"But she wanted me to visit England."

"You wanted to travel overseas. She was trying to be kind."

His words wounded her like they often did. Was she being selfish for traveling to England? Mom had said she wanted her to visit Europe, but perhaps Jenny had pressed too hard. Perhaps her mom really had wanted her to stay home.

"Please tell her that I called."

The line crackled. "You can tell her yourself."

Jenny leaned forward. "Is she home now?"

"No." A bell rang in the background. "I must go."

He hung up the phone before saying good-bye.

Jenny stared down at the receiver in her hand. Until that moment, she hadn't realized how desperately she wanted to speak with her mom, to sort out together all that was happening inside her.

She scrunched her legs up to her chest, feeling like an utter mess. She didn't want to go home yet and face either her grandfather or

Robert. Nor did she want to leave Adrian or the beauty here that fed her soul.

It seemed an impossible line for her heart to walk, this teetering between the past and her future, between the comforts of home and stepping out on her own. She wanted to be independent, yet she was homesick—not for Cleveland but for her mom.

How was she supposed to grow up when on nights like this she still felt like a kid?

A voice interrupted her thoughts, and she lifted the receiver back up to her ear, thinking her grandfather hadn't actually hung up the phone, but no one was on the other end.

The voice, she realized with a jolt, was coming from outside the house. From the front porch.

She moved toward the window, and through the sheer curtain, she saw the shadow of a man and woman. Perry and Cora.

Jenny stepped away from the glass, not wanting either of them to see her, but their voices were still clear.

"You have to help me, Cora, love."

"Why are you wet?"

"I had a bit of a swim."

"Are you drunk?" Cora asked.

"Of course not."

"Injured?"

"It was a small accident, nothing more," he said. "Please let me stay, just until morning."

"Go home, Perry, wherever it is that you live now."

"I'll sleep on the couch," he said. "Or the floor. The police want to interview me tomorrow."

Cora groaned. "You wrecked your car . . ."

"No." He paused. "It was my boat. I hit a crag in the fog."

She sighed. "You were on the island."

He didn't respond.

"There's nothing left to look for out there."

The doorknob began to turn. "There is, Cora, love. And when I find it, I'll split the profits with you."

Cora's laugh was bitter. "I hardly think you'll share."

Jenny rushed back toward the stairs, her heart pounding. Perry had been out on the island tonight, searching for something.

She paused at the top of the stairs and listened again. If only Cora would tell him once and for all that she wasn't his love. Nor was she going to help him. Perry needed to figure out a way to help himself.

"Did you get the money?" she heard him ask.

"I'm trying."

"Cora—"

"I'll be done with the window soon."

"Surely you have some in savings."

"You've emptied my resources."

"You know I adore you."

"Last I knew, you divorced me, Perry."

"We were no good together as a married couple."

"That's because you never seemed to realize that marriage is a partnership. It takes two people, fully engaged, to make a marriage work."

"I will never make a good partner for anyone," Perry said solemnly.

"That's a poor excuse."

"I suppose I'm a poor excuse of a friend, just like I was a poor excuse of a husband."

"We could try again," Cora said, her voice small. And Jenny felt sorry for the woman who was desperate to grasp for what might have been.

"It's too late for marriage, Cora, but I want to be a better friend."

It was a lie, Jenny knew, but did Cora realize it? Or would she continue clinging to the hope that he might change back to the man she'd once loved?

Jenny wanted to run out and rattle him for continuing to harass Cora. And shake Cora while she was at it. But instead, she slipped into her room and locked the door, her thoughts returning to the park.

What did Perry think was on that island?

She suspected it had nothing to do with ghosts or white horses or the legends about a curse.

CHAPTER 19

Liz eyed the stewardess's tailored dress suit and matching navy cap as the woman explained how to remove seat cushions and strap their arms underneath in the unlikely event the Boeing 707 landed in the Atlantic instead of on a runway in London.

How a cushion could save her life was beyond her, but the Pan Am stewardess seemed confident in its ability to double as a lifejacket.

Liz had greater things to worry about than a transatlantic flight. Or that's what she told herself on the train ride to New York. In her purse was a telegram from Cora. Jenny was fine, Cora had written, but she had been seeing a young man. A man Liz wouldn't like.

With Cora's words, Liz remembered another man that Cora had said she'd never like. A man she'd ended up liking very much.

She didn't want to impose on Jenny's desire for independence, but she also didn't want her caught up in a relationship that would break her heart when she returned home, especially since she was about to marry Robert Tripp.

The stewardess reached above the woman seated next to Liz and demonstrated how to turn on the fan and light in the panel overhead. Then she showed them how to secure the oxygen masks over their faces, if necessary.

Liz glanced out at the terminal.

She had no real gauge on how to mother an adult child not yet married. Her own mother had passed away soon after Liz had returned home from her summer in England, when Liz was a year younger than Jenny.

Her mother had been a good woman, but she'd been crushed by Stephan McAdam's penchant for control, spending more time with the committees she chaired than with her family at home. Now Liz was struggling to press up against her father's thumb before it crushed her and her daughter too.

She wanted so much more for Jenny than a proper marriage, like the opportunity to find herself before someone told her exactly who she needed to become. The opportunity to experience joy in life before the years passed in a blur of routine.

Liz had studied the mothering of other women, trying to emulate what they did well. Recently she'd even quizzed Mrs. Hamilton next door. The woman said Liz had to encourage her daughter to pursue her own dreams, but Stephan wasn't a big proponent of dreams, at least not ones that contradicted his plans. Even though she'd told him that she didn't want to remarry, he had been intent on finding a suitable husband for her and now for Jenny so they wouldn't concoct any grand schemes of their own.

Jack, her husband, had been a respectable man and good to her, but she didn't want Jenny marrying like she had for pedigree. Or out of desperation to leave their home.

More than anything, she wanted Jenny to marry a man of her own choosing, a man willing to dream alongside her and step into her world of wonder instead of trying to force her into walls built by someone else.

Unfortunately, Robert seemed to be terrified of Jenny and her dreams.

The stewardess, with her pleasant smile, checked Liz's seatbelt.

What would it be like to work for an airline company? To travel around the world and be respected by men and women alike?

Things were much different now, more than a decade after the war. Women had more choices about their future, or so she'd read in the papers. Stephan balked at Liz managing even the minute details of their household, but the oldest Hamilton girl was managing a chain of stores for her father. And Mrs. Hamilton was quite proud of her accomplishment.

That's what she wanted for her daughter. Respect and choices. Heaven forbid, if Jenny ever lost her husband, Liz didn't want her to have to run back home.

She'd insisted that Jenny attend college, and when Jenny returned from England, Liz would urge her to finish. It was more than just academics. Jack had left their daughter an inheritance that would provide for a lifetime of dreams once Jenny turned twenty-one and finished her degree. Jenny didn't know yet about the trust fund. If it was ever made public, Liz feared that multiple men, gold diggers, would vie for matrimony.

Jack would have wanted their daughter to marry someone within the family of McAdam Industries, but he would never have wanted anyone to marry her solely for money.

When the airplane began rolling backward, Liz wrapped her fingers around the upholstered armrest of her chair.

The passenger next to her was older, her forehead rippled with lines. The woman took a last puff from her cigarette, then crushed it in the ashtray between the seats. The curl of smoke lifted, mixing with the gray film that already coated the ceiling.

"First time flying?" her neighbor asked.

Liz nodded.

"Me too, but my husband said it's safer than driving. Not that there's a bridge over to London."

"I'd prefer to take a ship." And Liz would have if she could have secured passage this week, but all her agent could purchase was a ticket on this new transatlantic flight.

"I suppose we have to trust our pilot and the good men who built this plane."

Liz didn't know much about airplanes, but she'd been around cars her entire life and knew well that the men who built them weren't always good.

As the airplane moved forward, her neighbor slipped another cigarette out of her silver case. "My name's Sarah."

"I'm Mrs.—" She stopped herself. "Lizabeth, but please call me Liz."

"Why are you visiting England?"

"My daughter is there for a few weeks. She turns twenty-one on Sunday, and I want to celebrate with her."

Sarah sighed. "Doesn't the time pass quickly."

"Much too quickly," Liz agreed. "You have daughters?"

"Three of them. All grown up and married now."

"My daughter doesn't want to get married."

Sarah laughed. "She just hasn't met the right man yet."

"Do you really think there's a right person to marry?"

Perhaps the question was too personal to ask a stranger, but it was one Liz had wrestled with for a long time. She couldn't discuss her thoughts with an acquaintance in Cleveland.

"I don't know about only one person, but I definitely think it's a choice we need to make carefully and prayerfully, if you don't mind my saying."

"I don't mind." Liz glanced out the window as the airplane cruised slowly to the end of the runway. "I think prayer is the best place to start. The trouble is when the people deciding for you aren't the praying sort."

"Does your husband have someone in mind for your daughter to marry?"

"No," Liz said. "My father does."

The woman looked confused. "Her grandfather?"

"There's a man who works for him—"

"Oh, honey. He shouldn't be deciding about marriage for you or your daughter."

Sarah made it sound so simple, but it wasn't simple at all.

Liz had thought it perfectly normal, back in 1936, to marry the man her father had selected. Her heart had belonged to another at the time, but love had failed her. She'd decided that she couldn't trust the flighty whims of her heart, so she'd stepped into a marriage without love, even though she and Jack had grown to care for each other deeply in their own way.

It was a gift to give her daughter the legacy of a business and financial security that would extend far into the future, but Jenny didn't seem concerned about such things. She'd been born after the Great Depression and was so young during the Second World War that she didn't remember the pains that had gone along with the turmoil. Liz had tried to cushion her from all of it, a cushion that was now about as durable as the one on her seat.

Jenny, she knew, needed to learn how to thrive on her own. That's why Liz had encouraged her to spend a season in England. The world in Jenny's eyes was a very small space, bounded by a fifteen-mile perimeter. Liz wanted her to peel back the curtain and see beyond it before her inheritance blurred everything.

The airplane rolled faster down the runway until they were skimming the ground. Liz clung to both armrests as the wheels lifted off.

Then they were soaring above the buildings until the city of New York disappeared, brushed away with a stroke of blue outside her window. Ships appeared on the water below, a dozen specks dotting the blue. Her stomach turned, and she wished she'd waited for passage on one of them.

"Makes you feel small, doesn't it?" Sarah asked, leaning across to look out the window.

"Minuscule."

"Almost makes some of the things that worry us seem small as well."

When she finished her cigarette, Sarah leaned back and closed her eyes, but Liz's gaze was fixed on the ocean. Perhaps she did worry too much. Instead of letting go of Jenny, perhaps she needed to let go of her concerns for her daughter's future.

She'd celebrate Jenny's birthday and meet this boy and hopefully avoid seeing Gilbert Kemp altogether before she returned home.

In the distance, another airplane flew the opposite direction, its metal skin reflecting in the sunlight. And her thoughts wandered away from Jenny, back to the man she'd loved long ago.

She and Cora had corresponded regularly for about a decade after Liz's visit. Cora had told her that Simon was killed in the war and that Enchanted Isle never opened again after her summer there. But she never mentioned Gilbert, and Liz never dared ask.

Had Gilbert survived the war? If so, was he still in the Lakes? He probably had five or six children, all of them working together on his farm.

She'd thought about him over the years, more often than she liked to admit. In their summer together, she'd fallen head over heels, thinking that Gilbert loved her too. When he asked her to marry him, she decided to step out of her father's clearly defined boundaries and embrace a new life as Mrs. Gilbert Kemp.

Then everything had fallen apart. Gilbert had terrified her with his rage the night after he'd proposed, breaking her window with the rocks he'd thrown and then telling her to go home. And she'd left before making the worst mistake of her life.

In hindsight, she and Gilbert had been naïve thinking they could make a marriage work in spite of their vast differences. She'd been caught up in the strangeness of it. The glamour. The idea that she could remake herself into someone new instead of remaining the person she was meant to be.

Sweat beaded on her forehead, and she fidgeted with the controls overhead until she turned on the fan.

Why was it so hard to be satisfied with the ease of her life? With the things that her father deemed important?

It all seemed meaningless sometimes, like Solomon had written long ago.

And Jenny, more than anyone Liz knew, craved meaning.

"I feel terrible about last night," Adrian said before he started the car.

Jenny clutched her wounded hand, hidden under a strip of gauze and her winter glove. "You shouldn't. I enjoyed seeing the park."

"If you want to cancel today, I understand."

She shook her head. "I don't want to cancel."

They drove through the village and then up the winding mountain pass called Hardknott to photograph the Roman ruins. The Ford shuddered each time it hit a rut, shooting another stab of pain up her arm. The aspirin she'd taken that morning had dulled the worst of her pain, but the medicine was beginning to wear off.

"It was Perry on the island last night," she said as he shifted gears.

He glanced over. "How do you know?"

"He showed up at Cora's house late last night saying he'd wrecked his boat on the crags."

Adrian swore. "He was trying to chase us."

She nodded. "He spent the night on Cora's sofa."

"Did he say why he was on the island?"

"He was searching for something." When Adrian slapped the wheel, Jenny glanced at him. "What is he trying to find?"

When he looked back at her, she saw the solemnness in his gaze, as if he wanted to entrust her with something else.

"I can keep your secret," she said.

He nodded, his focus back on the road. "I think my dad might have found something at the park."

Goose bumps trickled down her arms. "Like the artifacts in your attic?"

"I don't know," Adrian said, trying to maneuver around the holes and debris in the road. "Perhaps like the coin he left behind."

"That would explain why Perry won't sell the island."

Adrian parked near a mountain peak. "Emma thinks a hidden treasure is another one of those dreams that Dad blurred with reality."

"What do you think?"

"That he should have told someone what he found."

Wind rocked their car as he handed her a pair of black wellies, and she slipped off her saddle shoes to pull on the boots. When she tried to open her door, the wind pushed back, ramrodding her into the vehicle. Adrian yanked the door open from the outside, and she stepped out in the awkward wellies that covered the bottom of her trousers, her camera dangling from the strap around her neck.

Her boots sank into a boggy field as she moved toward the fort. Adrian reached for her good hand, and they battled the wind together until they reached a crumbling stone wall.

"When the Romans marched between the coast and Ambleside, they stopped at this fort to rest," he explained.

"It must have been a terrible march in the winter."

"Legend has it that they had hot water here for their baths."

"This is a land of legends, isn't it?"

"It's certainly a land of stories. Ones that span back for thousands of years." He picked up a smooth stone and rubbed his hand over it. "'King Eveling stood by the Azure River, when the tide-wave landward began to flow; and over the sea in the sunlight's shiver, he watch'd one white sail northward go.'"

She leaned against the wall. "Who's King Eveling?"

"The ruler of fairies. Local legend has it that this was once a fairy rath before the Romans built their fort out of stone. King Eveling held court in a mystical throne room."

She saw the fairies flitting between walls made of glass. A king propped up on a golden throne.

"I love fairy stories."

"My favorite one is the legend of Eden Hall," he said. "Henry Wadsworth Longfellow translated a German poem about it."

She grinned. "Pray tell."

"Eden Hall is located north of here near the town of Penrith," he explained. "The legends center around an ornate Syrian glass owned by the family who lived there. Supposedly this glass was stolen from fairies about five hundred years ago, and these fairies said if the goblet ever broke, the luck of Eden Hall would crumble as well."

"Did it ever break?"

He shook his head. "Eden Hall was dismantled about twenty years ago, but the glass is locked away safely in a London museum."

"Perhaps," she said, "the fairies still live on the estate."

As they stepped inside the wall of the old fort, Jenny felt as if fairies might still live here as well. Others might only see the debris, but she saw a legacy in these ruins.

With her good hand, she adjusted the shutter speed on her camera and began snapping photographs of the amber-colored peaks that swept up to the backdrop of pale-blue sky. The silver river cutting through the valley below.

She imagined Roman soldiers marching through her viewfinder, hundreds of them following this path of river through the mountains, searching for a respite from the freezing wind that had settled into their bones. Their feet probably ached. Perhaps some of them were injured, forced to endure their wounds and serve whether or not they supported the empire.

She lowered the camera. If only she could capture the legends, the history of this place, on film.

"Did the Vikings live here too?" she asked.

"I don't believe so, but they lived in the village of Buttermere."

"Where your parents met."

He grinned. "Exactly."

She pressed against her glove, trying to stop the pain throbbing through her hand again. Her aspirin was in her handbag on the floor of the car. "Is that village close by?"

"Close enough," he said. "Would you like to see it?"

"Yes, but don't you need to work this afternoon?"

He shook his head. "Emma told me to take the entire day off."

"Then I would love to go."

As they began driving down the other side of the mountains, she snuck two tablets from her handbag and swallowed them. Adrian didn't notice. He was slowly maneuvering around the minefield of ruts, pointing out things as he drove. Brooks that he called *becks*, dales instead of valleys, and a pristine mountain pool named a *tarn*. Or bathing pond, she thought, for the fairies.

An hour later, she and Adrian drove through a hamlet, parking near the lake of Buttermere. A brood of chickens bobbed their heads as they crossed the street, and several Herdwick sheep grazed the fells outside town.

With a blanket under his arm and a picnic basket in hand, Adrian blazed a trail for them around the perimeter of the lake through the scrubby broom. The roots gnarled above the damp soil, and Jenny stepped carefully around them so she wouldn't trip again. Water splashed into the lake from a nearby fall, but other than that, the afternoon was silent.

Adrian spread the blanket over a patch of grass and unpacked a loaf of malt bread, a block of cheese, and a thermos with sweet tea. Several clouds rolled over the fells across the lake, unfurling like a white carpet toward them as Adrian cut the brown bread. When he handed a piece to her, she removed her gloves, hiding her bandaged hand under the sweater beside her. "Do you have a napkin?"

"We call them *serviettes* in England."

She groaned. "Do you have a serviette?"

"No," he laughed. "You'll have to wash your hands in the lake. Or wipe them on your slacks."

"Perhaps I'll borrow your sleeve." She took a bite of the soft bread filled with raisins and scanned the hill across the lake as they ate. Near the top, a black gash scarred the rocks and brush. "What's that?"

"An old mine," he explained. "There are dozens of them around here."

"Gold mines?"

"No. Mostly copper, coal, and slate. Perhaps my dad found his coin in one of them."

"I wonder where Curtis got the money to build Enchanted Isle."

"Emma thinks he was born into a wealthy Irish family," Adrian said. "My dad and Curtis both took a risk when they started the place. After Curtis's death, our family would have lost the inn if Perry hadn't purchased the island . . . at least, that's what my mum said. She eventually married a man who could provide well for her without the hassle of the inn, so she passed along the hassle to Emma."

"Emma doesn't seem to mind."

"You're right," he said. "She loves taking care of the place and all the people who come through there."

He unwrapped wet newspapers from a glass jar and handed her a spoon. "Have you ever had damson and custard?"

She shook her head before taking a bite of the creamy sweet-and-sour mixture. Then she reached for her camera and took a picture of him eating from the jar, a purple streak threading the stubble on his jaw.

She pointed at his chin. "You seem to have missed your mouth."

"Perhaps you should feed me," he quipped.

She shook her head. "I'm going to take pictures of the lake."

He followed her down to the water's edge, where she photographed the rounded stones forming a foundation underneath the surface and the algae swaying in the undercurrent. Then she turned her camera and snapped another picture of him, his eyes intent on the lake as if he'd lost himself in another memory.

She sat on a rock and removed her borrowed wellies. "Let's put our feet in the water."

"It will be freezing cold."

"It'll also wake us up."

"Did you stay up too late last night?" he asked.

She grinned at him. "Someone kept me out long past my bedtime."

She tucked her camera back into the bag and peeled off her white socks. Then she began rolling up her slacks. Before she finished, he dug his bare foot through the water and splashed her.

"Adrian!"

"You looked as if you needed a shower."

Huffing, she reached down to return his splash with her hand, but the moment her bandage hit the water, she shrieked. He caught her wrist and lifted her hand, turning it to examine her bandage. "You've hurt yourself."

She shrugged. "It's starting to feel better."

He glanced back up, searching her face. "Is this from your fall?"

"The octopus's crown."

"Why didn't you tell me that you injured it?"

She forced a smile. "Should I have told you when we were running from Perry? Or when we were in the boathouse?"

He flushed. "Today would have worked fine."

"You already felt bad about what happened on the island . . ."

He gently unwrapped the cloth and flinched when he saw the gash. "I'm so sorry."

"And now you're apologizing when I was the one who tripped."

"We have to get you to a doctor."

She shook her head. "I don't like doctors."

He shook off his feet and replaced his socks. "Finally, we found something you don't like."

"I really don't need to see one," she insisted.

"Dr. Blyton will have to decide whether you need to see him or not."

CHAPTER 20

Unfortunately, Dr. Blyton sided with Adrian, concurring that Jenny needed medical care. After scolding her for neglect, the dreadful man cleaned her cut with a liquid that resembled water but burned like fire. Adrian held her opposite hand, but it didn't diminish the pain.

"You're only getting two jabs," Adrian said.

"I don't want to be jabbed once or twice!"

"You'll prefer it to an infection," Dr. Blyton said as he prepared the two shots. Then he threaded an additional needle.

Jenny tried to focus on the man holding her hand beside her, on the fort she'd seen today, on the people strolling past the office window in the village of Grasmere. But even when she tried to distract herself, the image of two needles inflated in her mind, battling each other like dueling swords, metal clanging, the silver edges gleaming.

Curse her imagination for wandering away on its own.

Dr. Blyton injected the first medication to relieve some of her pain; then he stitched up her wound, adding a tetanus shot for the encore.

When the ugly ordeal was over, her hand wrapped in a new bandage, she and Adrian stepped back onto the sidewalk. The sun was setting over the stone buildings around them, making their gray walls glow orange.

Adrian pointed toward a red kiosk. "Should we phone Cora?"

Jenny shook her head. "She's in Carlisle again today."

They stepped off the curb. "Would you like to join me for supper at the inn?"

She smiled. "I suppose that depends on what the chef is making."

"Haggis and black pudding."

She rolled her eyes. "My favorites."

"I hope you won't be too disappointed if the menu changes to roasted chicken and crackling."

She sighed, feigning disappointment. "I'll acclimate."

"Very good," he said. "Before we drive to the inn, there's one more thing you need."

Her eyebrows climbed. "Does it involve needles?"

He shook his head. "Hopefully we're done with needles for the day."

A block down the street was an ivy-clad shop displaying the sign *Grasmere Gingerbread*.

Adrian guided her toward the stucco building. "My mum used to bring me here after every visit with Dr. Blyton."

"I can't believe you went more than once!"

"He's a good doctor, even if he's a bit abrupt."

She tilted her head. "He's more than a bit abrupt."

"You deserve something sweet for surviving the encounter."

The white walls inside were lined with shelves displaying preserves, biscuits, and paper sleeves. Adrian purchased two of the sleeves, and when they stepped back outside, he pulled out what looked more like a cookie than cake.

She slipped the gingerbread slowly out of the bag and sniffed it. Then she took a bite. It tasted like brown sugar and butter and perhaps ginger, though it seemed more like cinnamon to her. "This is delicious."

He laughed. "How's your hand now?"

"Significantly better." She took a second bite. "Though it might need more gingerbread."

"I think we could accommodate that."

He bought her two more pieces, and the gingerbread erased all memory of the needles.

"Thank you for taking care of me, Adrian."

He smiled as they walked toward the car park, but even as her pain diminished, memories seemed to return to Adrian. The tree line along the shore broke, framing the water of Grasmere, and he paused, his gaze skimming the surface as if he'd forgotten she was beside him.

"Is this where Tom died?" she asked quietly.

"Near the other side." He pointed at the trees on the opposite bank. "I haven't been back since that night."

When his voice broke, she reached for his hand.

She could tell him again that Tom's death wasn't his fault, but assigning fault seemed to be of no comfort. He missed his friend, and she decided to wait beside him, giving him the space to remember on his own.

An hour later, Adrian parked his uncle's car in front of the Herdwick Inn. He hadn't talked much on their drive back, but he smiled at Jenny now as he opened her door.

She stepped into the cool air, looking out toward Windermere at the waning moon that emerged over the island. This evening the skies were clear, so unlike last night. "Do you think Perry will return to the island tonight?"

"Perhaps."

"Strange, isn't it, since he owns the land."

"Not so much if he's trying to keep a secret."

Emma met them in the dining room, her short hair brushed neatly to the side. About twenty people filled the tables behind her.

Jenny extended her good hand, and Emma shook it. "I hope you're joining us for supper."

"If there's room for us," Adrian said.

"I wish I could invite you up to my home for a meal, but I'm afraid Frank and the boys are having tinned soup."

Adrian glanced at Jenny, and she responded with a short nod.

"If there's enough soup, we'd like to join them," he said.

Emma turned toward her. "Do you know how to use a tin opener?"

Jenny laughed. "I mastered that in college, but not a gas stove."

Adrian winked at her. "I can assist if necessary."

"Then there's plenty of soup to go around. Before you go"—Emma stepped between them, threading her hand through Adrian's arm— "would you check on room four? The occupants said their lamp has burned out."

"Where's Oscar?"

"He had to leave an hour ago."

"I suppose I can change a light bulb."

Emma stepped toward the corridor. "Did I mention you're the best brother ever?"

"I don't recall that."

"You are," she said, nudging him forward.

"I'll change the light bulb after we eat."

"Better to do so now." Emma nodded toward a table at the far end of the room. "The occupants are just now finishing their meal."

He eyed Jenny. "I won't be long."

"There's no need to rush," Emma said, smiling at him.

Jenny chided herself for her nerves, but it seemed to her that Emma's insistence involved much more than the changing of a bulb.

After Adrian disappeared down the corridor, Emma directed her to a square table near the entrance. "We can wait for him here."

Jenny sat on the cushioned chair, resting her sore hand as Emma took the seat across from her. Then Emma scooted her chair closer to the table and placed both elbows on it, cradling her chin in a nook between her fingers.

"I'd offer you tea, but I'm afraid there isn't time."

"Time for what?" Jenny asked, glancing back toward the arch that separated the dining room and corridor. Hopefully it wouldn't take Adrian long to replace the bulb. His sister clearly had an agenda, and Jenny wasn't certain that she wanted to be privy to it.

"I like you a lot, Jenny Winter."

"Thank you," she replied skeptically.

"But I've been worried lately about my brother."

A waiter bustled by them, balancing two plates with some sort of meat and boiled potatoes. Emma didn't speak again until the man began talking to other diners three tables down.

"I want what's best for him, and Ohio is an awfully long way from our lake."

"I'm aware of that." Painfully so.

"Have you talked about the future?"

Jenny squirmed, bumping her hand against the table. Pain shot up her arm again, and for the first time since she'd arrived in the Lakes, she wished that she were back in Ohio. "I think you should ask Adrian about that."

"He's had a rough go at it since our father died." Emma inched back in her seat, dropping her arms onto the tablecloth. "He isn't one to give away his heart easily, and I want him to be happy."

"What will make him happy?"

Emma contemplated her words before speaking again. "Being with someone who respects and cares for him. Someone who helps him to forgive himself."

"He's an amazing man, Emma, but—"

"Who's amazing?" Adrian asked as he slipped up beside them.

Emma sighed, her gaze lingering on Jenny before she looked up at her brother. "That was quite fast."

"It was the oddest thing . . ." He reached for a spare chair from another table and situated it between Emma and Jenny. "I couldn't find a single light bulb in the entire room that needed to be changed."

"Now, why would they have told me that one of their lamps was broken?" She glanced across the room to her guests, as if they were to blame.

Adrian cocked his head. "I can't imagine a single reason."

"I'll phone up to the house and tell Frank that you'll be joining them for soup," Emma said as she stood.

He pointed his sister toward the door. "A word outside, please."

"Not now, Adrian." She turned to the kitchen instead. "I have to help the cook."

"She means well," Adrian said after his sister rushed away, though Jenny felt as if she'd been backed into a corner, no place to run.

"She clearly loves you."

"Still, I want to know," he persisted, "what were you planning to say after the part about an amazing man?"

Jenny shook her head. "You shouldn't be eavesdropping."

"How else would I discover the truth?"

"Perhaps you need to ask another way, Adrian."

He smiled. "Perhaps I shall."

CHAPTER 21

Adrian locked the door to his uncle's kitchen before handing Jenny a stack of newspapers. Together, they covered the linoleum on the kitchen floor, coating the entire room in black and white, like the pictures they were about to develop.

His nephews had fawned over Jenny that evening as if she were Queen Elizabeth, examining the five stitches in her hand, studying her blonde hair. He admired how graciously she'd treated them. How she found joy in everything except perhaps the visit with Dr. Blyton today.

Adrian started to shoo his nephews away, but Jenny had smiled and told him they were fine. And all had been fine until Ronnie asked Jenny if she liked his uncle. In that moment, Adrian had wished he'd taken Jenny to one of the pubs in Ambleside for supper, a meal of fish and chips instead of bean-and-bacon soup. Between his sister and her son, he was sunk.

Jenny had successfully sidestepped Ronnie's inquiry, saying she needed to help Adrian in the kitchen. And they'd left soon after.

As they'd walked up to the farmhouse, Jenny still wouldn't tell him about the conversation between her and Emma, so he'd be knocking on his sister's door later tonight, after he took Jenny home. Emma, he suspected, in her sweet but conniving way, had been trying to coerce information from Jenny or convince her to do something. Either way, Jenny—he also suspected—wouldn't be coerced. And he prayed that she wouldn't run away.

He covered the Formica on the kitchen counter with newspaper and pulled the shades over the window to complete the darkroom.

"Will you turn off the lights?" he asked after lining up the stainless steel tank, a reel, her canisters of film, and a pair of scissors by the sink.

"What are you going to do?"

"We have to develop the film first, and then we'll print your negatives onto paper."

"Magic," she said before turning the lights off.

Once the room was dark, he unrolled her film and wound it onto the reel of the tank. After securing the top, he asked Jenny to flip the switch again, and in the light, he explained to her the familiar process, how to add the working solution, stop bath, and fixer, slowly turning it to agitate the film and solution in perfect time before filling it with tepid water.

"It's the science behind the art," Jenny said.

"Exactly. Both have to work together to create a masterpiece. Science and art along with darkness and the light."

After the final wash, he stood close beside her at the sink to uncoil the film, and then he held her hand up, demonstrating how to hook the film on the line he'd strung between cabinets, the wet film draining. His hand resting over hers, he turned her slowly toward him, his heart beating fast.

"Jenny," he started, but his mind went blank.

"Yes?" she asked softly, not moving her hand from his.

"What did Emma ask you?"

She glanced over at the vine of film dangling beside them. "She asked me about the future."

"Just the future?"

She hesitated. "Our future."

"It's none of her business."

"I couldn't quite tell her that."

He lowered his hand, still cupping hers inside it. "It's not Emma's business, but it's very much mine."

"Do we have a future, Adrian?"

Her question weighed heavy on his mind, teetering with the balances. A future with her he wanted very much indeed, but what if he snapped one day like his father had done? What if he were doomed to fail? "I'm afraid I'll bring more harm to you than good."

"Oh, Adrian. I feel completely safe when I'm with you."

"But your hand."

"You didn't force me to fall on the crown. Just like you didn't give Tom the cocaine or force him to take it before he swam."

She looked so beautiful smiling at him in the kitchen light, her cobalt eyes like jewels, contrasting with the black-and-white newspaper print that concealed everything around them.

"You're a healer, Adrian. I saw it when you helped that ewe. She trusted you implicitly, and you brought life not harm to her and her lamb."

Her words washed over him slowly, like a balm, changing the image he'd thought permanently frozen in the silver salt of his past.

He cleared his throat. "Should we develop your next roll?"

"We should," she answered, inching back from the sink, but her eyes were still on him.

Instead of reaching for the canister, he pulled her close, and she folded into him. He kissed her hair first, then her lips, just like he'd wanted to do back in the boathouse. And she kissed him back.

Someone jostled the knob to the kitchen door. "Adrian?"

"Blast," he muttered.

Jenny's cheeks reddened as she scooted away, but he didn't move.

His uncle knocked. "Are you in there, Adrian?"

"Just a moment," he called back.

"I need to speak with you now."

Jenny reached for a towel and turned away from the door, wiping off the tank and bottles of solution.

Adrian moved slowly toward the door and unlocked it. Frank and Gilbert were on the other side, both their faces somber.

"What's wrong?" Adrian asked.

"You need to come with me," his uncle said.

"Where are we going?"

"We'll discuss it outside."

Adrian glanced back at the kitchen and saw the concern in Jenny's eyes.

Frank stepped forward. "The boys and I will drive Jenny home."

"Thank you," Adrian said as he reached for his coat on the rack.

A policeman stood near the front door, dressed in a dark-blue uniform and helmet, a wooden truncheon secured at his waist. Then another officer came from his left, escorting Emma.

The man motioned him toward a waiting car. "We need to speak with you at the station."

"There was an accident on the lake last night," Inspector Dixon said from behind his cramped desk in the Ambleside police station, his black toupee slightly askew.

Adrian glanced over at his sister and uncle beside him, but it seemed neither was aware of Perry's accident. Did the man know Adrian had taken Jenny to the island?

"A boat hit one of the crags, and when my men cleaned up the wreckage, they . . . they found something."

"What exactly did they find?" Gilbert asked, his voice tense.

"We believe it's the body of Curtis Sloan."

Emma gasped, her hand flying up to cover her mouth.

Instead of shock, Adrian felt nothing. A vast crevice of emptiness. He reached for his sister's hand, enveloping it in his. "Why do you think it's Curtis?"

"We found a ring engraved with the Sloan family crest on the body," the inspector said.

Gilbert shifted in his chair, his forehead falling to his hands. "It's probably Curtis," he said grimly.

The inspector lifted a manila file from his stack and opened it before eying Gilbert. "According to our records, you said you found Curtis's body on the island in 1935, but you didn't report this until the summer of 1946."

"I should have come to the police straightaway." His voice broke. "I was in shock, seeing the body beside my brother that night, and Simon, he had a knife in his hands . . ."

The inspector leaned forward, skepticism flashing in his eyes. "You waited two years after your brother died to tell us."

Gilbert's chin plodded up and down, his nod a wary admission.

"Did you kill Curtis Sloan?" the inspector asked Gilbert.

"No."

"Did you assist with the murder?"

"I answered these questions before."

The inspector glanced down at the file before looking back at Gilbert. "In light of what's happened, I'm afraid I must ask them again."

"I don't know what happened that night—" Gilbert choked on his words.

"But you decided to hide the body," Inspector Dixon said.

Gilbert shook his head. "When I returned, the body had disappeared."

"Why didn't you phone the station?"

"Because I was afraid." No one spoke, waiting for him to explain why. "My brother was already broken; a trial might have killed him. And any trace of evidence was gone. People already thought he was mad."

The inspector drummed his hands on the table. "Do you think Simon might've returned before you to dump his partner's body into the lake?"

"I don't know how he would have made it back to the island before I did."

"Why would Simon have killed him?"

"You don't know that our father killed him," Emma said. "And Gilbert certainly didn't."

"We're going to find out what happened." Inspector Dixon tapped the tip of his pen on a file folder, circling the top with a ring of dots.

Pain throbbed between Adrian's temples, and he leaned back in this chair, pressing the bridge of his nose, the accusation of murder pounding in his head. He wanted to protest the accusations, say that his father would never have killed anyone, but the evidence seemed to prove what their family already suspected.

Nothing at Dr. Blyton's office could take away this kind of pain.

The officer drove the three of them back to the inn.

"Don't leave the Lakes," he warned Gilbert before he left. Then they stood huddled together in the parking lot like lost sheep, afraid to speak.

"I should have gone to the police the night I found Curtis," Gilbert finally said.

"You were trying to protect Dad," Emma told him. "And us."

"Still . . . I'm sorry."

Emma kissed his cheek. "None of us know exactly what happened before you arrived on the island that night."

Adrian felt as if he might explode. "Dad was holding the bloody knife, Emma!"

"That doesn't mean he killed Curtis."

Gilbert pointed up the steps. "Let's go home, Adrian."

But instead of climbing the stairs, Adrian roared away on his motorbike.

CHAPTER 22

Fifty feet of stained glass decked the cathedral's East Window. Jenny craned her neck to study the clover-shaped windows at the top, her gaze trickling down the colored fragments of glass as she studied each depiction from the life of Christ.

"The original pieces are from the fourteenth century," Cora explained, standing beside Jenny in the choir.

"It's magnificent."

"The ability to create stained glass from that era is a lost art," Cora said. "We can repair it, but the old glaziers took the secrets of their craft to their graves. And so much of their work was destroyed during the Reformation."

Jenny shook her head, her gaze lingering on the glass. "I don't understand why anyone would want to destroy art."

"Because they didn't see the beauty. Only what it represented." Cora sighed. "Hundreds of years passed before people began appreciating glasswork again."

In spite of Cora's earlier objections, her restoration work was exquisite. She'd cleaned the glass on a circular-shaped window that depicted a pilgrim and replaced the corroded pieces before hemming it back together with lead came, the seam bridging together the old and new. Then she'd waterproofed it all with linseed oil.

Cora's heels clicked on a brass plaque in the floor as she stepped away. "I need to speak with the curate."

Cora seemed much happier now that this window was finally restored. Or perhaps it was because of Perry's visit. Either way, she'd invited Jenny to see her work in Carlisle today.

And Jenny was plenty happy too. Adrian's kiss sealed the feelings that had been raging in her heart. *Love* seemed like a presumptuous word to attach to it, but she cared much more for Adrian Kemp than she'd ever cared for any other man. And she wanted to spend every possible moment of her time left in England with him, exploring the lakes and fells when he wasn't working.

She'd hoped he would phone last night or this morning to tell her why Gilbert had whisked him away, but she hadn't heard a word. If he didn't call this evening, she would bicycle down to the inn first thing in the morning.

As she waited for Cora, Jenny toured the building with her camera, slipping around scaffolding in the places where the workers were restoring windows and plaster and stone. She photographed the carvings of angels and the arches along the sanctuary, wishing that Adrian were here to enjoy it with her.

After a half hour, Cora returned, her face lit with a smile. "They paid me for the window."

"Congratulations."

"I'll treat us to lunch."

Jenny climbed into the Fiat. "Is Perry coming back tonight?"

Cora's long earrings, trimmed with glass bananas, apples, and grapes, brushed over the shoulders of her sweater as she leaned forward to open the glove compartment. "I'm planning to stop by his house on the way home."

"I didn't think you knew where he lived."

Cora pulled a red booklet out of the compartment. On the cover was a crown emblem above the words *Driving Licence*. "He left this behind when he spent the night. I found it between the seat cushions on the couch."

Jenny opened it up and saw Perry's address in Penrith. The name slowly registered with her—the town was near the house of the fairy glass.

She looked back up. "How far away is Penrith?"

Cora shifted to first gear and drove out to the street. "It's on our route home."

"Do you want to see Perry?" Jenny asked, struggling to understand.

"I need to give him his license."

"But why won't you just mail it to him?"

"There's no reason to do that," Cora said. "We're practically driving right by his house."

"And you want to see where he lives now."

Cora shrugged.

An hour later, an attendant at a petrol station directed them to the address on Perry's license, but before they left the station, Cora stopped to fix her hair and reapply her lipstick. Then they drove along a river until they found a stone cottage with a spindly sycamore tree growing in the front lawn. Cora parked along the lane, watching the house from the car, as if Perry might emerge to greet them.

Jenny nodded toward the door. "You're supposed to knock."

"In a moment," Cora replied, but she still didn't move.

"Do you want *me* to?"

"No . . ." The front door had opened, and a middle-aged woman dressed in capris and a tight pink blouse stepped outside. She carried a spade and a potted plant.

Cora's perfectly painted lips dropped open, but no sound emerged, not even a gasp.

Jenny rechecked the house number on the license. "Perhaps this is his old address."

Cora nodded once before speaking. "Surely."

Jenny opened her door. "Would you like me to check?"

"You may as well."

Jenny stepped out of the car, the red license in hand, and walked to the house. Minutes later, she returned and slipped quietly into the passenger seat.

Cora shifted the car into first but didn't drive. "Who is she?"

Jenny pressed her hands together, wishing she were anyplace else but here.

Cora turned toward her, eyes glazed. "Jenny?"

"She said she's his wife."

Memories flooded back to Liz as she rode the public bus around the lake, between the railway station at Windermere and the center of Ambleside. Several white sails furled in the breeze, and she thought back more than two decades to the summer that she'd spent at her aunt's cottage along the water, where she'd lost herself in the depths of Windermere and the eyes of Gilbert Kemp.

She'd fallen for Gilbert as they'd sailed together across this lake, exploring the coves and islands like the swallows and amazons in the book he'd loved as a boy. She'd never told him about her phobia of fish, so he'd tried to teach her how to catch the trout as they passed through here, swimming toward the Irish Sea. She'd refused to touch the creatures that ended up on her fishing line, but she'd fallen hook, line, and sinker for that man and his gentle strength.

They'd been so young, but she'd thought the bond between them indestructible. Gilbert had snared her heart, and when she'd returned to Cleveland, she had left a piece of herself behind with him.

After a safe landing yesterday, she'd spent the night in a London hotel and took an early train from Euston Station, traveling north for most of her day. Now the bus passed the Herdwick Inn, and she wondered if Gilbert's family still owned it or the island on her left that once housed Enchanted Isle.

So many memories were rooted in that park. She and Cora had spent hours playing there while Gilbert worked with his brother, Simon. Even though she'd been new to her craft, Curtis had asked Cora to create glass for several attractions, and her friend had been so proud of her work on the railway station and the magnificent carousel.

No matter how long she lived, Liz would never forget that carousel. The Magic Lagoon. It was like nothing she'd ever seen before—a masterpiece of art and engineering. But more than the novelty of it, the carousel was where Gilbert had proposed.

She hadn't anticipated his proposal—and he hadn't planned to do it—but on that warm August afternoon, he'd asked her to become his wife.

And she'd known, more than anything else, that she wanted to spend her life with him. That they fit together like two wedges of Cora's glass, two distinct colors and yet complimenting each other in what she'd thought was a beautiful piece of art. Even her aunt, whom she'd adored, had liked Gilbert. Liz hadn't cared whether or not they lived here or in Cleveland; she'd just wanted to spend the rest of her life with that man.

Over the years, she'd racked her brain trying to figure out what had changed between them that afternoon, what she could possibly have done to infuriate him. Or if he'd simply panicked under the weight of his foolishness, in the realization that he'd committed to spend the rest of his life with her.

Perhaps she shouldn't have come back to the Lakes, reawakened these memories. Perhaps she shouldn't have encouraged Jenny to come for that matter, especially so soon after leaving school. The sweetness in her daughter's soul, she feared, might sour if she left a portion of her broken heart here as well. She wanted Jenny to embrace the life God had gifted her, no matter where she was or whom she was with.

She'd celebrate Jenny's birthday and perhaps convince her to return early. Or finish her holiday in London.

Luggage in hand, Liz stepped off the bus and found a driver available to hire. It was a homecoming of sorts, returning to Ambleside, but it felt strange to be here alone.

CHAPTER 23

Cora flung her long coat toward a hook on the rack, but it dropped into a heap on the tile floor. She'd fumed the entire car ride home, mumbling about a blooming fool, though Jenny wasn't certain if she was talking about Perry or herself.

Jenny whisked the coat off the floor and hung it beside her own. She didn't fault the woman for her anger. The scales had finally fallen off her eyes, it seemed, and the reality was excruciating.

Jenny reached for the kettle and filled it with water. "Let's make some tea."

Cora tore the first two matches by striking too hard, but the third one flickered between her fingertips. Jenny placed the teapot on the burner.

When the doorbell rang, Cora's hands flung up above her shoulders, as if she could press the sound away. "I swear, if it's Perry . . ."

God help him if it was.

As Cora stomped toward the corridor, Jenny reached for two cups. Perhaps now that she knew the truth, Cora could begin to move on as well. Or at least stop financing Perry's new marriage. Jenny didn't think she could bear to hear Cora kowtowing to him again.

But then she heard Cora screech, followed by laughter, and Jenny rushed toward the front room. Perry wasn't paying them another visit. With Cora was her mother, wearing a wrinkled Chanel jacket and skirt along with a matching white hat, a piece of luggage on each side of her.

"Mom!" she shouted, hugging her. "Why are you here?"

Her mom glanced at Cora before looking back. "I wanted to celebrate your birthday."

Jenny tilted her head. "And?"

"Why must there be another reason?" Her mom slipped the gloves off her hands, slapping them together against her palm.

But Jenny knew there must be something else. They'd already celebrated in New York.

Was her mom worried about her? Or had Cora told her about Adrian?

The teapot whistled in the background, and Jenny swept back toward the kitchen to pour the tea. At first, she tried to balance the handles of all three cups around her fingers, but her right hand screamed back at her, the consistent reminder of her trip to Enchanted Isle.

What would her mom say when she told her that Adrian had taken her to the abandoned park?

She carried the cups out on a serving tray with her good hand, and the three of them sipped tea together, the two older women reminiscing about Liz's summer here.

"I thought I was so old back then," her mom said. "So composed."

"You were composed. Unlike me, who fell apart at the drop of a hat." Instead of sipping her tea, Cora held the cup a few inches below her lips as if she'd forgotten it was there. "And fell for the wrong man. Perry and I divorced almost a year ago."

"I'm sorry, Cora." Her mom placed her cup back on the tray.

"Don't be. Our marriage was a disaster."

"I envy you and your space here to create." Her mom turned back toward Jenny. "Did she show you her glasswork?"

Jenny nodded. "Her studio is filled with art."

"I'll never forget the lovely windows you created for Enchanted Isle," her mom said to Cora.

Jenny scooted forward. "I didn't know you designed glass for the park."

Cora shrugged. "Only for the railway station."

"And the carousel," Liz reminded her. "That was my favorite ride."

"I hardly remember what they looked like."

It was strange, Jenny thought, that Cora hadn't told her about the glass when she'd asked about the park. Then again, she hadn't yet told Cora that she'd been on the island.

"The glass was a cranberry color, set along the top of the carousel like trinkets, between the painted scenes from the sea." Liz sipped her tea. "Don't you have a photograph of it?"

Cora shook her head.

"It's too bad," Liz said sadly. "It was a beautiful ride."

"It still is beautiful," Jenny said slowly.

"Still?" Cora groaned. "Perry would have your head if he knew you were on the island."

"I'm not planning to tell him."

The telephone interrupted them, and the three women stared down at the black receiver. "I probably shouldn't answer that," Cora said.

Jenny leaned over and unplugged the jack from the wall. "A good choice."

"Perry has his driving license now. I don't believe he needs anything else from me."

"I'm sorry," Liz said again. "It hurts to lose someone you love."

"It will all work out in the end." Cora nodded toward the steps. "You two will want to catch up on your own before bed."

Jenny stood and reached for one of her mom's bags.

"Thank you for hosting us," Liz said as she picked up the other suitcase.

Upstairs Jenny and her mom took turns in the bathroom, changing into their nightgowns before returning to the bedroom. Liz collapsed onto one of the beds. "I've missed you."

"I've missed you too."

"I wasn't sure if I should come."

"But you were worried."

"Perhaps a little," Liz said.

"I've been doing fine on my own."

"That's not what I was worried about."

Jenny hung her sweater on a hanger and lit the paraffin heater. "Did Cora tell you about Adrian?"

"I really did want to surprise you for your birthday, but, yes, she mentioned you'd been seeing a boy."

"He's not a boy, Mom. Adrian is practically twenty-three, and I wanted to tell you about him on my own."

"I don't want to intrude like—" Liz stopped herself, but Jenny knew exactly what she'd intended to say. She didn't want to intrude like Stephan McAdam often did. "You've already grown up in these weeks, Jenny. Or perhaps I should call you Jennifer now."

She shook her head. "Only Grandfather calls me that."

Liz scooted to the edge of the bed. "What are you planning to tell Robert?"

"That I can't marry him."

"He'll be disa—"

"No, he won't, Mom. He'll be relieved."

Liz glanced down at her hands. "Not because of you, Jenny."

"He was only marrying me because Grandfather wanted him to."

Liz smiled when she looked back up. "So tell me about this Adrian."

Jenny sat down beside the writing desk. This was a conversation she would have preferred to practice a time or two, but it was too late for a rehearsal now. She reached for the envelope of pictures, the ones she'd developed at the chemist. "Let me show you some of my photographs."

Her mom opened the envelope and thumbed through the photos of the moon and the lake. "These are extraordinary."

"Adrian taught me how to use my new camera."

Liz studied one with reeds that framed the edge of the water. "You have an eye for photography."

"He has an eye for it as well and the ability to capture it. And he's super smart. He graduated with a degree in business."

"Perhaps you could finish your degree in photography."

Jenny fidgeted on the chair. "I'm not smart enough to do that."

"Yes, you are." Her mom held up the photograph. "You just see the world through pictures."

Jenny pondered her words. She would certainly enjoy taking photography classes, but would she be able to pass them?

"How is Adrian using his degree?"

Jenny took a deep breath, trying to determine exactly how to tell her mother about the connection with Gilbert. "Right now, he's helping his sister at a local inn called Herdwick, but he's planning to move to London."

Her mom's lips pressed into a perfectly shaped *O* before speaking again. "I've been to the Herdwick."

"I know," Jenny said. "Gilbert told me."

"How—" Her mom's voice trembled with her question. "How do you know Gilbert?"

"He's Adrian's uncle."

"I see." Her mom leaned back against the pillows, closing her eyes.

"Simon Kemp was Adrian's dad."

She opened her eyes again. "Cora said that Simon died during the war."

Jenny nodded. "Adrian stays with Gilbert when he's home."

"Does Gilbert know you're my daughter?"

"He does now."

"I should have told you about him before you came to England." Liz pulled the blankets over her. "In some way, I suppose, it felt disrespectful to your father to tell you about this man I once loved. A man I thought had either died in the war or moved away."

"Dad would want you to find love again."

Her mom shook her head. "It's too late for that."

Jenny turned off the lamp and climbed into the second twin bed. "Are you going to ask me about Gilbert?"

"No."

"Aren't you the slightest bit curious?" she pressed.

"You're curious enough for both of us."

Jenny bunched up one of her pillows to get comfortable. "Gilbert never married, Mom."

Silence greeted her in response.

She tossed a second pillow onto her mother's bed. "Did you hear me?"

"Good night, Jenny."

Jenny was smiling as she fell asleep.

The rock pinged off Jenny's window, then made a scuffing noise when it hit the ground. Adrian had tried to telephone multiple times this afternoon and evening, but no one answered. He'd only wanted to talk to Jenny, tell her about Curtis before the rumors spread.

Everything had changed since he'd walked out the door last night with Gilbert. He'd spent much of the night and morning riding through the Lakes, stopping at Grasmere again before taking the bone-jarring road over to the ocean. He'd thrown sticks and stones into the tide, anything he could find to throw, and he'd wondered what it would be like to climb aboard a steamer and cruise away from England, start again in a new place where no one knew anything about him or his family.

He threw another rock toward the glass and waited.

Gossip about Curtis's death would spread like quillwort on the floor of a tarn, the dense weeds covering up any hint of truth even if it emerged. All fingers would point back to his dad and now Gilbert too.

The window above screeched as it opened, and Adrian stepped forward.

"Jenny?" he whispered, not wanting to wake Cora. Her Fiat was parked outside, but her bedroom window and the studio were dark.

Jenny's face appeared in the window frame. "Adrian?"

"Why is he throwing rocks?" a woman asked from the other side of the window.

Adrian stepped back. "Is Cora with you?"

"No, it's my mother."

"Your mum?" Adrian repeated, confused. "I thought she was in Cleveland."

A second head appeared in the window. Jenny's mother, he assumed. "I've been wanting to meet you, Mr. Kemp."

He brushed his hands together. Mrs. Winter was actually the last person that he wanted to see, at least tonight when he was throwing rocks at her daughter's window. "Please call me Adrian," he finally said.

"I believe it would be preferable for you to come through the front door," Mrs. Winter said.

He took another step back. "I can return in the morning."

The two women conversed together, though he couldn't hear their words. Finally, Jenny spoke. "We'll meet you downstairs."

They opened the front door for him, both dressed in their robes and looking more like sisters than mother and daughter. Jenny's face was scrubbed clean of any makeup. And she looked beautiful.

Jenny offered to make tea, but he shook his head before taking the seat offered to him.

"It's a pleasure to meet you, Adrian," Mrs. Winter said.

"You as well, though I'd hoped to make a better impression."

"Do you throw stones often at my daughter's window?"

Jenny jumped. "Mom!"

"It's my first time," he replied, embarrassed. "I'm afraid something has happened."

"What is it?" Jenny asked.

He took a deep breath, knowing he must tell her no matter how hard.

"When Perry's boat hit the crags, the divers who cleaned it up found . . ." He searched for the best way to explain, but there was no good way to cushion the news. "They found a corpse snagged in the rocks below."

Both of the women's faces turned pale, and he wished more than anything that he didn't have to deliver this news. "They believe it's Curtis Sloan."

Jenny gasped, and Mrs. Winter looked stunned as well.

"I'm sorry, Adrian," Jenny said.

He dug his hands into his coat pockets. "The police have asked us to keep quiet for now, but it will be impossible for them to keep that news secret for long. Before word leaks out, I wanted you to know."

"We won't say anything," Jenny assured him.

"Curtis Sloan," Mrs. Winter said slowly. "He owned the park."

"He co-owned it with my father."

"How did he die?" Mrs. Winter asked.

"They aren't certain yet, but the police think my father killed him." Mrs. Winter gasped.

"Gilbert found my father with Curtis's body, back in 1935. And he was holding a knife."

"When exactly did he find Curtis?" Mrs. Winter asked.

"The night the park closed for the season."

"I see."

He stood, and Jenny walked with him toward the door. Her mother seemed to fade into the background, though Adrian suspected she wasn't far.

Was she as concerned as Cora about him? She was right to be worried, he supposed, especially knowing now what his father had done.

"You don't know for certain that your father killed Curtis," Jenny said.

"You sound like Emma."

"Fight for the truth."

"I fear the truth died with both men."

"Then fight for your dad."

CHAPTER 24

Liz wrestled with her pillow. She was bone tired from her travel, heart tired from old emotions flaring again, but a branch kept brushing up against the glass, stealing away her sleep. The last time someone had thrown a rock at her window, it had been Gilbert, and he'd been raging mad.

A cool breeze stole up from the valley and edged through the window, the tiniest of slivers like the opening in her heart. But much could come through even the smallest of spaces. The wisp of wind or a forgotten memory. The branch brushed over the glass again, the sound recapturing the memory of a rock thrown in anger.

Even though she'd searched her heart that night and for months after, she'd never been able to discover what she had done to make Gilbert so mad, but now she knew why he'd turned from Dr. Jekyll to Edward Hyde that night. His own heart had been crushed by what he'd found in the park.

Gilbert had no right to bruise her with his words, but now she understood. In his own pain, he'd wounded her.

She'd braced herself over the years for news that he'd been killed in the war, like his brother. If not, she felt certain that he had married a British woman and was a splendid husband and father. She'd never really considered the possibility that he wouldn't marry.

What would it be like to see him again, knowing at least some of the truth?

Not that the truth mattered much anymore. She'd married Jack Winter, and she had no regrets in that regard. Together they'd borne and raised a daughter that they loved. A daughter she didn't want anyone to hurt.

What if Adrian declared his love to Jenny and then changed on a dime, like Gilbert had done? What if Jenny gave him her heart and he misused it?

But then again, Adrian wasn't his uncle. She'd liked his authenticity tonight and how he seemed to respect and care for her daughter. Jenny looked as if he'd hung the moon.

Jenny might say she didn't want to marry, but it seemed that she wanted to find love. And that's what Liz wanted for her too—for Jenny to discover love on her own and one day marry without interference from her or her father.

Finally, Liz fell asleep and didn't wake again until she heard Jenny shuffling beside her. When Jenny left to dress, Liz padded downstairs in her robe to find Cora reading the newspaper at the table, a cup of tea and rasher of bacon beside her.

Cora lowered the newspaper. "Good morning."

"A good morning to you as well."

Liz poured herself a cup of tea, remembering the days when she and Cora used to linger over the breakfast table talking about their previous evening often spent on Enchanted Isle.

What would Cora say when she found out the police had recovered Curtis's body? Liz wished she could tell her friend, but Adrian had asked them to keep it in confidence for now.

"Where's Jenny?" Cora asked as Liz sat across the table from her.

"Getting herself ready for the day."

Cora took a sip of tea. "She's been seeing Gilbert's nephew."

"I know."

"I tried to warn her," Cora said.

"She's capable of making her own decisions."

"After what Gilbert did to you—"

"I know, it was dreadful."

"He shattered a pane on your window!"

Liz sighed. "None of us should be bound by the choices of our family." Nor should they be bound by their family to make a wrong choice.

"Adrian has made bad choices on his own."

"What are you going to do about Perry?" Liz asked, wanting to decide for herself about Adrian Kemp.

"He called again last night, and we had a long talk." Cora wrapped her hands around the cup. "He's decided to sell Enchanted Isle."

"What made him change his mind?" Liz asked, wondering if he knew about Curtis.

"I've been loaning him money since our divorce, and I told him that I wasn't going to give him another cent."

They were both silent for a moment.

"Will you miss him?" Liz asked.

A tear fell down Cora's cheek. "Terribly."

Liz reached across the table and took her friend's hand, squeezing it. Cora had given this man her heart, and he'd stomped on it so often that Cora must feel as if it had been flattened.

"You should come back to America with Jenny and me," Liz said. "You'd like Cleveland in the summer."

Cora shook her head. "I need to lose myself in my studio. At least there I can repair what's been shattered."

"Your heart will heal, Cora."

Her friend smiled weakly at her. "So will yours."

Gilbert wiped down the kitchen counters twice before he returned to his room. Not that Liz cared how he and Adrian lived, but he didn't want her thinking they were two sloppy bachelors, buried under food scraps and grimy dishes. He'd wanted to show her that they were respectable men, for Adrian and Jenny's sake. Even if he was being investigated for murder.

His mind rolled again at the thought, and he quickly stamped it out. Adrian had invited both Liz and Jenny for dinner, but this time, Adrian asked—commanded, really—that Gilbert dine with them.

Tonight, he had to focus on their guests.

Adrian told him this morning that Liz had lost her husband four years ago, and the news did the strangest things to his heart. He'd grieved silently for Liz, his heart wrenching at her loss. And then the news stirred something inside him as well. Hope, perhaps, that he'd finally be able to ask her forgiveness for what he'd done long ago.

He combed his hair again and took to his knees beside the bed, praying that God would give him the words to say and restore some of what had been lost.

Adrian stepped through the open doorway. "They'll be here soon."

Gilbert didn't move. "I'm going to pray until they arrive."

Minutes later the doorbell rang, and he heard Adrian greet their guests. He had never thought he would get this chance again, and yet here it was, staring him in the face. He needed every bit of the courage he'd lost over the years. God had sufficiently, and necessarily, humbled him, but tonight he needed to face what he'd done with humility and grace, no matter what Liz said.

Taking a deep breath, he walked down the steps and into their front room.

Liz Winter was standing near the window in a tailored gray dress and matching slip of a hat pinned over her blonde hair, a double strand of pearls around her neck. She looked just as lovely as the day he'd asked for her hand in marriage, and for just a moment, it almost seemed as if nothing had come between them. As if he'd never thrown the rocks at her aunt's window.

But he had, of course, and he needed to mend the bridge between them the best he could.

Adrian took Jenny's hand and led her toward the kitchen, the two of them talking as they walked, though the words were muffled in Gilbert's ears. Liz shuffled her oyster-colored purse between her hands, her gaze on the ground as if she were scared. It tore him up inside to think she might be afraid of him.

"Liz—" His voice broke. "I'm so sorry."

When she glanced up, her eyes were warm, but she still didn't speak, waiting it seemed, for him to explain. The story spilled out in a barrage of words, like dandelion seeds blown into the wind. Or bullets flying across the room, hitting nothing. More sound than substance.

He didn't know if he was making sense, but he wanted her to understand that he'd never wanted to harm her.

"I was drunk out of my mind when I threw those rocks, angry at what my brother had done." He clutched his hands together in front of him, wishing again that he could crush the memories. "And I didn't stop drinking for years. I drank myself through the war until God stopped me in my path and sent me on a new journey."

"You shattered more than my window." Her eyes filled with tears, and he wished he could pull her into his arms like he would have done years ago. "You shattered my heart with your words."

"I'm not making excuses for what I did," he said. "But I wanted you to know—"

"Why didn't you apologize earlier?"

"I sent you a letter right after you left. And then a dozen more."

She shook her head. "I never received your letters."

"I didn't know if your father had intercepted them or if you were ignoring me, but I had to find out. A year after you left, I bought passage on a ship to New York."

Her hand flew up, covering her mouth.

"I found your parents' home in Cleveland, but the housekeeper said you were in Bermuda."

"My honeymoon," she whispered. "I should have asked you what was wrong before I left."

"No—I was angry, but not at you, Liz. I was angry at myself for what I'd done." He stepped forward, wishing he could take her hand. "Please forgive me."

A tear trickled down her cheek, and he reached up, brushing it away. "If I could, I'd go back in time and change everything."

She took a handkerchief from her purse and dabbed at the edge of her eyes. "I forgive you, Gilbert."

And with those simple words, a torrent of peace swept through him. Salvation had been a gift of God, one he hadn't deserved. This forgiveness from Liz was another gift.

His own eyes teared. "Thank you."

She stepped forward, pushing up onto her toes to kiss his cheek. "Thank you for asking."

He placed his hand on the slender small of her back, as he'd done so many times before, and guided her toward the kitchen. Jenny and Adrian were laughing as they stirred the rice pudding on the cooker, overcoming any gloom that lingered inside this old house.

The four of them ate broiled trout and cabbage for supper as Liz told them about her life in Cleveland, of her work representing McAdam Industries at a number of events. Her voice feigned a light-ness, but Gilbert knew her, or at least he knew the twenty-year-old version of her, and she sounded as if she were trapped on a hamster wheel, spinning endlessly but never actually going anywhere.

When they finished eating, Adrian turned to the sideboard and opened a drawer, pulling out a cardboard envelope. He set it by Jenny's place. "I printed your pictures."

She took the envelope. "Are they awful?"

"You tell me."

She opened the envelope, and a look of satisfaction edged across her face when she leafed through the black-and-white photographs.

"You can see the contrast in the fells and lake," Adrian said, pointing at one of the pictures. "Perhaps you could publish your photographs one day, so people in Cleveland and beyond can visit our Lakes."

Liz leaned forward. "I agree."

Jenny smiled at both of them as she tucked the photographs back in the envelope. "Perhaps I will."

A stack of ledgers loomed tall behind Jenny, ledgers that Emma had found with the album in her basement storage. Gilbert had reviewed them before Maria sold the island to Perry, but he'd only given them a cursory glance. With Simon gone—and Maria anxious to move on—he'd decided that nothing in the books could change the past. But now he and Adrian both wanted to review the ledgers again before turning them over to the inspector in the morning.

Liz followed Gilbert's gaze toward the sideboard. "What are those?"

"The books from Enchanted Isle. Adrian and I are going to look through them tonight to see if we can find out what went wrong between Simon and Curtis."

"Can we help?" Jenny asked.

Liz shook her head. "They don't need our help."

Years ago, he'd wanted to partner with Liz for a lifetime, but perhaps the four of them could work as a team for the night, trying to find answers together.

"Actually, we're glad to have the help." He lifted one of the books and handed it across the table to Jenny. Then he gave books to Liz and to Adrian. "There are thousands of entries in three years' time."

"What are we looking for?" Liz asked, brushing her hand across the cover.

"Any large sums of money spent or deposited."

He opened his book and skimmed through the first lines, praying the answers they needed were somewhere inside. Something that would clear both himself and his brother.

CHAPTER 25

It was the unusual bits of accounting that Adrian noticed first. At university, his professor had said when someone wanted to embezzle money from an organization, he or she typically siphoned it in small increments, so Adrian focused mainly on the farthings and pence sprinkled throughout the pages. The shillings to buy paper serviettes. The money spent in maintenance fees when Gilbert did most of the work.

At first, he tried to track the figures in his mind as he read them, but he quickly resorted to scratching them on a separate notepad. There was almost too much detail in these ledgers, as if someone had wanted to hide something within the overwhelming catalog of expenses.

On the flip side, the profits were oddly consistent for a business that generated revenue in ticket sales.

"How much were the tickets?" Adrian asked his uncle.

"It cost a shilling for some rides. Two shillings for others."

But every day, income had been entered at two hundred pounds. It wasn't possible that the park had sold the same number of tickets each day for months on end. Either someone had been sloppy or—

"How many people visited the park each summer?" Adrian asked Gilbert, his mind spinning.

"About four hundred thousand."

"Does anyone else have an unusual amount of line items for serviettes?"

Mrs. Winter and Jenny each scanned several pages before concurring.

"Perhaps they had a lot of messy guests," Mrs. Winter said.

"Perhaps," he replied. "Or perhaps someone was taking the extra money to line their pockets."

It was almost a perfect scheme, really, running the sales of something illegal through the park's income. The ticket profits would be hard to dispute. Instead of paying someone for the serviettes or maintenance or food, the bookkeeper could simply deposit the extra shillings in his pocket. No prying eyes or questions as to where he'd obtained it. A little at a time, patiently scheming.

Gilbert rested his elbows on the table, scanning the handwriting in front of him before he looked up. He didn't seem shocked at Adrian's words. "You think Curtis or Simon was laundering money through the park?"

Adrian wrestled with the possibility. "I think an amusement park could be a front for seemingly legitimate profits and expenses."

"Your father rarely touched the books," Gilbert said. "He was the creative mind behind the place."

"But if he found out that Curtis was running money through the business . . ." Adrian leaned back in his chair, the weight returning to his shoulders. "He might have a motive to kill his partner. Or Curtis might have tried to kill him first."

"We need more than speculation," Gilbert said.

But it would be hard to find the facts with a world war separating the demise of the park and their questions about accounting errors. None of the sellers listed in these ledgers, if still in existence, could possibly tell him how much Curtis and Simon had actually spent.

"What if someone other than Simon knew about Curtis's scheme?" Mrs. Winter asked.

Adrian turned the page. "If only we could go back in time and find out what they were hiding."

When he glanced up, Jenny was looking at him, and he knew exactly what she was thinking. What if the men were hiding gold coins?

Better to dig in these books, though, for answers, than dig in the trees.

With the wireless turned on, they listened to "Armchair Theatre" as they each recorded expenses that seemed odd. Then Mrs. Winter closed her ledger. "My eyes are swimming with numbers."

Gilbert stood up from the table. "I believe tea is in order."

"I'll help you," Mrs. Winter said. She strung her hand through his arm, and he escorted her out of the dining room.

"I believe they just might discover they need one another after all," Jenny whispered. "Though they may need a little prompting."

Adrian groaned. "Why must women get involved with someone else's relationship?"

"Because sometimes it takes a bit of a nudge." Jenny inched her chair closer to him. "Adrian?"

"Yes?"

"Could I glance at those photographs again?"

He turned and retrieved the envelope, handing them over to her. "What are you looking for?"

She opened the envelope. "Whatever else Curtis Sloan was trying to hide."

Magic sea creatures circled in Jenny's mind as she stared down at the carousel before her, the black and white on the photograph turning into the most majestic of hues. The mist had obscured most of the carousel in her picture, but she remembered pieces of it, the glass around the top that looked like shells, stained red from the powder of gold.

The glass splintered inside her head, a cranberry-colored liquid pouring out of the shells, spilling onto the ground. And gold followed, hundreds of nuggets flooding down, crusting the ground with golden snow, a crowd of leopards staring up at her.

What if there were more coins hidden on the island?

The image changed into the carousel's octopus, chopped in half, and it swelled at a frightening pace, its tentacles grasping in a wild fury to capture whoever had destroyed it.

Adrian's dad, it seemed, had been much too clever to hide any sort of treasure under a platform or in a hole in the woods. If he'd hidden the coins, he would have done it in seemingly plain sight.

Colored glass changes or even hides the light.

That's what Cora had said, that the stain of glass could hide things.

What if Simon, when he'd designed the park, had asked Cora to create the perfect hiding place for his cache—one caged in glass made of gold?

Finding a treasure like that might convict Adrian's dad, but it could be exactly what Adrian needed to clear his uncle of any crime.

Standing, Jenny walked down the sloped corridor, the photograph in hand, and stepped outside. She leaned against the painted railing and breathed in the cool air. Sheep bleated on the hill below, and the moon shot a silver ray across the lake's surface, like the path of an arrow targeted to hit Enchanted Isle.

The door behind her opened, and Adrian stepped outside. "What is it?" he asked.

She told him about the cranberry glass that Cora had designed for the railway station and carousel, the possibility that the red glass might mask something of worth.

He glanced down at the lake. "Perhaps Gilbert and I will take the boat over—"

"I want to go too."

He shook his head. "Not after what happened last time."

"I can help you."

"If Perry is on the island . . ." He clenched the rail. "I'd never forgive myself if something else happened to you."

And how could she argue with that?

"I'll stay here," she agreed reluctantly, "but only if you will phone me the moment you get home."

CHAPTER 26

Liz woke suddenly, her heart pounding at a memory of Perry Banks that had interrupted her dreams. In her summer here, the four of them—she and Gilbert, Cora and Perry—had piled into Perry's fancy Jaguar for an awkward evening that included dinner and a cricket match. At some point during the night, Gilbert had left to retrieve drinks for all of them. She couldn't remember if Cora had remained behind, but she clearly recalled her annoyance at Cora's date.

In Gilbert's absence, Perry had bragged about his new automobile, but apparently Liz hadn't been as impressed as he'd thought she should've been, so he'd told her that the Jaguar was only the beginning. Not only did he have big plans for his life, he'd found the money to finance it. And she'd wondered briefly how he'd accumulated it. But then Gilbert had returned, and she'd promptly forgotten that Perry was even there.

Downstairs, the grandfather clock chimed once, and Liz scooted up on the pillows, looking toward the opposite bed to see if Jenny was in the room. She must still be downstairs, sketching the pictures that had already drawn themselves in her head.

If Adrian was correct about someone filtering money through the park, could Perry have participated with whoever had been taking the money? Had he received a portion of it too?

Cora and Perry hadn't married for another three years. When Liz had received the announcement, she'd hoped for Cora's sake that Perry had changed and matured—Liz had certainly changed since her summer in England.

Did Cora know where Perry had gotten the money for a Jaguar and who knew what else? For that matter, where had Curtis obtained the money to invest in Enchanted Isle?

Liz reached for her robe, wrapping it around her before padding down the hallway. Light filtered out under Cora's bedroom door, so Liz knocked, hoping her friend was still awake. Cora called for her to come in.

Cora was in bed, reading *Vogue*, her face smeared with cold cream and her hair hidden under a bright-pink cap that fit snugly across her forehead. The aroma of witch hazel had settled across the space cluttered with clothing and magazines.

She lowered her magazine. "I thought you'd be asleep by now."

Liz stepped carefully over articles of clothing and shoes dropped like globs of cookie dough on a tray. Then she collapsed onto an upholstered chair near the window. "Don't you have a dirty clothes basket?"

Cora shrugged. "There's not much of a reason to pick up my room anymore."

Liz nodded in understanding, though she'd reacted much differently after she'd lost Jack. Instead of avoiding her chores, she'd become obsessive about keeping her bedroom neat, as if cleanliness would tidy up all the clutter inside her head.

She pulled her knees up to her chest, wrapping her arms around her legs as though she and Cora were twenty again, staying up late to talk.

"I woke up after the strangest dream," she said. "And I remembered something Perry had said when I was here before."

Cora pushed herself up on the mound of pillows. "What did he say?"

"That he'd found something that was going to make him rich."

Cora clenched the edge of her comforter. "Did he tell you what he found?"

"No, he was very mysterious about it."

Cora shook her head. "Perry says the oddest things sometimes to get attention."

"That's what I thought at the time, but now I wonder if he really did find something of value."

Cora glanced toward her window before looking back. "I can assure you that he's not rich."

"It would have taken a lot of money for Simon and Curtis to build a park like Enchanted Isle."

Cora didn't say anything.

"Do you know where they obtained the money to finance it?"

Cora shrugged again, focusing back on the magazine she'd dropped on the bedcover. "I don't see how that would matter."

"Perhaps Perry loaned them the money."

"My guess is that Curtis obtained it through a bank loan."

Liz studied her friend. Why was Cora lying to her? "It seems that this would be a risky investment for a bank."

"The park was quite lucrative in its time."

"Another curiosity, really, since it should have taken years to recoup the money they'd spent to build it."

"What are you suggesting?" Cora asked.

Liz didn't want to break Adrian's confidence, but if she found out who was taking money from the park, perhaps the police could discover who'd killed Curtis. Besides, she couldn't possibly expect her friend to be truthful with her if Liz wasn't in turn. "Did you hear that the police found Curtis's body in the lake?"

Cora's voice trembled. "No . . ."

"I wonder if Curtis and perhaps someone else was using Enchanted Isle to hide something."

The strength returned to Cora's voice. "It's a rumor, I'm sure, propagated by the Kemp family."

Liz sighed. "We used to be honest with each other. The best of friends, remember?"

"I don't want to lie to you, Liz. There are just things I can't say."

Liz moved to sit at the edge of her friend's bed. "Why not?"

Cora brushed her hands across the covers. "It's complicated."

"Jenny thinks there might be something still on the island."

"It doesn't matter if there is," Cora said. "She can't return to that place."

Jenny stepped through the open door, and she looked as if she were about twelve again with her ponytail and pajamas, running into Liz and Jack's room after a nightmare. "What do you think would happen if Adrian visited the island?"

When Liz heard a tremor in her voice, she moved toward her daughter. "Why are you asking?"

Jenny rubbed her hands together, her voice tight. "Gilbert and Adrian were planning to go there tonight. Adrian was supposed to call me when they returned."

"Why didn't you tell me?" Liz asked.

"I didn't want you to worry."

"Has he phoned?"

Jenny shook her head.

Cora flung back the covers. "I have to find them."

"We'll go with you," Liz said.

"No"—Cora dug through a pile for clothes—"someone will get hurt."

Liz cringed at her tone. "What's on the island, Cora?"

"I can't tell you."

Liz stepped toward the door. "You're not going there on your own."

240

Gilbert hadn't been on Enchanted Isle in more than twenty years, and he wasn't at all certain that he wanted to go tonight. But if he didn't, Adrian intended to search alone. He couldn't let his nephew do that, especially now that Curtis's body had been found.

He shook his head. He didn't put much stock in any sort of treasure on the island, but someone had taken Curtis's life, and greed was a powerful motivator. Someone might still be desperate to hide what they'd done.

He and Adrian would check behind Cora's glass and return quickly to shore.

The moon doused Windermere with light as the two men motored around to the private beach where Gilbert had often gone to meet his brother, past the crags that had snared Curtis's body.

Once on land, they moved swiftly through the forest, carrying a ladder, rope, and screwdriver along with their torch as they followed the railroad tracks that circled the park. When they reached the railway station, Adrian shined their torch up at the red glass, but the glass was exposed on both sides of the wall, nothing hidden behind it.

The path on the other side of the railway station led into the park, now a graveyard of rides. As far as he knew, Simon had never returned to the island after Curtis's death. Before the ownership of the island transferred hands, Gilbert had reluctantly volunteered to clean up a few things, but Perry had wanted everything left on the island in its existing state.

Gilbert missed his brother deeply, but he was glad that Simon never saw this ruin of a dream. If the war hadn't taken him, the sight of this destruction would surely have stopped what was left of his heart.

Gilbert and Adrian stepped up to the Magic Lagoon, an old gem that had lost its luster. The last time Gilbert had ridden this merry-go-round, he'd proposed marriage to Liz. And now, by God's grace, Liz had forgiven him for what he had done. No matter what happened after tonight, he was grateful that he'd been able to tell her that he was sorry.

Glass was embedded around the crest of the carriage, red shells dividing the scenarios of mythical sea creatures. Adrian helped him balance the ladder on the platform so Gilbert could climb up and pry off one of the glass plates.

"I'm quite certain this would be categorized as vandalism," he said as Adrian handed up a screwdriver.

"And trespassing."

"Neither amendments I want added to a murder charge."

"You haven't been charged," Adrian said. "Only under suspicion."

"Let's hope no one followed us here because of those suspicions."

The weathered lead around the glass detached much more easily than he'd anticipated, and he removed a pane with his screwdriver. "Can I borrow your torch?"

Adrian handed it up, and Gilbert scanned the crevice that extended back into the ceiling of the merry-go-round. It would have been the perfect hiding place for small items, but he didn't see anything inside.

"How many red panes are there?" he asked as he climbed back down onto the platform.

"Three on this side and probably three around back."

With the draping branches and leaves on the opposite side, it would be tricky to access the panes.

Adrian carried the ladder to the next pane, and they leaned it precariously against a large wooden seashell partially cracked through its middle.

It took them twenty minutes to check the other two panes in front, but Gilbert didn't find anything inside except an old bird's nest. Even with the torchlight, he couldn't see how a bird had entered the space.

He handed Adrian the torch before picking up the ladder and rope. Adrian held down the branch of an oak tree that had hooked itself around a coiled bronze rod, but as Gilbert stepped back into the grove, a beam from another light pierced the darkness.

"What exactly are you searching for?"

Gilbert cringed at the familiar voice, but he didn't turn around. "Hello, Perry."

"You didn't answer my question."

"I don't believe it's any of your business," Gilbert said as he rested the ladder against the cresting. Even as his face turned toward Perry, he reached through the leaves and found what he hoped was Adrian's shoulder, shoving his nephew away.

"Anything that happens on this island is my business." Perry lowered his torch, and Gilbert saw him leaning against a lamppost. "It's been much too long since we've talked."

Gilbert folded the ladder. "I was just leaving."

"Actually, I think I'll borrow your ladder first, have a glimpse inside the merry-go-round for myself."

Gilbert stepped away from the platform. "Whatever was up there is gone now."

"It wasn't a request." As Perry moved closer, Gilbert saw the pistol clutched in one of his hands, its nickel barrel gleaming in the light. A German Luger—he remembered that gun well from the war.

"It was you," Gilbert said, his eyes frozen on the pistol. Blood didn't stain the barrel, but it might as well have been the knife he'd found beside his brother. The truth of what happened unfolded like a worn map, directing him down a path he'd never considered before. A path that had been in front of him all along. "You stabbed Curtis and then stole the island."

"I didn't steal it. I purchased it quite fairly from Maria and paid her a handsome sum for it."

"But you killed Curtis . . ."

"He should never have conspired against me," he said as if Curtis Sloan was to blame for his own death.

Gilbert's stomach rolled, partially with relief, partially in fear over what Perry had planned tonight. If Perry was willing to talk, it would give Adrian extra time to get the police. "Where did you get the money to buy the island?"

"I found it."

"Did the Romans leave it behind?"

"There are too many people searching for Roman treasure for it to be of much worth." Perry stepped forward, the gun pointing at his chest. "Give me that rope and your screwdriver."

Gilbert slowly slipped the rope off his shoulder and handed over both items. Perry nudged him toward a lamppost with the pistol; then he tied Gilbert's wrists behind his back and tethered him to the post.

Perry returned to the merry-go-round and unfolded the ladder. With his torch, he examined the inside of the opened compartments like Gilbert had done before moving on to the next pane, but instead of prying off the glass, Perry shattered it with the gun's grip. Gilbert cringed at the sound—one more piece of his brother's dream in pieces.

Perry searched the compartment; then he swore and climbed down, continuing his search.

Had Perry convinced Curtis and perhaps Simon to run some sort of racket through the place, or had they collaborated from the start? All these years he'd thought that his brother had killed Curtis, but Simon must have been in as much shock as Gilbert after finding the body.

The cold air settled over him, but he barely felt it with the adrenaline pumping through his veins. As Perry worked, Gilbert tugged at the rope tied behind his back, trying to free himself from the binding. Hopefully Adrian was cruising toward the mainland now, and the police would arrive before Perry finished his search.

Gilbert stopped struggling when he heard Perry push aside the branches and circle the ride's platform, marching back toward him without the Luger. He shined his torch on Gilbert's face and then down on a gold coin in his hand. Latin was inscribed around it, a stately king seated with a scepter in the center. It didn't look like a Viking or Roman artifact.

Perry lifted the piece up to Gilbert's face. "Where are the rest of these?"

"I've never seen a coin like that before."

Perry clubbed him across the cheek with the aluminum torch. "Don't lie to me."

Gilbert wiped his lip on his sleeve, his face throbbing.

"This bit is worth at least fifty thousand pounds."

"Then one bit is plenty for you."

"I've lost nine of these, and I want them back."

"Why would Simon and Curtis hide your coins?"

"Simon didn't hide anything." Perry lowered the coin and glanced at his watch. "Though he somehow managed to find out that his partner was cheating him too."

Perry retrieved his gun and returned to the post. "You maintained this place well, Gilbert. Did you know some of your rides still run?"

Gilbert didn't respond. Perry had changed his tone, his voice laced with an eerie enthusiasm. "I haven't done much in the way of upkeep, but I've managed to keep the lights on so I can search. Yet somehow the coins have managed to stay hidden." Perry glanced toward the north edge of the park. "How would you like one more ride on the roller coaster?"

"I've already ridden it plenty of times."

"I rather think you might try it again." Perry untied the rope that bound Gilbert, then pointed to the Torrid Typhoon. "Come along."

If Perry thought Gilbert actually had the treasure, perhaps he might have a chance at surviving this night. "Your coins are no longer on this island."

Perry stopped walking. "What do you mean?"

"I mean they're at the farm," he said boldly, as if believing the lie himself.

Perry hesitated. "Then why was this one in the merry-go-round?"

"Because w—" He paused, silently chiding himself for almost saying *we*. "Tonight I was searching for the one I left behind."

"Don't insult me," Perry said harshly. "You don't have my coins."

"You're right," a woman said behind them.

At first Gilbert thought it was Liz, and his heart collapsed at the sound of her voice. Perry, he feared, wouldn't hesitate to kill both of them.

But instead of Liz, Cora stepped into the light.

"Gilbert doesn't know the location of your little hoard," she said. "But I know exactly where it is."

CHAPTER 27

Liz felt ridiculous crouching near the entrance of a ride until she realized Perry was holding a gun. She stayed hidden like she'd promised Cora before her friend marched confidently toward Perry and Gilbert, as if she were immune to any bullets aimed her way.

"Why are you here?" Perry demanded after Cora emerged from the trees a good ten yards away from Liz.

"To give Gilbert a ride home."

Perry laughed, sending icy shards down Liz's spine. "Are you in love with him now?"

"Don't be ridiculous."

"Where are the coins, Cora?" Perry asked, his voice altering into a sickly pleasant tone.

Cora's tone wasn't pleasant at all. "You should have told me that you married again."

Perry tilted his head. "I didn't want you to be vexed."

"How long have you been with her?"

"Only six months. We eloped up in Gretna Green."

"Splendid," Cora replied. "Were you seeing her before we divorced?"

"See, you are angry."

Liz strained her eyes, wishing she could see Gilbert's face in the dim light, but all she saw was the strength of his shoulders. Thankfully, they weren't sloped in defeat.

Cora spoke again. "If you're married, why do you keep asking me for money?"

Several moments passed before Perry spoke again. "Kate might think I have a bit more income than I currently have."

"*You* think you have more income than you currently have!"

"Cora, love—"

"Where does Kate think you are the nights you're on the island?"

"Traveling for my business."

"And what business is that?"

"Where are my coins?" he repeated, his voice now sharp as a blade.

"Do you remember the times we all spent together in this park?" Cora swept her hand in front of her as if she were painting the scene, completely unfazed, it seemed, by Perry's gun. "You and Gilbert were friends then. We were all friends until Curtis died."

"I adored you." Perry inched closer to Cora, wavering again in his voice. "Still do."

"And then there was Liz and you." Cora stepped toward Gilbert. "You loved her, didn't you?"

Liz strained her ears this time, trying to hear his response.

"Very much," Gilbert said.

Perry snorted. "If you loved her, you wouldn't have let her go."

"It's one of my biggest regrets."

Perry turned back to Cora. "Tell me where the coins are."

Cora ignored him, talking to Gilbert instead. "Do you still love Liz?"

"This is irrelevant," Perry insisted, but Liz still heard Gilbert's words under Perry's exclamation, simple but profound.

"I'll never stop loving her."

And something sparked inside her as Gilbert's words replayed in her mind, a flicker of feeling that she thought had died ages ago. He still loved her, and she wondered if she just might love him as well.

"That's what I thought," Cora said, before addressing Perry again. "Your coins are back at my house."

He glanced at each of them. "Now you're both lying to me."

Cora shook her head. "I loved you, Perry, with all my heart, but I've never lied to you."

He scrutinized her. "How did you get them?"

"I took them—after Curtis hid the coins away."

"In the merry-go-round?"

She nodded.

"You knew I was searching."

"The pieces I found are still intact, all of them in pristine condition. I've hidden them well for you."

"More like from me."

"If I hadn't, you would have sold them all at once with nothing left for our future," Cora said. "Let's go retrieve the coins, and we'll forget all this nasty gun business."

Perry didn't move. "Or you could tell me right now where you hid them."

"You won't find them without me," Cora said, but her voice sounded strained this time, as if she didn't quite believe her own words.

"Come along," Perry said, pointing his gun toward the roller coaster.

Gilbert didn't move. "If you hurt Cora, you'll never get your money."

"If you don't hurry, I'll shoot both of you now."

Liz trailed Cora and Gilbert up the midway, under the cover of the trees.

Jenny's heart raced so fast she thought it might take flight, speeding across the lake without a boat. Before they'd left the mainland, her mom had taken charge, dictating like Grandfather would have done. It was almost as if her mom had found her voice again. As if she finally knew what she needed to do.

When they realized that Gilbert and Adrian were still on the island, her mom had called the police station, but the policeman hadn't seemed as alarmed as Liz, saying he'd send someone to visit the island soon. Cora had borrowed this boat from a friend and shown Jenny how to start its engine in case they had to leave in a rush.

Someone ran out of the woods, and she ducked back down in the boat. But when she glanced up again over the side, she recognized the man rushing by.

"Adrian," she called quietly.

He stopped. "Jenny?"

She stepped out of the boat, her saddle shoes scraping the pebbles on the beach.

"Why are you here?" he whispered.

She moved up onto the rock-strewn shore. "Cora was worried about what Perry would do if he found you here."

"She was right to worry."

Her heart beat faster. "Is Gilbert okay?"

Adrian shook his head, his voice trembling. "Perry has a gun."

The image flashed on the beach before her, Perry wielding a gun, his gaze fierce. She blinked him away. "We already phoned the police station, but they didn't seem to be in much of a hurry."

"Perry's gun will persuade them to move faster," he said, pointing toward the reeds. A boat, she assumed, was hidden among them. "Come to shore with me."

She shook her head. "I have to wait for my mom and Cora."

"If he hurts Gilbert, I don't think I'll ever be able to forgive myself." In his words was a silent debate, as if he knew he must go but didn't want to leave her.

"I understand," she assured him. "I wouldn't be able to forgive myself if I left when my mom needed me here."

"I'll hurry back." He disappeared in the trees along the shore, but she didn't climb back into the boat. If Perry had a gun, they were all in danger.

Jenny glanced again over the water's surface and thought about the stories of the ghostly white horse who watched over this lake. About the legends of the people who'd fought and died in the fells around them. About the fairies and the glass.

If only they had an army of fairies to wreak chaos, like the ones from King Eveling's court up at Hardknott. In her mind, she saw dozens of them waking from their sleep, causing mischief in this enchanted land. A gun certainly wouldn't scare them.

Then again, perhaps she didn't need fairies after all.

"Adrian," she whispered toward the reeds, but he didn't respond. He must have already left for shore.

She closed her eyes, thinking for a moment. Cora said that sometimes people saw lights on this island. Perhaps they were powered by electricity that Perry had kept on.

This was a park, after all. Perhaps she needed to play.

She smiled until she heard the voice of her grandfather pound in her head.

Life isn't a game.

Yet the fairies in her mind were perched in the dark trees, waving her forward. Tonight wasn't a game, she knew that, but she might be able to stop Perry. Or at least distract him so Gilbert could get away.

All she needed was some light.

She wove quickly back to the park, staying hidden in the copse of trees. When she reached the main strip, she saw the beacon from a flashlight—Perry's, she assumed—near the roller coaster.

Instead of following the flashlight, she hurried toward the carousel and turned on a switch. For a moment, nothing happened, but then several bulbs flickered on the carriage overhead. A brass bell rang, followed by music from the band organ hidden inside the carousel.

"Fairies," she whispered.

And the park came alive.

Adrian set the throttle on the boat before pulling the starter cord, but the engine didn't respond. Balancing himself against the stern, he tried a second and then a third time before flipping back the cover, checking with his torchlight to see if the spark plug wire was loose.

Then he groaned. The wire was fine, but the spark plug had corroded, carbon coating the silver. He'd need his ratchet and torque wrench from the boathouse to change it. This boat wouldn't be crossing back to the mainland anytime soon.

He ran back across the beach toward Jenny. Somehow, he'd have to convince her that they needed to use her boat to fetch the police before Cora and her mum returned.

"Jenny," he called into the darkness as he drew close to her boat, but she didn't answer. He switched on his torch, shining the light across her motorboat and back toward the forest. She was no longer here.

His stomach plunged, and for a moment, he froze. Then he scanned the trees behind him. He'd never find Jenny in the darkness, and he wouldn't dare turn on his torch inside the park.

He eyed her boat, but even if he was going for the police, he couldn't leave the three women and his uncle without transportation. If they were running from Perry, they'd have to leave quickly. And if Perry chased them in his boat, they'd never make it swimming to shore.

Turning back, he studied the strip of water in front of him, his heart thundering in his chest. It was about a thousand feet from here to the western shore of Windermere, six laps of the pool at Durham. In years past, he'd swum this length without hesitation, but now . . .

Now he had no choice.

Taking a deep breath, he prayed for strength. Gilbert needed him and so did Jenny and perhaps Jenny's mother as well.

A light filtered over the trees, across the lake. He didn't see Jenny or the source of the light, but it prompted him to move.

As he stripped down to his pants, he could almost hear the voice of his coach telling him to clear out his mind, breathe. Still, fear washed over him when he dove into the water.

Focus, his coach would shout. *Pull.*

It was a familiar rhythm to him. Arms overhead, transporting him to the other side. More familiar than the fear.

He had to focus on the rhythm, not the depths below or the distance to shore. Not his leg that plagued him or the memories of that last night with Tom.

Heat fueled his body as he kicked through the water and light.

And his leg didn't ache at all.

CHAPTER 28

Lively music swept through the park, curling up to the platform of the roller coaster like a ewe with her lamb, offering a strange sense of comfort in the chaos. "The Midnight Flyer." One of the songs from the organ's music roll.

For the briefest of moments, the music transported Gilbert back more than twenty years, to the days he'd worked in the park and the hours spent riding alongside Liz on the Magic Lagoon.

Perry swore at the interruption, but with each note from the organ, hope soared inside Gilbert. Someone else was on the island with them. Someone, he hoped, who could help stop Perry.

The man butted the barrel of his pistol into Gilbert's neck, pushing him toward the covered platform of the Torrid Typhoon. Several trains of cars sat idly inside, as if they'd been waiting for decades to take another ride.

Of all the rides in the park, this one had been the most difficult to maintain. Gilbert had feared that someone would be injured by flying out if their buckle broke loose or a car lost its traction on the rails.

He wished he could turn around and look Perry in the eye, as if he could somehow decipher the man's plans. Clearly Perry wanted to threaten them, but did he really want them dead?

The image of Curtis's body flashed through Gilbert's mind, an image forever seared in his memory. If Perry had killed Curtis Sloan, Gilbert doubted he would hesitate to kill again.

He eyed the two strands of cars in the dim light. If the electricity still worked on this ride, a chain would pull the train up the first hill. Kinetic energy replaced the strength of the chain on the other side, plunging the passengers down without any sort of mechanics.

Perhaps Perry would just send them up, expecting the rotting planks to collapse under them or the old tracks to derail them on the downside. If all else failed, Perry could simply neglect the brakes as the cars flew toward the platform. They'd crash into another train of cars at about forty-five miles an hour.

But if Perry was planning to kill them, why didn't he just shoot them and be done? He would be free to search for his cache at Cora's house and run far away with it.

Then again, he could be planning to just kill Gilbert, thinking he could jar Cora into leading him directly to the coins.

For an instant, Gilbert debated telling him that the police were on their way, but he feared Perry would simply speed up his work. Slow and steady is what they needed. And more time to find a way out of this mess.

New lights flashed in his peripheral vision, but Gilbert kept his gaze forward, the chill of metal burrowed into his neck as he walked up the platform steps. Adrian, he prayed, would return soon with the police.

Perry lowered the gun when they reached the last step. Cora didn't speak, but when Gilbert glanced over, her eyes were wide. Stunned, it seemed, that her ex-husband hadn't decided to follow her home.

Perry pushed him toward one of the cars. "Get inside."

Neither Gilbert nor Cora took a step forward. The circuit to operate the cars was on the opposite side of the dark platform, behind the wall. It would only take seconds for Perry to switch it on, but seconds were all Gilbert and Cora needed to hide.

Perry scanned the platform with his torch, as if trying to determine exactly how to start this ride while keeping them firmly in his control.

"This way," he started as he nodded toward the wall, but his words suddenly stopped. The train before them had begun rolling forward.

Perry swore again, pressing the pistol into Gilbert's head. "I'll kill you if you don't get in that car."

"Don't do this, Perry," Cora pleaded.

The front of the train began climbing up the hill, wheels clacking against steel rails as the chain pulled it upward. Gilbert supposed he'd have a better chance to survive by riding up. If the planks held, he could climb out at the curve.

A light flickered on at the top of the hill, eighty feet in the air, and then he heard the clanging sound of bells, like the Chair-O-Plane used to make when passengers flew up over the trees.

Perry swiveled, lowering the gun for an instant.

Gilbert nudged Cora toward the moving car. When she didn't move, he whispered, "Climb out the—"

"Stop talking," Perry said, the barrel thrust back against Gilbert's shoulder.

The platform lamps flickered above them, and in the shock of light, Gilbert shoved Cora into the car. Her eyes grew wide again, questioning at first and then realizing. She swiftly slid across the bench and hopped over the metal door onto a second set of rails.

"Cora?" Perry shouted, swinging his gun away from Gilbert.

A shot, and then a second one, pierced the air. But Cora kept sprinting across the opposite platform until Gilbert couldn't see her any longer. She disappeared into the darkness, down under the posts that held up the rails.

Perry lowered the gun. The man, Gilbert suspected, hadn't conserved when he'd filled the magazine. If it had been fully loaded, six rounds remained.

The last car began crawling past them. "Get in that car, Gilbert, or I swear, I'll shoot you right here."

Gilbert stepped into the car, planning to sprint over the other side like Cora had done, but Perry hopped in beside him.

His skin crawled. He hadn't expected an escort to the top.

Years ago, he'd thought he would die during the war, but God had given him another chance to redeem his life. He wished he could do certain things over again. Wished he could see Liz one more time, tell her that he had never stopped loving her. And he wished he could tell his nephew that he was confident God had a plan for his strength and confidence, that with God's forgiveness, Adrian could forgive himself and love others with a full heart.

He glanced up at the top of the hill, and the light reminded him of the one he'd seen so long ago outside Berlin, except this time he was sober. Either God was calling him home tonight, or it was a sign that God would walk with him through the darkness.

Either way, he felt peace. In the light, all would be well.

The car moved up past the fifteen-foot mark as Perry pressed the gun into Gilbert's side, the lap bar locked uselessly upright.

"None of us want your coins," Gilbert said. "You can fetch them tonight."

"That's exactly what I plan to do."

He changed tactics. "Cora will report you to the police. They'll apprehend you before you leave town."

He snorted. "A few thousand quid will clear that up."

The cars climbed higher now, past the ceiling of trees. "How are you planning to find your coins without Cora's help?"

"She'll tell me when you and I are finished here."

"She's done succumbing to your charms."

Perry shook his head. "Cora will do what I say."

Gilbert wanted to laugh in the face of the man's arrogance. This time, Cora, he hoped, would remain strong.

"They say vengeance is sweet," Perry said.

"Not in my experience." The car shuddered as it continued to climb, and Gilbert thought it might come loose from the rails. "Did Curtis steal your coins?"

"He lied to me about the profits from his sales and then refused to tell me where he'd hidden our stash. I decided to find it for myself."

"But you never found it."

"Not until tonight."

Gilbert's fingers folded over the side of the car. Bracing himself wouldn't help much if they plummeted backward, but perhaps he could jump over the side.

The lights of Waterhead and then the village of Ambleside breached the treetops, the promise of help so far away.

"Why didn't you kill Simon with Curtis?" Gilbert asked.

"Your brother discovered Curtis had been taking extra money from the accounts, but he didn't know about the coins."

What would Simon have done if he'd found the treasure? Or what if Gilbert had found the coins himself, in the months before he'd have married Liz? Even though he'd like to think differently, he didn't know if he would have reported his find.

"So you decided to frame Simon for murder?"

"I had no intention of framing anyone," Perry said. "I just didn't anticipate you or your brother discovering Curtis's body after he fell."

Gilbert glanced over the edge of the roller coaster, and then back at Perry. "You were still here that night . . ."

"You can see a lot from up here," Perry said, nodding toward the railing.

"But the knife?"

Perry shrugged. "Curtis needed some motivation."

The details from that night hammered themselves into place. "You forced Curtis over the edge and then dumped his body in the lake before I returned."

"In quite the rush, I might add. Simon didn't know what happened, and I thought you'd return within the hour. I couldn't have the police finding Curtis or me."

"I thought I was going mad," Gilbert said to himself.

Perry snorted. "You weren't alone. I asked Simon once what he thought happened to his partner, and he said Curtis moved to Morocco."

The roller coaster reached the peak and began the slow curl around the top. Next was the plunge toward the lake.

"This is our exit," Perry said, yanking him to the right. The two of them stumbled out onto the narrow platform.

Gilbert could see the stately crowns of trees below them, but he couldn't see the ground. He knew the distance, though—almost eighty feet. Instant death for anyone who fell over the side.

Perry pointed the gun at him. "Do you like the view?"

"Not particularly."

Perry tapped the top plank of the wood railing beside him. "I've always liked it up here."

The wooden frame trembled as the cars barreled down the other side, and Gilbert braced himself for a crash. The entire ride shuddered in response, but the train continued on its journey.

Perry shoved two rotted planks of railing, and they both tumbled off.

"Why don't you just shoot me?" Gilbert asked.

Then he saw in Perry's eyes what he'd seen many times on the ground in France. Cowardice. Perry wanted Gilbert dead, but he didn't want to shoot him.

In that moment, he found a strange camaraderie with the man. God hadn't meant for one man to kill another, neither today nor back in the days of Cain and Abel.

The cars rattled in the distance as they raced up the second, smaller hill.

Perry nodded toward the open space, at least a yard wide, in the railing. "This is it, Gilbert."

He shook his head. "I'm not going over that."

The gun shook in Perry's hands. "Yes, you are."

But Gilbert refused to move. If Perry was going to kill him, he'd have to pull the trigger.

"I don't want your coins." Gilbert pointed toward the steps along-side the track, trying to reason with Perry one last time. "Why don't we go back down and discuss what happens next?"

"There's nothing left to discuss."

Perry leaned forward then, as if he were going to force Gilbert off the side. Instead of recoiling, Gilbert stepped toward him, startling Perry. The man moved swiftly to his right—where the railing once stood.

Wind crested over the hill as Perry teetered on the edge of the coaster, his eyes widening as if he'd forgotten the wooden planks had fallen to the ground.

Then, without another sound, Perry Banks was gone.

Gilbert lowered himself down onto the platform, sitting carefully beside the rail. Wind shook the roller coaster again, clearing some of the shock from his mind. He wasn't out of danger yet, but Perry would never have survived that fall. At least now Gilbert could think beyond Perry and his wretched gun.

He'd climbed the narrow steps beside the rail multiple times in the past while helping maintain these tracks. The wood was weathered now, and he prayed the bolts were still intact, at least secure enough to descend.

He'd find Cora, and they would get off this island.

Then he'd wake up Liz.

Liz screamed when she heard the thud in the trees, her stomach reeling. The music and lights that flooded the park earlier had filled her with hope. Prompted her to move. She'd found the electric box that operated the roller coaster and with the flick of several switches set the train of cars in motion, a distraction so Cora and Gilbert could break free. It had worked for Cora, but she'd never imagined that Perry would force Gilbert up the hill.

Cora reached for her hand now, the two of them propping each other up.

Had someone fallen off the roller coaster? Or had a piece of the frame collapsed onto the ground?

If Perry was still alive, they needed to hide, right away, but Liz couldn't seem to move. If Gilbert had fallen . . .

She couldn't bear the thought of losing him again.

Cora patted her hand and then stumbled back into the trees with the torch. The train of cars looped around the track, climbing up the hill again. Liz couldn't see if someone was still onboard, but if Perry hadn't stepped off, she needed to stop the ride before he emerged back on the platform.

Racing back up the steps, across the planks, she found the electric box again and ran her finger across the board of switches, turning each one off. When the rattle from the cars stilled, the lights gone, she sank onto the platform, and tears poured out of her eyes.

In those moments of darkness, she mourned the loss of Jack, the man who'd been so good to her even when her heart had traveled to another place in their first years of marriage.

Had she lost Gilbert tonight as well?

A new grief began pouring out.

Liz stood quickly when Cora stepped back onto the platform, wiping off tears with her sleeve.

"Perry didn't survive the fall," her friend said grimly.

Relief shot through Liz even as reached for her friend's hands. "I'm sorry."

"He got exactly what he deserved, but still . . ." Cora glanced up at the roller coaster. "We need to find Gilbert."

Near the top of the roller coaster, they saw the shadow of a figure slowly descending the steps, and Liz rushed toward the rickety stairs to help him. Before she reached the steps, Jenny and Adrian joined her side. Adrian's hair was dripping, his clothes wet.

Liz wrapped her arms around her daughter, hugging her tightly.

"Where's Gilbert?" Adrian demanded. When Liz nodded toward the top of the roller coaster, he gasped.

"I don't know what condition he's in."

Liz climbed onto the first step, but Adrian stopped her. "Please let me go."

"Of course," she said, moving away.

"The police are coming," Jenny told her. "At first, I didn't know what to do, so I—"

"You started the music."

Jenny nodded. "Anything to make Perry stop."

"He's been stopped," Cora said quietly behind them.

The three women watched Adrian and his uncle meet halfway up the wooden steps and then finish their descent together.

CHAPTER 29

Cora placed her clunky vase with its stairstepped colored glass on the coffee table. A crowd of seven circled around it, including the two constables who'd arrived on the island soon after Adrian had phoned from the shore.

"It wouldn't have been hard for Perry to find the coins," Cora told the small audience. "If only he'd looked."

Adrian raked his fingers through his hair, still trembling from the adrenaline that had coursed through him with every stroke across Windermere. His nerves felt as if someone had electrocuted them, each one laced with fire. He'd never thought he would swim again; yet not only had he crossed the lake, he'd felt God's presence with every stroke.

While God had given Jenny a vivid imagination, the creativity to help both Cora and Gilbert survive the night, He'd gifted Adrian with a fire that drove him to move. Diving back into that cold water had surged life back into him, energy that he wanted to use for good.

He glanced over at Jenny, her gaze on the vase. Soon he would tell her all that surged through his heart, but first they needed to find out what had happened tonight and perhaps two decades ago as well.

"Where exactly are the coins?" Harold, one of the policemen, asked as he glanced inside the vase. Adrian knew the man well; they'd been in the same year at grammar school.

"Step back," Cora said, lifting the glass off the table. All of them moved into the corners of the room, not quite certain of her intentions, and Adrian reached for Jenny's hand. Her soft skin seemed to meld into his, like colored glass and lead.

"'If this glass doth fall,'" Cora quoted from the old poem translated by Longfellow, "'Farewell then, O luck of Eden Hall.'"

Then she dropped the vase.

Splintered glass flew across the carpet, her work shattering. Only a lead skeleton remained, and when Cora lifted it, seven gold coins dropped out of the bottom.

She gathered the gold in her hand and held out the pieces, her palm now smeared with blood from the slivers of glass. "I sandwiched them between two plates."

"You were supposed to report any treasure," Harold said as he took them from her.

"I know."

Adrian stepped closer, studying the coins in Harold's palm, and then he glanced back and forth between Cora and Jenny. They were identical to the one his father had found, except the dual leopards now reminded him of Perry and Curtis, setting themselves up on a throne to reign over someone else's kingdom.

"What kind of coins are those?" Harold asked.

"Cursed ones," Cora replied.

Adrian sighed. "I'm afraid my father had one as well."

"Where is it?" Harold asked.

"At the bottom of Windermere."

Harold huffed before placing the remaining coins inside a metal box and clasping it shut. "We'll have to take this case before a court."

Cora nodded, resigned to her fate.

"Do you know where Perry found the coins?" Harold asked, taking notes on a small pad.

"At Eden Hall, before it was demolished." Cora placed the lead frame of her vase back on the table. "He and Curtis were searching for anything the family left behind, and they found thirteen of them buried near the garden."

She collapsed onto the sofa. "Perry wanted to sell all of them off secretly so they didn't have to share with the government or the landowner, but I think the coins were more valuable than they anticipated. Curtis, I suspect, didn't trust Perry. He said he'd keep their coins on the island and sell one or two a year to avoid unnecessary attention. Curtis hid his portion well by investing in the park, but Perry told people he'd inherited money and then openly spent his half of the profits."

Harold glanced up from his notes. "Buying this house?"

Cora shook her head. "I purchased this house with my income."

"Then what did Perry buy?" Harold asked.

"Two cars and a house south of here. It was never enough for him, though. He kept asking Curtis for more cash until the man disappeared. I thought Simon had killed Curtis because he either found out about their scheme or wanted the coins."

Adrian glanced back and forth between Cora and his uncle. "Did Perry kill Curtis?"

"I don't know," Cora said, but Gilbert nodded.

"He forced Curtis off the roller coaster."

Adrian rubbed his arms, the heat draining from him.

"According to Perry," Gilbert said, "Simon surprised him that night. He may have discovered that Curtis was siphoning money through the park, but Simon didn't kill him. Perhaps he found one of the coins with Curtis."

Adrian shifted forward, wanting to run away on his motorbike and process this new information, but Jenny squeezed his hand, anchoring him back again.

"I suspect Curtis told Perry to wait for his money." Cora picked a piece of glass off the ground and fingered the edge of it. "Perry never was one for waiting."

"How did you find the coins?" Harold asked her.

Cora looked back up. "When Curtis built the park, he commissioned me to design red shells for the carousel's rim, but unlike the windows for the railway station, he wanted to fit the glass into the panels himself.

"I didn't find out about the lost coins until after Perry and I married. By then, he'd sold his house and used the remainder of his money to buy the island so he could search for the coins."

"But you suspected where they were," Harold said, prompting her.

She nodded. "At first, I thought Curtis had taken them and left the Lakes, but Perry was convinced they were someplace on the island. While he was deployed, I found seven coins behind the glass. I didn't know what happened to the others."

In that moment, Adrian no longer cared about the coins. The real treasures in this life were the people he loved. His uncle across the room and Emma, his nephews and—

He stepped toward the door, and Jenny followed him. They slipped away from the house and down the quiet lane as the first rays of dawn began to warm the valley below.

"All these years, we thought my dad killed Curtis," he said. "He should have told the police what happened so Gilbert wouldn't have had to carry the weight of his guilt."

"I'm glad you know the truth."

He nodded. "I just wish I wouldn't have tossed the coin."

"How deep is the water under your boathouse?" she asked.

"Not very deep." He sighed. "I suppose I have to find it and give it to the police."

She reached for his hand. "Does it matter so much?"

"Now it does. To me, anyway."

"Your dad made some poor choices, Adrian, but you can make it right."

He glanced over at her. "The courts may not let me keep the coin, but I know someone who could photograph it for me."

They stopped beside an ancient stone fountain framed with ivy, the words *James' Well* carved above the trough.

"It's named after one of the apostles—James, the Son of Thunder." He dashed his hand through the trickling water. "When I was younger, I wanted to be full of thunder like him. People pay attention to thunder."

Jenny smiled. "I always preferred the flash of lightning."

"Your storm certainly distracted Perry."

Her smile faded. "I didn't like the man much, but I never wanted him to die."

"None of us did, but he was willing to risk everything for a handful of coins."

She rinsed her hands in the clear water. "Perhaps he and Cora might have had a glimpse of happiness if the treasure hadn't come between them."

He nodded slowly. The man had been so wrapped up in the gold he'd tried to hide that he'd missed out on the love of a woman wholly devoted to him. He could have built something instead of spending half his life searching for what he'd lost.

"It's almost six," Adrian said, checking his watch. "Which means that your birthday is officially tomorrow."

"I'd almost forgotten."

He put his arm around her, and she leaned her head on his shoulder. "If you could have any gift for your birthday, what would you ask for?"

She looked at him curiously. "I suppose I'd want two things."

"What's the first one?"

A grin lit her face. "Enchanted Isle."

"What would you do with the island?"

"Make it come alive again."

"If anyone could do it, Jenny, I believe it would be you." They turned together, moving back toward Cora's house. "And the second?"

She glanced over at him. "I believe I'll keep that one to myself."

"Perhaps one day you'll share it with me."

"Perhaps." She smiled up at him. "I have an idea for my party tomorrow night."

"What is it?"

"I'll have to speak with Cora first and then Gilbert."

"Speak to them about what?" he persisted.

Before they went back inside, she told him what else she wanted for her birthday.

Liz reached for the lace doily on the nightstand and smoothed the delicate edge of the material between her fingers. Cora had decided to stay overnight in Kendal to be close to her solicitor's office, so Emma invited Liz and Jenny to be her guests at the Herdwick Inn.

As Jenny settled under the covers, Liz reached for her brush on the nightstand and began brushing out her hair. "Your birthday's tomorrow."

Jenny rolled toward her. "I'm glad you're here to celebrate with me."

"I was hoping to do something bigger than just a dinner."

"A dinner with friends is exactly what I want."

Liz switched off the lights, and as she edged down under the covers, starlight streamed through the window, brushing strokes of an icy white across her bed. "Are you excited about returning home?" she asked.

Silence met her question, and for a moment, she thought Jenny had fallen asleep. Then she answered, "I think I'd like to get an actual job in Cleveland and my own apartment."

"And finish school?"

"Perhaps."

Liz smiled. She'd tell Jenny soon about the trust waiting for her, but not yet. Not until she and Adrian decided if they had a future.

"Your grandfather won't be happy about you launching out."

"I know."

Liz took a deep breath, knowing she had to release her daughter from chains that would bind her. "But I would be thrilled for you."

Jenny turned on the light by her bed and scooted up on her elbows. "Really?"

"Really," Liz assured her. "I want you to fly, Jenny. Wherever you'd like to go."

"I don't know what I want to do exactly," she said slowly. "Perhaps take pictures for a magazine or teach children that art is a gift to be embraced, just as important as numbers and words."

"You can do either of those if you'd like. Or both."

The world had changed dramatically in the past twenty years. Jenny could embrace her own dreams now, alongside the dreams of her husband if she chose to marry. Liz should have been encouraging her daughter more, especially in these past few years, to pursue the gifts that God had so clearly given her.

"Now that Dad is gone," Jenny said tentatively, "what do you want to do?"

Liz forced a smile. "I don't know."

"Something new," Jenny persisted. "Something you would enjoy as well."

"Something I would enjoy . . ."

"What do you enjoy, Mom?"

She thought for a moment. "Gardening, I suppose, and entertaining when the guests talk about something other than automobiles."

Jenny laughed.

"What's so funny?" Liz asked.

"Gilbert owns a Ford."

Liz laughed with her. "If your grandfather found out, he would never let us speak to him again."

"And Gilbert also happens to own a garden."

Liz stopped laughing. "Of course he does."

"It's a lovely garden."

"He cares well for it, I suppose."

"It seems to me that he needs someone to help him care for his garden and his home."

"Jenny . . ."

"Good night, Mom." Jenny flicked off her light, ending their discussion, but Liz couldn't sleep. Her mind wandered back to the ominous corridors of her father's mansion on Euclid Avenue.

She didn't miss the house, just as she hadn't missed it when she'd visited the Lakes years ago. Her mother, she'd missed, and her friends at the time, but here there was room to breathe, clean air to fill her lungs, an unrivaled beauty to brighten all that had dulled in her mind. All that would dull again when she returned to her calendar and carefully planned days and nights. No room in either time or place to simply enjoy.

Here she'd begun to remember again who she was in her heart, a daughter of God as well as the daughter of both Stephan and Violet McAdam. A woman who loved to watch things grow, to be outside and appreciate the richness of God's soil and land. That was one of the main things that she had loved about Gilbert long ago. He valued fixing the broken things of life, making the world right again.

Her father might disinherit her if she didn't return home, but if her mom were still alive, she'd understand. Liz had never wanted the burden of the Winter inheritance anyway.

Even though Jack had been passionate about the automobile business, he'd respected it wasn't her passion. She'd supported him to the best of her ability, raising their daughter and caring for their home and listening to him rant when he thought Stephan's hesitation against change was holding the company back. And he'd supported her love of gardening and Pepper, the cocker spaniel she'd adored.

Her father didn't tolerate dogs of any kind, so she'd found Pepper a good home on a farm outside Cleveland, a farm she visited at least once a month. Nor did he tolerate her working in the garden. A gardener was employed to work outside, just like the cook was responsible for the food. Everyone else in the house had an occupation except for her.

But she couldn't blame just her father. She'd lost her own vision for the future over the years.

Her father would be furious if she did try to get a position someplace, like Jenny, as if insulted that she didn't trust him to provide for her until she married again. But it wasn't about provision. It was the fact that she'd begun to think her life was over. A widow at the age of forty-three with no prospects for her future.

She climbed out of bed and pressed her hand against the cold window. In the starlight, she could see the spindly branches of trees outside the glass. A glimmer of water. The sight filled her with the sense of belonging, a feeling that had been fleeting in recent years.

The thought of living the rest of her life in her father's dark house felt overwhelming. Like prison with its many closed doors. Her own mother, she felt certain, would be pleased to see Jenny embark on a new journey. And she would probably be pleased for Liz to embrace a new adventure as well.

Her heart had begun to long again for the things of her youth—to partner even with the man she'd once loved and create a home of her own not governed by someone who had opposing plans for her life. Gilbert had said he still loved her, but that didn't mean they had a future together. Was it too late for the two of them?

If only he'd come back one more time, throw rocks at her window like Adrian had done for Jenny—without the rage from twenty years past. It was a romantic notion, of course, but her mind wandered to a picture of Gilbert standing below, pelting stones at the glass, smiling instead of yelling, asking her to join him downstairs.

Even if Gilbert still loved her, how could they merge their lives together at this age? If he came to Cleveland, she doubted that he'd settle easily into the lifestyle of the city. Her father and Gilbert would probably rub each other raw, two cogs swirling in opposite directions.

What if she stayed in these Lakes? If she did, she'd want to be more than a mistress of Gilbert's farmhouse. She would want to partner with him in his work, spend most of her day outside instead of confined behind doors.

Her heart fluttered at the thought, the idea taking wing.

Smiling, she crawled back into her bed and closed her eyes. Late into the night, she dreamed of blossoming flowers and the sweet smell of dirt. A dog sleeping on the rug and a certain man sleeping in the bed beside her.

When she woke again, she knew she couldn't stay in bed another moment. She slipped out before the sun rose, knowing exactly where she wanted to go but not sure what she would say when she arrived.

CHAPTER 30

Gilbert saw Liz on the hillside below his bedroom window, partially hidden in the misty rays of dawn. She was kneeling beside Winston, petting the dog.

He'd already known as he'd crept down from the roller coaster that he wouldn't let Liz go back to America without speaking his mind. If he didn't ask for her hand again, he'd regret it for the rest of his life.

He dressed quickly and then hurried out the back door and down the hill. As he drew closer to Liz, he saw that two sheep had inched up to her and another one of his sheepdogs had nudged his way in between her and Winston. She was still on one knee in the damp grass, trying to pet all the animals. A grand party.

He cleared his throat, not wanting to startle her before he spoke. "The dogs are supposed to be protecting the sheep from strangers."

Laughter flickered in her blue eyes when she looked up. "I'm not a stranger."

"I suppose not." Neither of the dogs moved. "Apparently, you're their new best mate."

She scratched Winston behind his ears as she stood. The dog was as much of a goner as Gilbert. "We have an understanding."

Gilbert nodded toward the inn at the base of the hill. "You should be asleep."

She shrugged, her eyes flashing again. There was a spark of new life in them that he hadn't seen when she'd come for supper. As if the morning had awakened something new inside her as well. "I woke up early and couldn't stay in bed. My mind kept replaying what happened at the park."

"Sleep evaded me for most of the night," he said, though he didn't explain why. Part of it was reliving the event with Perry, but most of it was trying to figure out a way to convince Liz that he still cared about her.

In his youth and shock, he'd ruined it the last time. He wouldn't allow himself to mess up again. He'd wait patiently until tonight, not a moment longer. This time when he asked Liz to marry him, he wanted it to be close to perfect so she didn't think it was on a whim.

An awkward silence drifted between them, Winston nudging against Liz's hand. She obliged the dog's perseverance by petting him again.

"I missed seeing you yesterday," she said.

"I spent most of my morning at the police station and then the afternoon with Cora's solicitor."

"Can he help her?"

"I believe so," Gilbert said. "Cora says that she didn't sell any of the coins like Perry did. Unless someone proves otherwise, she didn't seem to benefit from keeping the treasure, at least financially."

"I was planning to phone her after breakfast." Liz paused. "Love makes people do strange things, doesn't it?"

Gilbert glanced out toward the lake and then looked back at her. He'd certainly done some strange things because he cared for his brother, not to mention taking a boat all the way across the Atlantic because he hadn't wanted to live his life without the woman in front of him. "I suppose so, including the perception of love. What we wish for sometimes takes over the reality of what is true."

She stopped petting Winston for a moment, and the dog licked her hand until she resumed petting him. "Are you coming to Jenny's party?"

He nodded. "She's asked me to do a few things to help prepare for it."

"I hope it's not an obligation."

"No obligation at all. An honor, really," he said, considering his next words. "Would you join me after the party? There's something I'd like to show you."

She eyed him skeptically. "What is it?"

"A surprise." If he could convince her to go back to the island with him.

She brushed an unruly strand of hair from her face, looping it back over her ear. "Okay."

He smiled. "Thank you, Liz."

Winston's ears perked; then he raced away.

"I suppose that's my cue to leave," she said, stepping toward the path.

Gilbert smiled as he watched her walk away.

Rarely did one get a second chance at a botched relationship. He loved this district, his farm, but he loved Liz Winter more than all of it. For her, he would step away from this place if he must. He hadn't liked the busyness in Cleveland when he'd visited all those years ago, but if necessary, he would acclimate. All he wanted was a quiet space where they could grow together.

When he whistled, Winston joined his side. And he kept whistling all the way back up to the house.

Yellow and pink crepe paper streamed from one side of the inn's dining room to the other, dangling like a parade of bubbles across the plaster ceiling while Nat King Cole sang on the record player. A long table had been set with silverware and porcelain dinnerware etched with a lacy design of turquoise and gold. In the center of each table was a vase loaded with daffodils.

Emma had worked alongside Liz for the afternoon to prepare a meal of roasted lamb shanks, Yorkshire pudding, and a tiered chocolate cake garnished with sprigs of fresh mint for dessert. Jenny snapped a picture of the fancy cake as she waited for the guests. It was a small party—Jenny and her mom, Cora and Gilbert, Emma and her family, Adrian and Mrs. Moore. Just what she wanted to celebrate twenty-one years.

Jenny gave Cora a giant hug when she arrived. "I'm so glad you were able to come."

"I wouldn't have missed it." Cora held out a lei made with white and pink blossoms and lowered it over Jenny's head, their sweet aroma settling over her sweater. "One of my magazines said a lei is fashionable party attire in America."

"It's perfect," Jenny said before pulling out a seat for Cora between her and Liz. "Did you meet with your attorney yesterday?"

Cora nodded. "If I hand the coins over to the Treasure Trove now, he's hoping there won't be any other penalty."

Jenny took her hand. "I'm so sorry that you lost Perry."

"I didn't think he'd ever harm me, but he would have killed me at the park if Gilbert hadn't intervened."

Jenny's eyebrows slid up. "You don't like Gilbert."

Cora exchanged a look with Liz and then smiled. "I've changed my mind."

When the remaining guests joined them in the dining room, Jenny's heart overflowed. Already these people felt like family, bound even closer together after the tragedy on the island.

Instead of a formal party, the ten of them laughed around the table, sipping punch and eating dinner together while Adrian entertained everyone with his stories. Jenny began opening her presents after dessert, savoring each one as she'd savored the cake. Gilbert gave her a giltwood frame for one of her photographs, made in Italy, he said. Then he stood, winking at Jenny before telling the others that he would return soon.

Mrs. Moore gifted her with hand-knitted gloves, a silk flower stitched to the wrist of each one. Frank and Emma gave her a violet scarf sprinkled with white polka dots. Cora's gift was wrapped in a blue tissue paper and held together by a dozen ribbons. Folded inside was a necklace shaped like a teardrop, made from red glass. "It's the fire I promised."

Jenny clipped it around her neck. "I love it."

Cora turned to Adrian. "Where's your gift?" she asked, though her attitude toward him had changed, the hostility gone.

Adrian grinned. "I'm giving it to her later."

Jenny glanced toward the windows. Dusk would fall in about an hour, and none of them wanted to be at the park after dark. "Let's go over to the island," she said, clapping her hands together.

"The island?" Liz asked, the only one of their group not yet privy to Jenny's plans.

"Gilbert cleaned up a ride or two for the finale."

"After all that happened," Liz replied slowly. "Why would you want to go back there?"

"Because I want to reclaim the good memories."

"I'm afraid we're going to have to bow out," Emma said. "Frank needs to get the boys to bed, and my guests will be ready for their supper soon."

Mrs. Moore scooted her chair back. "I'll help you clean up here, then."

Emma thanked her, but when Liz offered to help as well, Emma shoed her toward the door. "You need to finish celebrating."

A silent debate raged inside Jenny. Her mom didn't want to go back to the island—and Jenny couldn't blame her—but tonight was important. If Liz knew what they had planned, she would regret not going.

Cora turned toward Jenny. "I adore you, but I don't ever want to go on that island again."

Jenny hugged her. "I understand. Mom and I will go with the men."

Liz shook her head. "I don't know."

Gilbert stepped back into the room, and before her mom could protest again, he was beside her, holding out her coat. Liz smiled at him, and that smile was the best gift that Jenny could receive. Her mother had no desire to explore the world like Jenny. She belonged right here beside Gilbert.

Gilbert glanced over at Jenny, giving her a brief nod. "We should go now."

"Only a safe ride or two, Mom. Not the roller coaster."

Liz glanced up at Gilbert. "Is this what you had planned?"

When he nodded, she turned back to Jenny. "I'll go, if it's that important to you."

"It is." Jenny said. "Thank you."

The four of them—Gilbert, Liz, Adrian, and Jenny—hiked down to the boathouse and climbed into the motorboat. This time, they didn't have to wait until darkness fell to travel to the island or silence themselves when they stepped off the boat. This time, they were free to laugh as they walked through the old train station and down the path toward the rides, listening to Gilbert sing "Blue Suede Shoes." When Jenny glanced over, her mom was holding Gilbert's hand and smiling at him and his silly rendition of the song. Her fear about returning to this island seemed to have disappeared.

A pink wash of light slipped down over the treetops, spilling onto the broken cobblestones. Adrian squeezed Jenny's hand, and then he disappeared off into the forest. He had supported her idea from the beginning and so had Gilbert, though Gilbert only knew part of what she had planned.

When they rounded the bend, both Liz and Jenny gasped. The carousel looked exactly as she'd hoped, a beckoning glow in the midst of the ruins. The sea creatures on the platform had been scrubbed clean, the panels of marine life glistening in the fading sun. The trees behind the platform were trimmed back, and the red shards of glass had been swept away, the broken panes replaced with painted wood. The carousel looked like one of Cora's bracelets, dangling with jewels.

"Well done," Jenny whispered to Gilbert.

Liz turned to him slowly. "You did this?"

"It was your daughter's idea."

Jenny stepped up onto the platform. "It's the perfect end to my birthday."

Instead of rotating counterclockwise like an American carousel, the platform began turning the opposite direction, powered by a magical hand. Adrian, she knew, was hidden inside the panels, spinning it slowly like a record on the phonograph. Music from the band organ played, and it would continue playing on its own, long after Adrian slipped away.

Gilbert offered Liz his hand. "Shall we take a ride?"

"We shall."

Gilbert helped her mom climb up onto the back of a fanciful blue-and-green seahorse, where she sat sidesaddle along its painted wings, as if she might take flight at any moment. And Jenny liked that thought. Her mom and Gilbert taking flight together, over the park and the lake, far away from the confines that threatened to keep them apart.

Gilbert found a seat on a bench next to Liz, the carved back of it curled into a seashell and painted a glistening pearl-white and peach. The speed of the platform's rotation increased as Jenny inched away from them. Then the panel opened, and Adrian stepped out, taking her hand. When the platform rounded toward the trees again, they both hopped off the ride.

"Where did Jenny go?" was the last thing she heard her mother say before she and Adrian disappeared into the woods, the music setting sail behind them.

CHAPTER 31

"I believe we've been set up," Liz said. The seahorse rose high on the coiled rod and then dropped back down beside him, the decades seeming to roll away as the platform turned.

Gilbert moved forward on the bench, his heart racing. "It seems we have."

Liz tilted her head, and a strand of blonde hair escaped from the tie that held it back. "Did you know they were planning to run away?"

"No." He smiled. "But Jenny wanted the two of us to step back in time together. Try to remember what it was that we lost."

"I don't know if we can step back," Liz said sadly. "Too much has changed in our lives."

He weighed each of her words as if they were dusted with gold. Or perhaps they were toxic, like lead. He didn't want to let Liz go, but maybe it was silly thinking they had a future together when they were so different now.

"You're right, Liz," he finally said. "We can't go back."

The seahorse climbed up and fell back down again. The music ringing around them.

Did anything in this life ever stay the same? It seemed to him that everything changed, evolving with every minute they had on this earth.

He and Liz had absolutely changed in their years apart. He'd helped win a war and then settled into a life of work and reflection. She'd married and mothered a child and lived a life among a society as foreign to him as the trenches had once been in Germany.

The organ music began to fade, the platform slowing. Without an operator, the carousel wouldn't turn again, and he had no intention to move.

The seahorse lowered down next to him and stopped. Liz's eyes were focused ahead, as if she could see something that he wasn't privy to.

All he could see was her.

Even though the years had carved and shaped them both, she was just as beautiful—youthful, even—in his eyes as she'd been at the age of twenty. Back then, once he'd fought to overcome his fear, he had been overjoyed when she accepted his proposal. Unlike him, she hadn't thought of their differences as a wall to separate them, more like a hurdle to jump over.

He hadn't taken a risk like that in a long time, at least not in the area of relationships. With the exception of his time in the British Army, his last real risk was traveling all the way to the United States in an attempt to find her. A colossal failure that had sent him reeling, trying to cure his heartbreak with gin.

Perhaps Liz didn't think there was a future for them together, but he couldn't let her return home again, at least not without knowing that while he'd certainly changed over the years, his feelings for her hadn't changed one bit.

"Gilbert . . ." she said as she climbed down from the seahorse.

"Why can't we go back?" he asked before she could say anything more.

"What do you mean?"

"Why can't we go right back to where we left off twenty-three years ago on this platform?"

She shook her head. "I'm not the same person that I was—"

"We're both different people, but my feelings for you are the same." He paused, reconsidering his words. "I suppose my feelings *have* changed, but only because I know now, by God's grace, that I would never do something as foolish as blame you when I'm not able to contain my own grief."

Liz sat down beside him on the bench, the music quiet now. The rays of sun had faded with the melody, the bulbs he'd replaced on the carousel and lampposts lighting the park. She no longer seemed worried about staying after dark. Perhaps it didn't seem as frightening under the warm lights.

"I thought I'd lost you when Perry . . ." Her voice trembled.

"I don't want to lose you again, Liz."

She glanced across the platform. "This is where you proposed to me."

He nodded. "Right on this bench."

"I gave the ring to Cora."

He dug into his pocket and retrieved it. "She delivered it back to me after you left, along with a lecture unlike any other I've ever received before or since, even when I was in the army."

"She's a faithful soul." Liz stared down at his palm, at the silver ring crowned with a small diamond made from the raging heat of earth. A symbol of a promise but also of being grounded in more than emotions or feelings. A jewel representing strength and elegance in the midst of fire, exhumed from a place of depth and polished until its beauty shone.

He took her hand and wound her fingers through his. When she didn't resist, he inched closer to her. "I love you, Lizabeth McAdam Winter."

She nodded slowly, not fighting the words. He was determined now to stay the course unless she insisted that she didn't love him anymore.

He took a deep breath, fueling the steadiness in his mind and heart before he continued. "We may have lost a season together, but we've grown in these years. Changed in ways that I think will only add to the bond of our—" He stopped. "Well, what are we exactly?"

"Two kids hopelessly in love." A tear slipped from her eye, and he wiped it away with his thumb. It was a mixture, he supposed—he hoped—of love and grief.

"Jack and I had a hard start at marriage," she said. "But you need to know that I still loved him. I never want anyone to think I didn't."

Her words pressed against his heart, but they didn't pierce him. He'd have never wanted her to live all those years of marriage without love. This man he'd hated in his heart, a man he never knew, had cared well for Liz. And he was grateful for it.

"More than twenty years have come and gone," he said. "I don't want to live the next twenty years without you."

Her hand trembled in his. "It sounds so simple."

"It is simple," he insisted.

"We've both created separate strands in our lives."

"Strands we'll learn to weave together."

She glanced down again at the ring still resting in his hand. "Where would we live?"

His answer came quickly. "Wherever you'd like. If you'll have me as your husband, I can return to Cleveland with you."

"No. I don't want to go back to Cleveland."

He blinked, uncertain how to proceed. He'd intended to give up this place he loved for the woman he loved even more. It would be the greatest of gifts if she gave him both. "Are you certain?"

She nodded. "I would much rather stay with you here."

He held out the ring, just like he'd done all those years ago, and knelt down on one knee. "No matter where we go, I want to go as your husband," he said. "Would you do me the honor of becoming my wife?"

Her gaze remained frozen on the engagement ring, her lips silent, and his heart began to cave again. "You can think about it, Liz."

Her face slowly rose from the ring, her gaze finding his. "I don't have to think any longer," she said softly.

He braced himself against the metal below him, the solidity of it building a scaffold of sorts all the way up to his heart and his mind, ready to capture the pieces if her feelings didn't reflect his.

The bitter taste of gin settled like an invisible dew on his lips, calling to him, but he wouldn't—couldn't—turn back to the drink if she said no. He'd lock himself in his room if he must and wear out his knees in a waging of prayer to stop what he knew he couldn't stop himself. Turn to the One who gave him hope even when it was painful.

"I'd like nothing more than to marry you," she finally said.

The longing for gin evaporated as he slipped the ring on her finger. Then he lifted her off the bench, carried her off the platform, and spun her around twice before setting her back down.

Liz Winter had agreed to marry him, and this time he wouldn't let anything, including himself, stop them from becoming husband and wife.

Jenny and Adrian climbed into the canoe hidden in the reeds and buckled their lifejackets. Adrian handed her a paddle, and the two of them paddled back toward the main shore.

The sun hadn't quite set, the lake glowing with magic as if a thousand fairies were dancing underneath the surface. She could almost see them, emerging from the deep, peeking up at their boat, teasing them.

"What do you see?" Adrian asked.

She shook her head. "You'll think I'm silly."

"I've never thought you were silly."

She glanced back, tilting her head as if she didn't believe him.

"You have an extraordinary ability to see things that other people miss, Jenny. Most of us lose that sense of wonder and imagination when we slip into adulthood, but you've kept your gift."

"Flights of fancy, that's what my grandfather calls them."

Adrian pointed his paddle at the water. "Where did you just fly, when you looked in the water?"

"I saw hundreds of fairies," she said. "Like the ones at Eden Hall. I know they aren't real, but they are very much alive to me."

She braced herself, waiting for him to say that she was crazy, but he surprised her with his words. "Most people only see the white on a page and sometimes the black and white, but you see every color. It's like you can see an entire picture, Jenny, before it's developed."

She'd never thought of it as a gift like that, seeing pictures that no one else saw.

He pressed his paddle across the smooth surface as if one of the fairies might grab on to it and hitch a ride. "I wish I could see the pictures with you."

She closed her eyes, the breeze brushing strokes across her face, the fairies giggling in the background. If only there were a way she could invite others into her world, give them wings to soar in a flight of fancy. If only she could inspire others to dream themselves.

Then she turned carefully on the bench, facing him. "I'll help you see them."

"I'd like that."

Instead of returning to the boathouse, Adrian paddled their canoe onto the eastern side of the island and secured it between rocks. Then he helped her back out and sat beside her on the flat surface of a boulder, the last threads of daylight falling across the strand of water that separated them from the boathouse and inn.

She leaned back against his chest, content as she watched the dance of light on a steel-blue stage.

He wrapped his arms around her, pulling her close. "You got one of your birthday wishes tonight."

Her gaze rippled across the pewter surface of Windermere. "I haven't seen my mom this happy in ages."

"I've never seen Gilbert this happy in my entire life."

"They're good for each other, aren't they?"

"Very much," he said. "And we're good for each other too."

"I believe we are."

"You said you wanted the island for your birthday."

She closed her eyes for a moment, dreaming.

"I want you to breathe life into it again," he said.

She inched away and studied his face as if he were living in his own dream. "I don't understand."

"Until last year," he explained, "Perry and Cora owned this island together."

"So Perry's widow gets half of this place . . ."

He shook his head. "When Cora and Perry divorced, the solicitor worked out a settlement where neither of them was allowed to sell the land without the other's consent. And in the event of Perry's death, all the property rights transferred to Cora. The solicitor didn't know about the coins, of course. Given Perry's record of spending, he probably thought Perry would sell it on his own after their divorce to pay off his debts."

"Surely Cora will sell it now."

Adrian smiled. "She said it doesn't belong to her any more than it belonged to Perry or Curtis. Since Emma owns the family inn, Cora said she's returning the island to me."

Her mouth gaped. "She gave it to you?"

He nodded.

"That's marvelous, Adrian."

"The thing is"—he pulled her close again—"this island needs someone who can create beauty out of the wreck, someone who sees in pictures like my dad once did."

Her breath caught. "Who do you have in mind?"

"Happy birthday."

"Seriously?"

He nodded.

"Oh my . . ."

"What was your other birthday wish?" he asked.

"You, Adrian," she whispered. "I want to be with you."

"You need to go back to school, Jenny, and finish your degree in photography or art or whatever you'd like."

Her heart dropped. "And then?"

"Then I was hoping you could teach me how to see in pictures as well."

"I'd like to do that, very much."

On that rock, jutting out from the island of magic, the water lapping gently at their feet, he kissed her again.

And this time, no one interrupted them.

EPILOGUE

June 1960, The Enchanted Isle

The Ferris wheel streamed sapphire and ruby light across the black canvas, carousel music spreading like a tidal wave down the corridors of the empty park. The pattern of lights, Liz thought, would look spectacular in Jenny's viewfinder, but instead of taking photographs, her daughter and Adrian were at the restored railway station, waiting for the first ferry to arrive.

She prayed hundreds of guests would pour into the park for tonight's grand opening. That success would follow this grand risk of a dream that some might consider crazy, a dream Liz herself had considered crazy when Jenny and Adrian first explained what they wanted to do.

While Adrian worked at the bank in London, Jenny had completed her degree in photography—Adrian helping her study with pictures instead of just words. Then they had married last summer on this island—after Gilbert and a crew had dismantled what Jenny had renamed the Horrid Typhoon—becoming business partners as well as husband and wife.

After the wedding, Liz had given Jenny and Adrian the statement outlining the investments and monies Jack had left in Jenny's name. Using the inheritance as seed money, Adrian resigned his position in London and created a plan for the park to eventually finance itself, as long as others shared their vision. Her dad, Jenny had decided, would like having his money invested in something she loved, a park like the one they'd visited together when she was young. The revival of this place was a tribute, in part, to both Jenny's and Adrian's fathers. A legacy they'd somehow managed to freeze in time.

With Jenny's gorgeous designs and Gilbert's engineering, the Kemp family had restored most of the old attractions and built six new rides, all of them inspired by the legends of lake fairies and white horses and creatures from the sea. A fierce new roller coaster, built of steel, stood at the foot of the park, aptly adding a *w* to *rath* for its new name: Fairy's Wrath. And dangling on wire over the midway were dozens of colorful fairies created by Cora, each one with glass wings.

Last year, a jury ruled that Cora had to turn over her cache of medieval coins, called double leopards, to the British Museum, but because she hadn't sold any herself or received any money directly from Perry's coin sales, they refrained from adding a jail sentence or fine. And she'd returned quite happily to her studio, restoring again what had been broken.

More rides would come to this park, birthed out of Jenny's imagination as Adrian helped mine her dreams, polishing each one. But no matter what they built, Liz would always prefer riding the carousel.

Gilbert slipped up into the ticket booth beside her, taking her hand. She still loved being surprised by him, the bolt that shot through her skin whenever he reached for her, his desire for her alone. It was a gift she'd longed for years ago, a gift she'd never expected to receive.

She nodded toward the single loop at the north end of the park. "You're supposed to be operating the roller coaster."

"And you're supposed to be selling tickets to a crowd."

Her gaze wandered back down to the lampposts that lined the cobblestone path. Remnants remained from the past, yet it felt new. Fresh. A place for a new generation to dream.

"People will come, won't they?" she asked.

He pulled her close. "I hope so."

She and Gilbert had circled their own loop in the past two years, landing upright again. They'd married less than a month after he proposed, not wanting to waste another moment apart. Originally, they'd planned to stay here in England, living quietly on the farm. But then Gilbert had flown home for a reception that her father had reluctantly hosted in his home.

Gilbert and Stephan had begun talking about automobiles on that trip, and Stephan had convinced him to visit one of their factories. After that, Gilbert hadn't needed much convincing. He was as intrigued by the workings of McAdam Industries as he was about the workings inside the Ford he'd left in England. And he wasn't the least bit intimidated by his father-in-law. Stephan seemed to respect him for it.

So, Liz and Gilbert had traveled often between Cleveland and the Lakes as Gilbert helped Adrian with the park. In Ohio they lived miles away from her father's house, on a two-hundred-acre farm they'd purchased near Lake Erie. Mrs. Moore had moved into their farmhouse here, a local boy helping her care for the sheep when Gilbert and Adrian were away, though Adrian and Jenny were now thinking about buying a lake home so they could live in this district all year.

The band organ continued playing, but the rest of the park was quiet. Too quiet. The ferry should have been here by now, the people swarming up the midway.

Liz had dared her daughter to dream. What would happen if no one else except Cora and the Kemp family dreamed with her?

Old fears threatened to return but then a new peace overpowered the fear, a reminder of the good, rooted in the past. And her heart overflowed. If this park failed, her daughter would continue to dream, even if she shared the adventures in her mind with no one except her husband.

"I hear voices," Gilbert said, but Liz didn't hear anything over the band organ.

"Real voices?"

He nudged her. "Yes, real ones."

With their fingers laced together, he led her out to the middle of the walkway, and then she heard it too, a low rumble of activity, the clamor of laughter, stomping of feet.

Her heart surged as Adrian and Jenny emerged in the park lights, marching together hand in hand as if they were grand marshals in a parade. Maria Kemp was right behind them with Emma, Cora, and Mrs. Moore. And then dozens of people Liz didn't know.

Jenny released Adrian's hand and rushed toward them, her cheeks flushed. "A whole crowd is waiting to take the ferry from the mainland."

"Well done," Liz said, feeling her face flush as well. "You've made it a reality."

"With lots and lots of help."

Emma's boys raced past them, toward the roller coaster. A queue of people young and old grew quickly beside the ticket booth.

"Time for us to get to work," Gilbert said before kissing Liz. Then he was gone.

Jenny hugged her. "Thank you."

"I didn't do anything—"

"Yes, you did. You let me dream."

Liz hugged her daughter again and then turned back to the booth. Her heart full, she hoped each visitor tonight and in the days to come would dream alongside Jenny as well.

Acknowledgments

The magical park called Geauga Lake had celebrated almost a hundred summers when I first walked wide-eyed under the clock tower entrance and into another world. It was a place of wonder for me and generations of children, a place where we could dream. Sadly, this amusement park is gone now, but the memories of it, a gallery of pictures, are forever etched in my mind.

I wanted to write a story about a park once filled with beauty and wonder as well, an amusement park that had seemingly lost its way. And I wanted to set this story in a magical place.

My talented friend Diane Comer—who loves stories and all things beautiful—introduced me to the labyrinth of lakes and rich history hidden in England's Lake District. The mystical lakes and rugged fells, home of Beatrix Potter and William Wordsworth, have inspired the writers, artists, and tourists who've flocked there for more than a hundred years. As I researched these Lakes, my idea about a fictional park began to grow.

While I've tried to remain as faithful as possible to geographical and historical details, sometimes novelists must expand on the facts to create a compelling story. The island that houses Enchanted Isle was purely of my making, but Windermere's Belle Isle helped inspire it. Because the United Kingdom didn't officially adopt the metric system until the

1960s, I used British Imperial System units for measurement though Gilbert, as an engineer, might have been thinking in meters and grams.

The art and science of photography evolved rapidly during the 1950s and '60s. I tweaked several camera and film-development details to accommodate this story, and I also changed the launch of Pan American's transatlantic passenger service. Pan American didn't fly passengers across the Atlantic until October 1958, six months after Liz took her flight.

The lore about fairies and buried treasure in the Lake District is accurate. Roman and Celtic artifacts continue to be found today on the heathery fells and across England. In 2015 alone, the British public made more than 82,000 archeological finds.

Thank you to the many people who contributed to this story and encouraged me along my journey. A special thank-you to:

Erin Calligan Mooney, Colleen K. Wagner, and Natasha Kern for helping me turn the threads of my idea into a novel. You ladies are the best of the best. It's an honor to partner with each of you!

My amazing hostess, Diana Berry, who welcomed me into her home and opened the window to the incredible Lake District. Thank you for taking me on a grand treasure hunt and introducing me to many of your wonderful relatives and friends. Thank you, Auntie Anne and Uncle Pete, Jeanette, Phil, Jane, Jean Berry, and Fred and Alma Stobbart. It was a pleasure to hear each of your stories, especially the one about nicking the cat's eyes. Still laughing . . . And grateful both for Grasmere Gingerbread and to Jeanette for making sure I tried a Kendal Mint Cake before I left the Lakes.

Simon Berry, thank you for brainstorming about islands and treasure and sharing both your family's stories and the book your father wrote about Lakeland history. And for "translating," since oddly enough our two great nations, as you said, are set apart by one language. The Berry family owns three elegant inns in the Lake District—Waterhead,

Low Wood Bay, and the Wild Boar. The beautiful Low Wood near Ambleside is now almost 250 years old.

Lisa Wilcke, a glass artist and teacher extraordinaire. Thank you for inviting me into your world, teaching me the history of glass as well as how to cut, color, and create with it. Your passion helped inspire this story.

My friend Ann Menke for your encouragement and assistance in smoothing out the rough edges on my first draft. Aunt Janet (Wacker) for teaching me how to dream and for your many stories. John and Anne Shafe for sharing your lives with me over English biscuits and tea. Dawn Rhudy, sheep farmer extraordinaire, for helping me understand the complexity of these animals. Brad and Sarah Perron for your passion and knowledge about historic carousels in both England and the States.

My writer's group—Dawn Shipman, Julie Zander, and Tracie Heskett—for reading early drafts and graciously helping me grow this story. I rely so much on your collective wisdom and craft. My sistas for your prayers and for loving me on both good days and the not so good ones. Michele Heath, my first reader and friend for life, for your honesty and incredible ability to help me clarify my messy thoughts.

My amazing family, including Jim and Lyn Beroth, for your consistent prayers and support; Pop Dobson for helping me understand broken boats and broken tires; Drew Dobson for passing along your rowing expertise; and Karen Dobson for coaching me on all things swimming.

My husband, Jon Dobson, for not only giving me time and space to dream, but for dreaming alongside me—I couldn't write fiction without your support! My two daughters, Karlyn and Kiki, for embracing exactly who God created you to be and reminding me of all the wonder in our world.

Our Master Creator for breathing life into a beautiful world and every man and woman who occupies it, each one fearfully and wonderfully made.

Book Club Questions

1. What are some of the favorite places you remember visiting as a child, and how did those places mold you? Have you returned to any of those places as an adult?

2. Not everyone appreciated Jenny's inclination to step outside reality when her imagination sprouted pictures and stories on its own. What do you think are the positive aspects of having a vivid imagination? What are the challenges?

3. What were some of the other unique giftings of the characters in this story? What unique ways has God gifted you?

4. Did you have an adult in your younger years who appreciated your unique abilities? How did he or she impact your life? How have you encouraged those in the next generation?

5. Adrian was deeply conflicted about the love and loyalty that he had for his father and the reality of what he thought his father had done. Do you think Adrian was justified in his frustration? How do you forgive someone who has failed you?

6. In many cultures around the world, a good reputation is more valuable than any material possession. How can someone overcome a bad reputation tied to themselves or their family?

7. Mrs. Moore forgave Adrian for his part in Tom's death, but Adrian still struggled to forgive himself. What did he need in order to accept this forgiveness?

8. Why do you think the author used glass imagery throughout the book? What are some of your favorite symbols in the story?

9. The heart of this story is about repairing the shattered pieces of a relationship. How did some of the characters mend their relationships? And why did other characters refuse to fix what had been broken?

10. In the Bible, the prophet Isaiah talks about God caring for those who grieve by replacing ashes with a crown of beauty and despair with a garment of praise. Does anything in this story remind you of that verse?

11. Have you been able to accomplish any of the dreams you had as a child? How are your dreams for the future different now than when you were young?

Author Bio

Melanie Dobson has written seventeen historical, romance, and suspense novels—including *Enchanted Isle*, *Beneath a Golden Veil*, and *Catching the Wind*—and three of her novels have won Carol Awards. Her Underground Railroad novel, *Love Finds You in Liberty, Indiana*, won Best Novel of Indiana, and *The Black Cloister* was named *Foreword INDIES's* Religious Fiction Book of the Year.

Prior to her writing career, Melanie was the corporate publicity manager at Focus on the Family and owner of Dobson Media Group. She lives with her husband, Jon, and their two daughters near Portland, Oregon, where they enjoy hiking and camping on the coast and in the mountains of the Pacific Northwest. When she isn't hiking, practicing yoga, or reading with her girls, Melanie loves to explore old cemeteries and ghost towns.

Follow Melanie at www.melaniedobson.com.